GANGSTERS OF GANGNAM

JAMES WALSH

Published by Zebre Dreams

ISBN 978-1-8381452-0-0

This is for you.

Additional thanks to Ira Rebeca & Ms. Rust.

CHAPTER ONE: THE HOSPITAL

Time to work. Time to murder. The cool, calm dawn on an early October morning was the perfect timing for a criminal to initiate his daily deeds. Oculoplastic surgeon and complete sociopath Dr. Tarawa-Li Maska - also part of the Maska Triad based in Gangnam, South Korea, was on his way to claim his next sorrowful victims. Being a trained Oculoplastic surgeon, he specializes in procedures involving the patients (or in his case, "victims'") eye sockets, eyelids, and tear ducts. 'The Surgeon' has an impressive resume doing so, as he is no stranger to performing gruelling and barbaric torture, including slicing through a person's eyelids whilst they are completely conscious, sawing off a person's eyelids and forcing the victim to ingest them and most recently, gauging his victims' eyes out whilst the man's family was tied up in the operating room, watching this heinous act being committed.

'The Surgeon', the first out of the three triplets, is known as the underworld medical genius for anyone in the criminal underbelly of Korea. He operates many of his well-received services to anyone who has enough money. From dispersing untraceable poisonous pills for customers wanting to kill, right up to the barbaric torture he commits for anyone who is unlucky enough to be on a "kill list." The "kill list" is a term for the contract killings that are sanctioned by the Chairman to be completed by the three triplets - Tarawa-Li was the only one sadistic enough to perform killings commonly when off-duty hours struck.

That is where this cool October morning comes into place. Tarawa-Li investigates his work schedule to see who is on the list for today (he manages to operate as an Oculoplastic Surgeon in a Korean hospital as the Maska Triad pay billions a year for their own secret ward, disguised to the general public as 'Ward: Still in Development'). He looks down on his scrappy piece of white lined paper and sees:

Today's Kill List

Name: Solomon Sanders

Age: 23

Occupation: Journalist

Incident: Leaked false information regarding an unnamed Korean presidential candidate, including money laundering, tax evasion, arson, manslaughter, and fraud

Payment: 16 million won

Payee: Anonymous

Additional Requests: Take photos of him when deceased and then post to his family home address

Name: Aria Chung Lee

Age: 18

Occupation: Waitress

Incident: Caught being inappropriate with the Maska Triad Chairman

Payment: None (Maska Triad Exempt)

Payee: N/A

Additional Requests: Dispose her body however your normally do it, this victim is especially popular among the youth, so we may have some of her friends and family members on this list in the weeks to come

"Must be a quiet day at the office." Tarawa-Li mumbled, "Early morning is about to begin, so I have until noon until I have to be back at the house."

He puts the scrappy paper back into his pocket, washes his dirty dry hands and grabs the surgical equipment he desires for his torture rituals. His victims are heavily sedated and are already prepared for him in separate operating rooms. Thanks to the Maska Triad, the most challenging work is already completed for Tarawa-Li's benefit. Tarawa-Li slowly glances at both of his victim's rooms, deciding which he wants to lay down his wrath of torture onto first.

To his left, a bloody and bruised foreign journalist, with what already looks like a laceration around his left cheek bone. To his right, a still bleeding teenage girl, with two of her front teeth cracked and her jawline shattered. Sure, both people didn't do anything negative at all, but their presence negatively effects the triad. People who end up on the kill-list could be a firefighter or a salesman, they could be the nicest people on the planet, but being nice does not do anything for this world. Being vigilant, observant, and relentless does. Tarawa-Li does what is needed to be done in order for himself and his family to thrive. There cannot be any negative presences or roadblock, there cannot be any distractions or nuisances. The triad must gain as much power, status and money as possible, and if anyone disagrees, they get put to death at either the hands of Tarawa-Li or one of his other two twin brothers. The most feared three in Korea, some dub 'The Terror Triplets.'

Tarawa-Li enters the operating room to his left, slowly opening the door and then closing it behind himself.

"Hello, fine sir. I am your surgeon for today. I believe you are the man solely responsible for leaking false information regarding an unnamed Korean presidential candidate. The article you published included the candidate being involved in money laundering, tax evasion, arson, manslaughter, and fraud. Now, I don't know about you, but manslaughter is a pretty serious thing, huh?" Tarawa-Li exclaimed.

A few more chilling seconds pass by and he continues with his speech.

"You see, Mister.... Solomon Sanders.... you are a young man like myself! We have so much more to contribute to this world! Unfortunately, due to your narcissistic choices, your time to contribute to the world is over. Just make sure in your final moments of your beautiful life to smile please, friend; I must take some photos of your dead corpse to your family! I'm sure your wife misses you very much!" Tarawa-Li chuckled.

He grabs the metallic drill and turns it on. The screeching sound it gives echoes throughout the depressing four walls. The flickering lights inside the operating room would make it seem it is a scene from a gory horror movie. The wet floor consisting of blood and urine, the standstill sedated body, the sociopath surgeon. This is what he always dreamed of ever since he was a teenager: a place to rule with an iron fist and a no holds barred environment.

Tarawa-Li penetrates the poor soulless victim's eyeballs with the sickening drill, with a small smirk swiped on his unattractive face. He dug down just like normal, until the tip of the drill has eventually blasted through the entire skull. With the drill now unattached to the lifeless body, darkened red blood spewing out of control and a smile still on the face of the Surgeon, a camera is brought into the room by a security member who works for the triad. The

Surgeon crouches down on one knee, with his left shin being flooded in excess blood and urine. He turns the camera on to start taking pictures of the contract killings victim. He then proceeds to have a bizarre conversation with himself.

"You are so photogenic, Mister Solomon! Yes, exactly like that! Did your mother ever tell you how beautiful you are, or should I say were?" Tarawa-Li chuckled, "Now I hope you do not care that I'm adjusting your facial structure to put a smile on your sorry little face. I just think a wife prefers to see her husband smiling instead of frowning."

He takes a few pictures of the victim.

"Security, how many photos do you think I should take of my latest patient?" Tarawa-Li asked.

"Who knows, boss?" The security guard answered.

"Well, let me take a couple more, then I'll have to move onto my next patient." Tarawa-Li said.

After taking several pictures of the deceased target, he gives the security team the action to go ahead and dispose of the fresh corpse (placing the camera in the guard's back pocket). While doing so, the liquids of blood and urine tremble from inside of the operating room down into the hallway of the ward. Tarawa-Li places his metallic drill of death back into the surgical toolbox, removes his bloody gloves and unclogs the drains in the operating room so the excess blood and urine goes down the hospital room's drains. As he knows he still has masses of time before the sedation runs out on his next victim, he changes the lightbulb which kept flickering during the recent torture, pondering if the door can also be fixed. Quickly disregarding the old door, he enters the next room and focuses on Aria Chung Lee, the next customer to feel the triad torture. He enters the room with the girl and begins to have another conversation with himself.

"Good morning, madame. I am your surgeon for today. I believe the reason you are in this operating room on this fine October dawn is because you were caught being inappropriate with the Maska Triad Chairman. You may know him by the name Atheno-Li Maska? I know him by the name 'Father'. Now, do not get me wrong, my father is a single man. My mother passed away many years ago now in a very unlucky accident back in Hong Kong. However, being inappropriate with a man like my father with his power position and social status in a public place? Were you ever mentally stable if you ever thought that was a good idea? No need to worry now dear, your time is about to come to an end." Tarawa-Li said, now turning his voice into a quieter volume.

"Now. How would you like to die… how would you like to die…how would you like to die…?"

He let a few more seconds pass by until he continued with his conversation with himself.

"My other brothers prefer to be more 'gangster like' when they approach how to kill. You would have liked both. We are triplets." Tarawa-Li said, "One of my brothers is a chef. His name is Dan-Li, he likes to use knives. My other brother, Jing-Lee, he likes to use guns, guns are his favourite weapon of them all."

The sick smile remained on the face of the sociopath.

"What did you say, Miss Lee? Did you say that you want to die by an electric drill through your eyeballs and skull?" Tarawa-Li asked.

Tarawa-Li puts on a new pair of surgical gloves, pulls his long greasy black hair into a ponytail and exhales smoothly. With his palms ready and smirk set, it was about time for another torture to begin.

The young female victim laid on the elevated surface, clueless about what is about to come of her. If only she knew who she flirted with a couple of nights ago, this could have all been avoided quite that easily. There are many girls like this in Gangnam, pretty girls who only want to date rich old men so in a few years down the road they can receive a hefty life insurance sum when their partner passes on, only so they do not have to work to become financially dependent themselves. However, most people in this present day in Korea know all the triads the country has to offer to avoid any wrongdoing – there was only one major triad left in the country. That's how powerful and intelligent the Maska Triad had become – they were invisible and had become a folk tale of sorts. It is the only triad left in Korea where the criminal underworld can still not identify any member by their proper name, and to be honest, why would they want to? The Maska Triad is the near whole of the Korean criminal underworld in present day. Trying to identify a member of the Maska Triad instead of just referring them to their alias would be like buying a puppy and then feeding it chocolate.

Tarawa-Li opens his rusty old surgical box. Clattering loudly, he finds his electric drill and pulls it out of the box, staring at it the same way a kid would stare at a well-loved toy.

"That's enough staring, now let's get down to business." Tarawa-Li whispered.

The electric drill penetrates the girl's right eyeball instantly. Blood squirted viciously, almost if it was actual rain. The shooting red liquid quickly covered his unattractive face and surgical gloves, resulting in his vision becoming impaired, and the slippery surface of blood on the operating room floor did not make matters any better. Tarawa-Li takes his bloody surgical gloves off in a hurry, wipes his red face with his bare hands and controls the bleeding of the female. His senses are confused; through his thin nostrils he smells the metallic smell of his death drill, he hears the thick consistency of the girl's blood dripping from her exposed eye socket to the operating room floor, and he can see the absolute carnage of what the operating room has become. Yes, bleeding does happen in torture, but it is a very rare occasion for a blood slip-n-slide show for only one eyeball removed.

He talked to himself once more, almost as if he were speaking in a ritual form, "I am an oculoplastic surgeon. My speciality is eyes. I have never seen someone bleed so much from one of my torture mechanisms before, maybe I should follow in my two brothers' footsteps when it comes down to this type of stuff. Maybe I should become a 'normal gangster' with guns, knives, drugs and beautiful women surrounding me. But I guess that wouldn't be life of a criminal surgeon. I would just be a false advertisement. I love to see them bleed anyway, and I guess my job is great; I just hating tasting it when it manages to get in my mouth."

Tarawa-Li finished with the second torture victim, deciding to dispose of her body by getting the security team to assist him with positioning her into a barrel for a third-party delivery team to dump somewhere in the sea. He releases his ponytail back into the normal greasy mess it was previously and was preparing to go back to the triad house, as he normally does.

When planning to leave, Tarawa-Li receives a text message from Atheno-Li, his Father, Chairman of the Maska Triad, and Head of all Triad Operations. The message read:

Tarawa, increase your percentage of national narcotic distribution. Last quarters analytics have come through and we are no longer the highest narcotics distributor in Korea, a god-damn Taiwanese owned triad is now in front! You have got to be kidding me! A Taiwanese triad in Korea? Those fellas must have some big balls. Anyways, increase your sales if you want to become the next chairman.

Also, a totally unrelated note, but I have arranged a family gathering for an important announcement. The gathering is tomorrow. Everyone is going to be there. Well, everyone important is going to be there.

CHAPTER TWO:
THE RESTAUARANT

The cool, calm dawn on an early October morning was the perfect timing for a criminal to initiate his daily deeds. The second of the three triplets, Dan-Li Maska, owned (due to his father's money) a small yet cosy seafood restaurant in the heart of Gangnam, named 'Fancy Fish'. It's the most common eatery for seafood lovers in the city, always given service with a smile, food that awakens the taste buds and very reasonable prices compared to the local competition.

Dan-Li, not only the owner of this delightful establishment and a proud graduate of the Korea Culinary School, also does his "side hustle" inside the very restaurant he owns. Since he has optimal control for every square metre of the restaurant, he has made sure to tactically position everything to his comfort. Now, it may come as no surprise at all that Dan-Li also has a "kill list" to complete each and every day. What may come to a surprise, however, is that he performs these dastardly acts on restaurant grounds, even when there are customers present only mere metres apart.

Many of the sick, wicked acts of crime occur in the owner's office, due to the fact it's always guarded with security members from the beloved triad. The room and entire hallway floor contain zero security cameras, and includes the space home to his favourite weapons among other goods such as drugs and cash. Second of all places where these acts occur is the staff restrooms. Many of 'chef's' staff work continuously, (due to the rush hour like traffic of customers) there is normally never a sight to see when entering the webby walls of death. Knives are the main forte for this perpetrator, with the latter including brass knuckles and barbed wire smothered baseball bats. The main dependant factor of the killings is how Dan-Li feels on the day. Does he want to invite the victim to dine for free in the guest suite with oversexualised K-pop idols on the same floor as his office? Or does he instead tamper with the victim's food (most likely an extreme laxative dosage) and wait for the victim to rush to the public bathrooms and then wait outside the customer bathrooms, then to guide them to the staff restrooms for some extra care? By those two choices of maximum insanity, you can then recognise what feeling Dan-Li is in today: angry or sadistic.

If, again, you're asking yourselves questions such as "Surely you will notice someone missing from the restaurant, either when the act is occurring or if one of their close friends or family files a missing person's report?" Well, my friend, this happens a lot actually. The only difference is that the Maska Triad are the anonymous owners of the Korean Police Department. The beginning of this transition caused a spectrum of kerfuffle, it's done and dusted now. It was purchased roughly a decade ago for a whopping 500 trillion won. In actual fact the triad even attempted to buy the Vietnamese and Taiwanese departments, respectively, although this resulted in a failure. The expansion of the triad to these named countries never entailed in its proposed journey. If anyone reports a missing persons case to the Korean Police Department (or any criminal case in that matter) that involves buildings, people or services with any involvement with the triad, they will never be followed through or entered in the department's logs or databases.

Dan-Li finally finishes his commute and enters the lively and bright seafood restaurant he adores. Wearing a big smile on his small head, his black wavy hair dragged backwards, his trimmed Van Dyke facial hair making him look like a samurai, his cross-like scar beaming all shades of red around his left ear lobe. This man was ready. Not only to make money in the underworld, no, not at all: Dan-Li was ready to increase his profit margins with the greatest place he loved more than home, his seafood restaurant.

Whilst greeting the always satisfied regulars, he analyses his surroundings for any peculiar or unrecognised guests. He quickly approaches one of his waitresses before heading up to his office to seek his daily schedule.

"How many shrimp and scallop combinations have we sold this morning already?" Dan-Li asked.

"45 sir... I still don't know how so many people can eat seafood like this so early in the morning!" The waitress replied.

"Answer that question again when you're an elderly man with a retired life." Dan-Li chuckled, "Anyways, I'm heading up to my office now. Don't bother me unless it's something urgent, understand?"

"Yes, sir." The waitress replied.

He quickly walks up the squeaky, wooden, unmaintained stairs to go into his lair of evil, as he himself likes to refer to the place. With the second floor, as normal, the four security members guard the office and hallway. These "security members" never seem to last too long, so the Maska Triad decided upon themselves to never acknowledge their security detail by name, as they portray them to be worthless and irrelevant, only helping to serve a greater good to mankind. He opens his wooden door, asking as normal to be left alone unless an emergency occurs. There, placed on his unstable, cheap and unreliable object known to some as a 'desk', lay the daily agenda of his "kill list".

He takes a glance of who his daily victims are and decides on how his game plan for today will outcome.

<u>Kill List</u>

Name: Kung-Muni Choi

Age: 23

Occupation: Banker

Incident: Assault of three elderly men, two pregnant women and a disabled man

Payment: 20 million won

Payee: Former employer at the bank he used to work, was fired from his position after the allegations spread into the workplace

Request: I have requested your services before, so I know you guys easily get the job done, thanks again

Name: Jason Holland

Age: 18

Occupation: Intern Engineer

Incident: N/A

Payment: 50 million won

Payee: Unknown - I.P traces to a small town in Taiwan

Request: Let's see if you guys really live up to the job you claim

He checked the list again, and again, and again, and again.

"Must be a quiet day at the office." Dan-Li chuckled once more, but one name did catch his attention perhaps more than it should have. "Jason Holland.... Why does that name sound so familiar to me? Do I know this kid?"

He shook his head to stop thinking about whether he knew him or not. That's the worst thing you could do when you're a contract killer.

"Shit- I better not get myself into that zone again. Whoever payed 50 million won for this kid to be dead must want him dead really bad, so in turn, this kid must have done really bad." Dan-Li said to himself, closing his eyes. "Do not overthink this name. You are a master; you are a god! You can do anything you put your mind to. You are going to be the next Maska Triad Chairman, because you are inevitable."

Dan-Li decides on the office approach, enticing the victims with a free premium upgrade of dining, letting them enjoy the company of slutty idols (who were actually working girls hired by the triad) and free alcohol to accompany such a delight. He alerts his security detail, claiming today as an 'angry day,' and waits for his first victim to arrive. Whilst waiting a few minutes, his first victim came inside.

Kung-Muni Choi enters, with his nappy ginger afro-style haircut, a large nose with a slight crooked angle to his left side and a wart that looks to be spewing some form of liquid out of it. He already looks drunk or on some form of a substance, the saliva spewing out of the right corner of his mouth, his mumbled dialect and his pupils widely enlarged. This may be an easy kill for the Chef. He was notified by his minions about the victim entering and quickly signals to entice him with the free alcohol and girls. He enters his weapons wardrobe and there behold a vast array of choices for the kill.

"Brass knuckles for this one, I think!" Dan-Li said, picking up his desired weapon, "Since this punk is already drunk as a skunk, I think I'm going to have some fun with this one."

Whilst he was just approaching the finish of his weapons choice, his victim was enjoying the fine dining of the seafood establishment. The mouth-watering shrimp with garlic sauce, the flavoursome crab soup, the delicious lobster ravioli. It seemed like the aggressive banker achieved a lucky haven in his otherwise down-in-the-dumps life. Two beautiful girls in disguise of the triad fed him the food like he was royalty. The free bucketload of champagne tingled his taste buds additionally, and the comfy fine dining seats improved the ongoing back problem that he suffered from. This was to go on for approximately a quarter hour long, until the Banker was about to black out.

With the victim nearly blacked out, the girls left the room. Uneaten plates of seafood, open cans of beer and corked out champagne bottles flooded the area. Dan-Li enters the untidy space, with brass knuckles attached on his right wrist and a swiss army knife in his back pocket. Kung-Muni Choi, barely able to open his eyes, realised what his destiny was about to come. Unable to react due to his unresponsive system, he becomes standstill and waits for his death. Dan-Li stays silent and hits a knockout blow with his right-hand, locking onto the crooked nose of the victim. Then another blow with the brass knuckle loaded hand, this time breaking the jaw of the banker.

"You think that I'm the bad guy, huh, punk?" Dan-Li shouted, "You assaulted the elderly, you assaulted the pregnant, you assaulted the disabled! You get a unique experience today; you get to feel the sharpness of my swiss army knife!"

Dan-Li grabs the army knife from out of his back-jean pocket and slashes the banker's cheekbone. The deep laceration makes the skeletal frame visible to the naked eye. Another slash of the army knife, this time targeting the trachea. Kung-Muni Choi was deceased at this point, but Dan-Li was not finished with him. He takes the bloody metal brass knuckles off his scrawny right jaw and holds the army knife in a two-hand grip. With all his power, he uses the knife to carve lettering on the target. The dead body not only resulted in an absolute deformed nose, but also a cracked jaw which was never likely to be completely fixed, and a visible cheekbone with pouring blood and a dislodged trachea.

Using his knife, he carved a message into the body. It read: STUPID PUNK

He then left the room of murder. The security team disposed of the traumatic mess of the body, the waitresses quickly cleaned, and the triad working girls were waiting to entice the next victim. It became the waiting game again.

Another half hour went by and finally the second victim of the "kill list" entered. Wearing an orange designer sweater, skinny black jeans, and luminous orange footwear, sporting a luxury diamond watch and necklace, this target was notable in comparison to the norm of targets the restaurant would see in the morning.

"It sure is admirable how my father manages to always get daily victims to visit the restaurant for my benefit." Dan-Li said to himself.

With Jason Holland already being escorted to the second floor by the beautiful girls, with the fine dining room cleaned and ready for next use, it was again time for another restaurant murder. With no signs of being intoxicated or a lack of intelligence, Dan-Li already guaranteed this is going to be more difficult than the previous murder he committed not even an hour ago. He opened his weapons wardrobe once again and pondered on his choice this time, whether to take a cool approach with a simple pocketknife or take an insane approach with an axe contaminated with other victims' blood and demolished organs. He managed to reach a conclusion and decided to meet his contradicting voices in his head straight down the middle by choosing one of his favourites, his barbed-wire baseball bat.

In the fine dining room, the next victim was enjoying the company of the beautiful girls. He was a very lonely person most of the time, working triple the maximum hours a week someone of his age legally should. Intel discovered he had recently moved to Korea from the USA roughly only two months ago, with his sister and father after their mother passing away about a year ago. Whilst he was enjoying a mouthful of prawn and noodles, listening to one of the girls talk about her car problems, the Chef storms in, holding his prized-possession barbed-wire bat. Both girls immediately swarm out of the room, leaving only the hunter and prey together, once again in a now-locked soundproof room.

“Who are you?” Jason Holland asked.

"I am the person who will be sharing your last living moments with." Dan-Li said and smirked. "You are a wanted man, Jason Holland."

"How do you know my name?" Jason Holland asked.

Dan-Li just stared at the poor young boy for a few frightening seconds and began to smile. He rushes to the teenager, swinging the bat of death at the target, but failing. The intern engineer paces swiftly to the locked door, rapidly attempting to open it and save himself. Unable to open the locked door, the boy turns around, realising he has become trapped with the murderer waving his bat at the poor soul and nowhere to run.

"Sorry kid, it's just business." Dan-Li shouted.

After swinging the bat successfully this time, the barbed wire latched onto the teenagers' fleshy skin in a heartbeat. The beat-down continued for a good few minutes, with the victim becoming a liquefiable blood bath amassed with his vomit and spit. Dan-Li stopped the vicious attack, looking at his flesh covered bat and the near walls with the boy's blood covered handprints from when he still had hope to escape. The fine dining room looked identical to one of Tarawa-Li's operating rooms at the near hospital.

He went to the private bathroom to wash up, whilst the security were attempting to bring the remains of the dead body together to contain and then dispose. Whilst that was going on, the working girls were helping the security team out by going through a mass amount of cleaning products to remove any signs of human torture. After getting cleaned up, Dan-Li was about to go back to the house, when all of a sudden he received a new text message via his smartphone. It was from Atheno-Li.

Dan-Li, I know it must have been a tough day for you, since Jason Holland was indeed the son of the new Maska Triad Lawyer and the younger brother of Jing-Lee's girlfriend Zara. Some punk paid big money to see the little guy go, so he must have done something bad! Anyways, I heard that he was distant from his father and sister due to their mother dying, so do not feel too bad! Obviously, no need to mention about keeping the victim just as confidential as the others. Money is money, he was never even truly part of the family!

Just to let you know, I have arranged a family gathering for an important announcement. The gathering is tomorrow. Everyone is going to be there. Well, everyone important is going to be there.

He froze. Shocked at what he had just read, his whole body begins to stumble, making him fall down the restaurants harsh surfaced stairs. He lays there, stationary, unable to put into words about what has now become the harsh reality of a death so close to the family. With his father notifying him via text message, just like it is another day at the office, Dan-Li begins to feel intoxicated with masses of emotion. Anger towards his father, sadness towards his brother and regret towards himself. Has this really become his sadistic life? Killing anyone for money that is not even needed for the family anymore?

One thing is for sure, Dan-Li knew if he became the new Chairman, he would only kill for fine reasoning, not for some extra pocket money. Taking a few more minutes to meditate on the stairs before it took a security guard to ask about the man's wellbeing, Dan-Li heads home, undecided upon how he truly will act with the news of the victim being so close to his brother and other triad members.

"How could my father make me kill my brother's girlfriends' younger brother?" Dan-Li whispered.

CHAPTER THREE: THE AIRPORT

The cool, calm dawn on an early October morning was the perfect timing for a criminal to initiate his daily deeds. Jing-Lee, the highest prospect out of himself and his two brothers to ever become the next Chairman, was sitting down on his black leather office chair, drinking his daily cup of coffee.

Dressed in an all-black suit, the clothing and his appearance ironically resembles the grim reaper, especially when he has his death-like venting resting expression on his pale face. Unbeknown to some people, the grim reaper is the character they will have their first and last conversation with when visiting Korea.

Due to his sheer intelligence, being a trained aviation pilot, having a degree in aviation engineering, an air traffic controller and Head of Security Management and Immigration & Customs, the man some call 'Aero' really makes the most out of his daily life. That's not the only impressive content regarding this man and his resume: he can speak seven languages fluently – including Korean, Japanese, Mandarin, English, Arabic, Turkish and Norwegian – is a well-trained computing hacker and can even run a pace equivalent to an Olympic athlete. He is the complete package - making something such as "airport assassinations" sound like a low-key hobby for the guy.

He is the stereotypical gangster when it comes to his version of violence, though. He likes his guns, pistols especially, if they include silencing material to aid his stealth. Not only this, but he also has multiple secret businesses that are non-affiliated with the family triad. This has gone on for many years, too, without any suspicion of wrongdoing (as the sacred family rule prohibits such actions). From worldwide cocaine distribution to human trafficking, from owning his own private islands around the coast of Taiwan and New Zealand – all the way to mass murders of politicians, this is what you call 'seeing the bigger picture'.

Jing-Lee loves his girlfriend too; she is most likely the only person who he will ever fully listen to. They met a few months ago whilst she overheard Jing-Lee speaking blasphemy to a colleague in the immigration & customs department, where the man apologised in an instance and ending up gaining the phone number of the pretty girl. Since then, he made an eternal promise to keep her safe and happy, making her life filled with intrigue and adventure. The happy couple always met in a family-owned restaurant for dinner every single night together.

Having a life sounding like a movie, there's no surprise about how arrogant this man could get, especially in the different methods he experiments with when killing whoever's name is on the list of death.

Jing-Lee finishes his morning cup of coffee, placing it in the ever-so-filled trash heap besides his desktop computer. He quickly fiddles around with the daily national news, business stocks and weather, before reading his e-mails. Nothing new on that front, Jing-Lee perfects his short black hair to maintain his professional scary appearance, waiting for the list with the people he must kill on this fine day. Approaching the normal time of day he receives the list, a loud knock on his office door occurs.

"Come in." Jing-Lee shouted.

"Sorry to bother you sir, but there's a suspicious looking family in my office. They claim to only speak Mandarin, any chance you can give me a hand?" The colleague asked, coming into the office.

"Sure. Do you know where they are from, why they are suspicious, any prior convictions?" Jing-Lee asked.

"I believe they are all members of the Takani Triad. You know, the triad from Taiwan making their name in Korea nowadays?" The colleague stated.

Jing-Lee's eyes widen, and he swiftly leaves his office to rapidly approach the suspected criminals and most importantly, the main competition the family triad has seen in a prolonged time period.

He opens the office door wide, where the suspects are all sitting on the floor. In this room lay five Taiwanese males, all almost identical in every feature possible. All five men had the same brown hair swayed to their left side, the same darkish skin tone, big brown eyes, rotten yellow teeth that smelled like a year-old fish stew one would serve in prison, the same unbranded black cap to perhaps evade from security cameras, and they all carried with them fraudulent passports and identities. None of these men seemed like they were open to the idea of conversing with Jing-Lee, with all of them gazing at the man with dissatisfaction in their eyes. He motions for his colleague to exit his office so the man could talk Mandarin with the five men himself. When his colleague left the room, the five men stand together in unison, each of them clenching their fists, clicking their necks and actioning for some wanted violence, until one of the Taiwanese men steps forward from the rest of the pack.

“Let us into this fucking country and you’ll be able to live and continue to see your family and friends.” The Taiwanese man demanded.

“Ooh, five against one. This is going to be more of a treat than what my girlfriend gives me on my birthday!” Jing-Lee replied.

“We know exactly who you are. You and your stupid family have been the richest anonymous group of people in this world for a long time, but the Takani Triad is new blood and no matter what, we get our own way, punk.” The Taiwanese man said.

“What’s your name?” Jing-Lee asked, impressed that the mystery man knew that much.

“Sure, I’ll give you the benefit of the doubt as you’re the one who’s going to die. My name is Daro.” Daro answered.

“Hello Daro, nice to finally make your acquaintance. I am your grim reaper for today.” Jing-Lee chuckled.

“You are one funny person, considering you’re a dead man.” Daro chuckled.

“Unfortunately, I will not let that happen today. Instead, the Takani Triad will be losing five of their members, gladly for them its only five irrelevant yes-men.” Jing-Lee said.

“I think I’ve had enough of you talking. Let’s put this asshole to sleep!” Daro shouted.

“What’s with the bad language?” Jing-Lee sarcastically said.

The five men approached him with great speed and brute force, with the first man to approach Jing-Lee to get a knockout blow, hitting the corner of the right side of his head on his way down. The second man managed to send an impactful punch to the throat of Jing-Lee. After half a second of allowing the pain to sink in, the second man received a brutal takedown with a bonus of a crackled fracture of the man’s spine on the downforce to the solid office floor. The third man managed to strike a few mild punches to the already injured throat and a couple barely reaching the face, until he awaited his known fate. It was Aero rotating his neck 360 degrees until the pop and crack sound occurred. The fourth man had obvious martial arts experience, gaining the office wall for aid in some of the wall kicks he was attempting, which was very soon over as Jing-Lee kicked through the man’s skull with so much strength, the whole cranium was entirely detached from his body. The room was down to two, Jing-Lee and Daro. Jing-Lee looked almost unaffected, except from a small red mark where his trachea lay, the black suit perfectly intact as was his hair. The arrogant man even had time to smile about the four men trying to attempt to kill him.

"Not bad, punk," Daro said.

The moment to talk was irrelevant, the moment to kill was as bright as day. Reaching into his inside blazer pocket, he brings out his silenced pistol. Only to await him was Daro already aiming his pistol at the face of Jing-Lee. This situation was alarming and eye-opening; how was the weapon not confiscated on his departure? This has never happened to the most intelligent brother, ever. Was his future about to come to a tragic halt, just like that? Daro, still pointing his pistol that was directed in the path of Jing-Lee's now anxious but still pale face, decides to give a lecture.

"I have so many friends in Korea nowadays. You see, your family may own nearly everything in this country, but one thing you can never possess is the people." Daro said.

"Koreans never trust Taiwanese people; it is what it is. There's nothing you can do to change that." Jing-Lee chuckled.

"You cannot live in the past if you want to live in the present, if you want to live in the future. If you interrupt me one more time, I won't even give you this amazing opportunity of hearing me speak." Daro answered.

"Go on." Jing-Lee replied.

"The day will come when you and your whole stupid family will be caught off-guard, whether it's the members of our triad, or the members of your triad, the tables are about to turn majorly in our favour very soon. I suggest you to really appreciate your life, it won't last long." Daro counselled.

With the lack of focus and not living in the present, Jing-Lee manages to whip his silenced pistol out of his black blazer inside pocket, shooting multiple bullets towards Daro and jumping to the right to avoid any backfire. He was successful, Daro received multiple bullets to his head, throat and heart, instantly killing him. Daro still had an open mouth and his gun was still held in his right hand, hot as an oven, sitting dead. Jing-Lee disposed of the man's firearm, closed the daredevil's saliva-filled mouth giving home to a bunch of rotten yellow teeth, and smiled.

"You talk too much." Jing-Lee said.

With his colleague's compact office room playing the role of murder house, decapitated bodies left to right, Jing-Lee puts his pistol back into his inside pocket and leaves the room. When leaving the office, he walks past his colleague.

"So, did they speak Mandarin?" The colleague asked.

"Not any longer." Jing-Lee replied.

"I know what that means. I'll use the spare office for now then." The colleague chuckled.

Jing-Lee returns to his office, takes off his clothes for a quick shower (not ever liking to be sweaty on the job). He showers for ten minutes, gets changed into a new suit that his girlfriend bought him last week, styles his hair back into the handsome way he always desires, and checks any work related e-mails, as the list he receives for his killings can be either on his phone or work computer. Finally, after a tiresome morning with a mild killing spree sprinkled in for good measure, the daily list finally came.

<u>Kill List</u>

Name: Yousef Nahmi

Age: 37

Occupation: Lawyer

Incident: Attempted legal action against Maska Triad – former triad employee

Payment: None (Maska Triad Exempt)

Payee: N/A

Request: Be safe not sorry, easiest way to kill is via Immigration & Customs office. This will be on your hands if you risk another method to inflate your cocky ego [Flight Number: 264]

Name: Je-Song Kim

Age: 63

Occupation: Aviation Pilot

Incident: Has a huge life insurance fund, wife is too impatient to keep waiting

Payment: 17 million won

Payee: Vienna Stockdon

Request: Please just make it look like an accident [Flight Number 422]

"Would have been a quiet day at the office, if it wasn't for those Taiwanese punks." Jing-Lee said.

He opens his flight tracking software, entering the flight numbers in chronological order and glugging down his second cup full of hot coffee. Viewing Flight 264, he makes a discovery. Instant outrage occurs, realising the plane arrived at the Korean airport nearly an hour ago. Full of disgust, there was no time to sit and cry about it. Running out of the office in his brand new designer suit, this time with a buttoned white shirt, black trousers, black blazer and a ruby red tie, more of a hitman like dress-up in comparison to a grim reaper, Jing-Lee rushes to ask his colleague if he has seen the top target for the day.

“Have you seen an Egyptian guy recently?” Jing-Lee asked.

“Well, considering I was on passport control for a flight from Egypt not so long ago, I’m going to say no.” The Colleague said.

“No time for fun and games! I need you to help me track a guy called Yousef Nahmi, lawyer in his late thirties.” Jing-Lee replied.

“That’s the same thing the Korean Investigation Unit asked me to do earlier, strange that.” The Colleague stated.

“Don’t tell me that you let that man go into the hands of the only organisation my family doesn’t own!” Jing-Lee shouted.

"Calm down, the man never showed on his flight, he's still in Egypt, probably." The Colleague answered.

"That's one thing my father can never tolerate, a failed mission...thanks anyway." Jing-Lee mumbled.

"Not a problem, who were those Taiwanese guys earlier, if you don't mind me asking? Are they Takani guys?" The Colleague asked.

"If you ask me another question on the topic you can meet them in person. Just not in this world, in hell instead." Jing-Lee answered.

"No, thanks. Go back to your office, if I get any news on the Egyptian lawyer, I'll let you know." The Colleague said.

Jing-Lee quietly leaves the office to return to his own, playing with his eyebrows as the usual bad habit to cope as a stress relieving mechanism. He browses on his computer again to search for Flight 422, noting to himself of the arrival time, as it was not for about another hour. Time management and experience suggests that since the target is the pilot of the flight himself, it will most likely be a less surrounded area, which makes the situation more of a bliss to enjoy.

He turns his computer off, walks himself in front of the big glass mirror next to his desk and glances upon himself, contemplating the repercussions for not being able to kill one of the names on his list. No matter what the reason for failure is, failure is not taken lightly by the Chairman. It usually results in a form of punishment for whoever could not get the job done. He knew however that due to the sheer complexity of being an airport assassin, his father would never give him the full treatment compared to his other two brothers. In fact, it is no surprise to anyone that Jing-Lee is the Chairman's favourite son. The most handsome, the most charming, the most driven, the most intellectual, the most resilient, the most determined, the most optimistic. If the Maska Triad was in the public eye at all, even the general public would know that he has the most promising future compared to his two brothers, which is why Jing-Lee is so arrogant. He knows it too.

Now laying down on his comfy two-seater black leather couch, drinking a third coffee for the day, he begins to ponder about what the Taiwanese man said to him before he blew his brains out. Does the Takani Triad know something we need to? Are they planning an attack on the Maska Triad? How do they have intel on the most secretive and wealthy triad in the world, the only notable Korean triad left? All these thoughts and more entered his head, giving him a migraine thinking about all of these different scenarios, producing mass amounts of paranoia. He finished the last of his coffee, laid on the couch and rested his eyes for some moments, trying to release any upheaval caused in his feelings and replacing them with calm and collected thoughts.

He napped for a near hour. In panic, realising his next target was most likely in the airport by now. He rushed off the couch to sit at his office desk, almost tripping at the couch corner with the instant amount of adrenaline that he had gained. The flight has only just concluded, arriving at the airport a few minutes ago. Aero makes sure to tactically position himself to guarantee he has a clear and consistent view of the target. Soon enough, the Pilot was spotted. He was roughly 5 feet tall, very chubby with a double-chin or even a triple-chin in some angles, short grey bristles of hair only on the front portion of his wrinkled head, big watery brown eyes with a non-existent smile. It was almost like he was screaming a ‘my wife only wants me for my money’ look. The Pilot, looking the most depressed a man could ever be, waddles slowly to his destination, or so he thought. With the surroundings being as empty as can be, Jing-Lee approaches his next target.

“Je-Song Kim, how are you?” Jing-Lee beamed enthusiastically.

"Sorry pal, I have lots of trouble nowadays with my memory, who are you?" Je-Song asked.

"Oh come on, you know exactly who I am!" Jing-Lee chuckled.

"I'm really sorry, but I don't remember you. Especially being a pilot doesn't help the cause, I see so many faces each day of my life. I have been one for four decades!" Je-Song chuckled.

"How about a whiskey in my office, you may remember me if we chat like the good old times?" Jing-Lee beamed.

"Sure, why not, it's not like I have anyone in my life who loves me anymore. Let's drink until we blackout!" Je-Song approved.

An hour later, with his office filled with empty alcohol bottles, flamed out cigarette butts and pills, any small chance for the target to survive was dead in the water. He felt a sense of guilt regarding the life of this one target, a well-off pilot devoting his entire life to the aviation industry, all for it to be lost because his gold-digger wife wants the money he has spent his entire life into earning for a nice retirement? Letting the man enjoy his last moments, drinking from the bottle, smoking the finest tobacco, taking ecstasy, it was almost like he was living like he wanted to die.

The target was unresponsive and defenceless like a little baby. He laid on that very same leather couch Jing-Lee was resting on earlier in the day. He adamantly pulls out his silenced pistol from his inside blazer pocket and shoots the target dead. One bullet in the skull, one in the heart for good measure.

“Hopefully, you will have better luck in your next life, cap.” Jing-Lee whispers.

Staring at the dead man, Jing-Lee thinks once more about his life. Is love real? Is friendship real? Is family real? What is the purpose of life? What is right? What is wrong? The mixed emotions swarm in his mind once more, making him become queasy and dizzy. He leaves his office. Checking his phone, Jing-Lee realises he has a new message.

Jing, it turns out that shitbag lawyer, Yousef Nahmi, is dead. He killed himself apparently, although there is a great likelihood of him being murdered, as there were many people around the world who wanted that man to be gone. Also, is it true this morning you had an incident with some of the fresh blood in town? The Takani Triad? Did you make them spit any details of their daily operations? What do they know about us?

Actually, you know what, we all have better lives to live and not to hide or fear regarding an enemy. Let us be. Let's not murder anymore of them yet, let's hear a triad out for once, you know, unless they try to murder you for sport again.

Just to let you know, I have arranged a family gathering for an important announcement. The gathering is tomorrow. Everyone is going to be there. Well, everyone important is going to be there.

All my love,

Atheno-Li

CHAPTER FOUR: THE FAMILY GATHERING

The next morning quickly arose, where the three triplets were anticipating either a catastrophic or spectacular announcement from their father. He would never gather everyone for a family meeting if the news wasn't worth it.

The main reason why the Maska Triad are never distinguished as rich folk is the fact that the exterior of their property never holds home to lavish sports cars or security guards. Instead there were old, rotten, and overgrown weeds. All of the properties they live in are never more than two floors high and the tinted windows help them with their disguise.

Members are only allowed to own clothing, jewellery, vehicles, individual properties and other miscellaneous items if the pricing of them is equivalent to what a regular city commuter can earn or realistically loan on a salary.

One of the most sacred rules which every single person involved must comply to: surprise the people around you by what's contained inside you and not your outer shell. A pretty coating will never see true greatness within themselves. Tarawa-Li especially doesn't even think the damn thing makes any sense, he just pays extra attention to it, as he loves to express his spiritual side (you know, when he's not drilling out eyeballs).

Now, you may think since the main home of the Maska Triad is surrounded by an overbearing amount of brown, disgusting leaves, it's an ugly site to see. However, the architectural masterpiece is what is inside of the dull exterior. The beautiful home contains six king-size bedrooms that include a wonderful traditional style en suite and their own entertainment centre full of the latest technology, brought to them by an experimental tech company they own. The surrounding greenery is a wonderful sight to behold too, with a whole assortment of Korean plants and flowers. A huge wooden table with a dozen of wooden chairs all painted in an ice white colour was the mainstay for the family dining room, with oil paintings of each former chairman surrounding the four ivory coloured walls. The lounging area had the most exquisite attraction of them all, possessing a diamond covered chandelier, stolen from a former Chinese president's home many decades ago. That even became a published news story, printed on front page national Chinese newspapers. The lounging room also consisted of comfortable fluffy chairs and a coffee table, with the main purpose to engage socially with one another, avoiding the use of modern-day social media on phones. Lastly, but not least, were the escape tunnels, with the extension being added by the current Chairman, most likely due to increased paranoia from watching too many crime documentaries and dramas.

The family gathering had begun, with each relevant member who was invited sitting on the cool wooden floor, cross-legged with the chairman standing, as usual.

To the farthest left was Tarawa-Li, or as you may know him, the lunatic triplet. Wearing a casual white tee, denim jeans and barefoot, he was just waiting for whatever news this was, hoping it's not regarding the multiple personality disorder diagnosis from the test results he received last month.

To the right of the 'Surgeon' was his brother, Dan-Li. Dan-Li appeared to be emotionless, staring into a pit of death, wanting to be put down. He was wearing a black sweater, black jeans and black socks, not only feeling like death, wanting death, but also looking like and representing death. He has improved controlling his dark emotions since the incident yesterday, just hoping for no mention of it in the announcement today. Then again, Jing-Lee would kill him if he found out about yesterday's actions, and considering he wants to die, he began to be open to the announcement.

To the right of the 'Chef', the last of three brothers, the highest family prospect, sat Jing-Lee. This time sporting a maroon plaid suit (blazer and trousers), ice white buttoned up shirt and designer footwear, smiling, knowing he never gets punished by his father for his outrageous fashion choices, or for anything. Although in a visible state of seeming merry, he was indeed still in a great state of awe. Many, many overbearing thoughts in his precious mind make him to become dizzy once again. Takani Triad? Breaking the sacred rule regarding external business not associated with the family? New wife? All of these included in the scrambled mind of the most intelligent triplet.

To the right of 'Aero' was Yung-Ko Jang. The man in his late forties was of Chinese descent, working with the Maska Triad for over a decade now. Being muscular and 5 feet 9 inches tall, fairly tall for a Chinese man, he can definitely become a nightmare if you piss him off. Before working with the Maska Triad, he was a detective for the Korean Police

Department, solving a record amount of criminal cases in only a few years of being on the job. Shortly after his third year, he was offered the role of Head of Surveillance and Strategy for the Maska Triad. In quick fashion, the transition from detective to preventing any evidence for a crime scene became second nature to the man. He sat with the three triplets, only hoping for the announcement to not be about his recent lateness. He has loved this job right from the start and the passion is still equal in comparison from his very first day.

To the farthest right was Derrick Holland, lawyer for the Maska Triad (Father to Jing-Lee's girlfriend Zara Holland and recently deceased son Jason Holland, who was killed by Dan-Li). Being the newest official member of the Maska Triad, any negative energy is always directed into this man's way. 6 feet 3 inches tall, skinhead, full of arm tattoos and gold teeth, yet the man is easily the most insecure and vulnerable out of each and every one of them. Why? He's the outsider, with so much still yet to prove. Wearing his go-to white shirt with red stripes, brown trousers and black shoes. The man was just hoping this gathering would be finished sooner rather than later, so he could finish up some legal work with a few of the overseas businesses.

The last to mention member was the most important one of all, Chairman of the Maska Triad, Atheno-Li Maska. Standing there, only 5 feet 2 inches tall, full thick grey hair spiked up, wrinkles coating up every part of his aging face, he just smiled, appreciative of each member in the room right now. Atheno-Li and his late wife had these triplets at an age significantly older than the norm, but they were both so glad to have them. Wearing his usual attire, brown shoes made out of wicker material, brown trousers and blazer, with a black shirt, top button open for his breathing not to play up, he began to read the speech he had prepared for them all.

"Thank you everyone for being here on this fine morning. As you know, I never like to beat around the bush, so I'll get straight to the point. I have been living with an undisclosed illness for a few months now, hoping it was soon to evade away. Unfortunately, I must announce that I have terminal cancer. So in result of this, I must find the most suitable replacement for the role of Chairman of the Maska Triad. In order to do this, I have no choice but to put my three sons into an indefinite suspension with the jobs at the restaurant, surgery and airport, respectively. Not only this, but I am stripping yourselves of your personal properties, vehicles and weapons. I must ensure the next Chairman is competent in keeping the business out of the public eye, working anonymously and without a digital footprint. There is a reason we are the only remaining triad from Korean origin, and for as long as I walk on this planet, this legacy will continue! If you think a true gangster is fully dependant on his gun to succeed, then I have failed you as a father. A successful gangster only needs the two bare essentials to keep his business running: fists and persuasion. The next Chairman will be whoever can agree a deal to purchase this well-recognised company in the only major industry we have not dominated in. The sole leader in revenue, Korea's finest plastic surgery company, PlaciCorp, owned by none other than the Takani Triad. Buy PlaciCorp, you not only eject the single rivals we have in Korea, but you also become the Chairman of the Maska Triad. It's your choice if you three want to work together or individually, but if you all fail, then you have all failed me as sons. If you are true gangsters of Gangnam, all you need is to know how to fight and know how to cut a deal, hopefully in the other way around though. Yung-Ko Jang will help you with any intel you desire and all information regarding PlaciCorp, with Derrick giving you any legal advice at your request and any legal paperwork that is required. If I see any of you with your damn drills or brass knuckles or hippie pistols, then you are automatically disqualified in the race for Chairman. If two of you secure a deal or the three of you together, I will set up another challenge for you to complete until there is only one sole survivor, proving himself the alpha male." Atheno-Li lectured.

Everyone sitting down was frozen from head to toe, unable to take in the event that has just been announced. The Chairman is dying. Palms begin to sweat profusely, lips start to vibrate up and down, tears start to run down each two cheeks swiftly, causing a waterfall of sorrowful emotion. With no-one able to respond to such an impactful statement, Atheno-Li leaves to rest on his bed, waiting for the dark day to arrive him.

The accomplished man had nothing to achieve anymore. He had made the Maska Triad financially stable for dozens of generations to come, and he trusts himself enough that one of the three kids he created can follow in his father's footsteps. When he became the Chairman for the first time in his life, he made an eternal promise to stride for greatness until greatness wasn't needed anymore. He consistently hustled. From performing armed robbery to bounty hunting, he made sure he would do whatever it took for the triad to be financially dependent, investing the stolen money into small up-and-coming independent businesses at first. A few years later he even met his future wife at one of the independent businesses' offices. The Maska Triad quickly became the fastest rising business, leading to the eventual purchases of such services as: the Korean Police Department, Korean Fire Department, Korean Ambulance Service, Korean Military and the Korean Marines. What truly is the greatest part about all of these purchases, however, is the fact that no one knows about the Maska Triad having any involvement with any of these services. The prime example of this is when he gained such powers, he made such amendments: calling one of these numbers would cost a fixed rate of 1,000 won a minute, requesting the police, fire or ambulance services would cost the customer 10,000 won and if any seen abuse was reported regarding the new amendments, a 10 million won fine. It's guaranteed to say that if any one person knew who made the changes, they still wouldn't be alive. Atheno-Li never wanted to kill for the sake of killing. The man was only aligned with making more money and power. He would only kill when necessary, such as a new business proposition getting declined or a derogatory comment towards his wife. But the man was simply just waiting to die now, in hope of one of his sons truly being competent to take over the role he has done for so many years.

Finally after several minutes of the five men sitting on the cold wooden floor in cold silence, Yung-Ko

Jang and Derrick Holland leave the triplets to talk about the colossal challenge that awaits each of them. Jing-Lee is still crying at an alarming rate, trying to wipe his tears out of each eye every second. Dan-Li just sits in complete silence, not knowing how to even talk at this point of time, whilst Tarawa-Li is having a complete insane breakdown, attempting to talk to each of his own personalities in that crazy head of his.

"Did you know about the illness?" Jing-Lee asked, attempting to hide his upset tone of voice.

"No." Tarawa-Li whispered in reply.

Dan-Li still unresponsive. He closes his eyes and attempts to meditate, trying to calm himself down from the news just received. To the left of him sat Tarawa-Li, who offers his right hand to hold onto for comfort. To the right of him sat Jing-Lee who offers his left hand to hold onto for comfort.

"Today we learn. Tomorrow we conquer. For today we are boys, for tomorrow we are men! For today we become ordinary once more, for tomorrow and onwards we are what we have always been, fucking gangsters." Jing-Lee said.

The three triplets rise from where they had sat, making their arrival to the dining room, as there was some leftover pork rinds and white rice from the night before. Refusing to be completely bummed out, the triplets try and make the most out of their companionship together, as they rarely got to enjoy a midweek midday meal. The last time in fact was several years ago. Plating themselves high of the fatty pork and stuck-together rice, the triplets began to talk about their childhood, to the times when their father was the most happiest, as their mother was still alive in those days.

"Do you remember when we visited Spain that one time, and I got lost and somehow managed to end up in Portugal?" Tarawa-Li chuckled.

"Yeah, I think that was the most worried look on our parents faces. There can't be any that beats that." Dan-Li chuckled.

"You guys clearly don't remember the time when I broke my elbow and I was in the hospital, but ending up getting a knee surgery instead, well, until the nurses realised it was indeed my elbow in the god-damn cast." Jing-Lee replied.

"How about that time on my ninth birthday when that elderly stripper knocked on our door saying someone had ordered for their services." Tarawa-Li chuckled.

"We've clearly all forgotten the time when we all accidentally released that poisonous scorpion into one of the bathrooms. That one was both funny and painful." Dan-Li replied.

Reminiscing on the good times of the past, the triplets eventually finish their big and helpful servings of meat and rice, just daydreaming, thinking about how simple times back then where, especially with their mother around to make Atheno-Li happy. They all agreed upon this day to be a celebration instead of a gloomy one, attributing all the good memories shared with one another and their ever-so-loved parents, the time to talk about business would wait until tomorrow.

The three also agree on spending time with their other loved ones in the evening, each man taking their respective partners to a local food stand or cart, appreciating the small moments in life with the people they care about.

Not much else happened during the day. The three went to their bedrooms to have a nap on their comfy king size beds, wanting to be refreshed for their dates this evening.

"I'm thinking of taking Zara to a food cart that's pretty much a steakhouse, if any of you want to join me for a double or triple date?" Jing-Lee asked.

“Thanks for the offer, but eating steak hurts my teeth. I think I’m going to opt for a smoothie bar.” Tarawa-Li replied.

“Sorry, me and Mallory are having a rough patch right now, so if I want this wedding to still take place then I need to resolve the issues we’ve been having as soon as possible.” Dan-Li replied.

The three gentlemen were wearing identical dashing suits, the classic black and white look. After some time to wash up and get ready, it was date night for all three.

CHAPTER FIVE: BABY FEVER

The first to leave out of the three was Tarawa-Li, who walks roughly two miles to visit his favourite smoothie bar in the city. The narrow streets were lit up with rainbow coloured lights, a dark starry sky, and a full moon glowing in its clear white fashion.

However, unlike his two other brothers, he wasn't actually meeting anyone at all. He loved to be alone in times of sadness and rumination, reflecting on his life choices. The Surgeon was typically a loner anyways, even though in the mind he had, he was never alone. He had many various conversations with various different people in that crazy head of his. The condition he had was worsening day by day, often plaguing his identity awareness.

He enters the small yet welcoming smoothie bar he has loved ever since he was a young child, often being taken after school by his late mother. The smoothie bar hadn't changed a bit over the years, the six wooden tables and chairs tightly fitted against each other, the squeaky-clean floor and service with a smile, Tarawa-Li always felt like he was in heaven when he visited this place.

“Hello madame, please may I have three cherry-kiwi smoothies?” Tarawa-Li asked.

“Sure, not a problem. My colleague is just going to get more kiwi, so take a seat and I’ll give you them once they’re ready.” The waitress replied.

He sat down at the first table closest to the entrance door, with his face looking to the outdoors, noticing a stranger’s pet dog. Tarawa-Li has loved animals, especially dogs, since as far as he remembers. On his sixth birthday, as a gift from his parents, he received a Korean mastiff (the biggest sized dog breed in Korea and the friendliest). The dog was named ‘Dae’, which means ‘greatness’ in Korea. He would do anything in the world as long as his best friend Dae would be by his side, until one day when everything changed. After visiting a business conference on a glum weekday night, his father had returned to the family home. Once returning, he was perplexed to see that his dog was attacking one of the security guards of the triad, who was often known for abusing his own pet. At an instant, Atheno-Li grabbed his safety knife out of his left trouser pocket and attacked his beloved pet. Dae received all of the brutal impact of the knife, dying in mere minutes, with Atheno-Li citing self-defence for his cause of attack, banishing any pets at the family house for an eternity.

Being completely in his thoughts, one of the staff members interrupted him for a short few seconds.

"Hello sir, sorry about the wait. Here are your three cherry-kiwi smoothies. Enjoy." The waitress said.

After being completely side-tracked for a few moments, he began slurping the brilliant concoction of the fresh fruits through the small plastic straw, being full of gratitude that this bar has never left his life.

Tarawa-Li knew he was always the oddball compared to his two other brothers. Once Dae had died, he began to lose purpose in his life and stopped communicating with the whole of humanity (except his mother and brothers) for three years. His psychological condition worsened from the day his father killed his dog, not only becoming temporarily mute but also being diagnosed with social anxiety disorder (irrational fear of being watched or judged).

"Even if I were the successful brother, managing to secure a deal with the Takani Triad to purchase PlaciCorp, my father wouldn't accept me as the next Chairman. He would announce a retry due to some bullshit excuse in that phony mind of his. I just know it." Tarawa-Li said to himself.

"What was that, sir?" The waitress shouted, thinking he had said something to her.

"I was talking to myself; I think." Tarawa-Li shouted back to reply.

Reflecting back on his father's announcement in the early morning, he realised he doesn't even want to be the next Chairman. Not only would the job title be too much pressure for the man in a psychological point of view, but he doesn't want to be anything like his father. Maybe he should just quit everything once his father passes away.

"Gangsters always carry guns, that's why they are called gangsters...plus, I can be disqualified if I don't want to be the next Chairman in the first place, idiot. Maybe I should even pull my gun out on you." Tarawa-Li whispered.

Before finishing his third and final feel-good smoothie that seemed to be crafted by angels, flashbacks of his mother appear right in front of his very eyes. Specifically, the same very summers' morning that his father and mother were on their way travelling to Hong Kong to celebrate their special anniversary, only for one parent to return back. He vividly remembers sobbing that morning, pleading for his mother not to leave him.

“Don’t worry my little cutie pie, Mamma is going to be back before you know it.” Mother comforted.

“You promise me, Mamma?” Tarawa-Li asked, weeping heavily.

“Of course I promise, dear. I’ll even make sure to bring you back an extra souvenir, just for you. Just don’t tell your brothers.” Mother replied.

“I won’t tell anyone Mamma; I love you so much.” Tarawa-Li cried.

“I love you to the moon and back, cutie pie. I promise you that I’m going to be fine, I promise you. I have to go now. Mamma will miss you, but she’ll be back before you know it.” Mother consoled.

“I’ll miss you.” Tarawa-Li sniffled.

“I’ll miss you too.” Mother sniffled.

The flashback had ended, and he was back again in the real world. The smoothie bar was about to close, so he finished his last flavoursome gulp and exited one of his favourite places. Tarawa-Li loved his mother, but knew being constantly fixated on the fact that she’s dead will continue his depression further.

Instead he focused on the present, the sound of the cool breeze delightfully clashing with the tall trees, the clearest night sky with the bright white moon, the smell of the freshest air in the city. Tarawa-Li knew he had to live in the present to make his mother proud of him, because living in the past, mourning the tragic loss over and over, would make his life just as dismal as the death itself. The Surgeon walked back home quietly with the smallest smile on his face.

The second of the three to leave the house for their own respective date night was Dan-Li with his future bride to be, Mallory Reece. Mallory was originally born in Australia, however, permanently moved to Korea to be with the love of her life. As a graduate of a degree in Geophysics, she is indeed an intelligent girl. Her long, auburn coloured hair, glimmering bright blue eyes, perfectly white teeth and hourglass figure meant not only she had the brains in the relationship, but the looks too. The couple are planning to get married very soon, as long as their bickering towards each other comes to an end.

They both decide to meet in a seafood restaurant, different to the one Dan-Li is normally used to. This seafood restaurant was only a few minutes' walk from the property, boasting a large open space, intimate lighting and live music from a delightful pianist. The food offered on the alluring menu looked even more spectacular to Dan-Li's restaurant, with him thinking to steal some of the ideas from this place to convert into his own, if somehow he doesn't become the next Chairman.

"Waitress, we would like to order now." Mallory stated.

"Sorry Madame, what would you two like to order?" The waitress replied politely.

"I'll have the water for drinks, the spicy fish stew for my first course, the glazed cod for my second. If the food is up to standard, I'll then order a dessert." Mallory stated.

"I'll have the white wine for drinks, braised octopus for my first course and the glazed cod for my second course, too. Thanks." Dan-Li said.

"Thank you." The waitress replied, leaving the two to be in peace.

"Been off the alcohol for a while now, how have you been finding it?" Dan-Li asked.

"Good, thanks. Though I find it unbelievable we're getting married soon but still not living together any day of the week." Mallory bickered.

“Can we talk about it another time and just enjoy the company of one another?” Dan-Li pleaded.

“You told me on the night you asked me to marry you that you would leave the life you were living and focus all of your energy on me. Was it all lies?” Mallory asked.

“My father has cancer, terminal too.” Dan-Li said.

“Why didn’t you tell me?” Mallory asked, with her angry expression instantly turning into a concerned and worried look.

“Me and my brothers only found out this morning. We decided to spend some quality time together, like the days of my childhood, just a few hours to forget any problems we had in the real world.” Dan-Li answered.

“A death of one person is a birth of another.” Mallory implied.

“What are you talking about?” Dan-Li replied.

“Well, giving you the obvious hints for months hasn’t helped you in realising, so I’m just going to tell you now.” Mallory said, “I’m pregnant.”

About to burst into a whole range of contrasting emotions that even Tarawa-Li would be impressed to experience, their first course and drinks arrive, rendering Dan-Li's crazy reaction to passive. Both plates of the scrumptious seafood dishes were a great sight to see, it was just significantly dampened due to the event that occurred sheer seconds ago.

"I want to be married to you, I want to have your kids, I want to spend the rest of my life with you. I just need you to leave that crime-filled life behind, so you can focus on the one thing you promised to commit to, me." Mallory expressed.

"I am a friendly yet fatal man." Dan-Li teased.

"What does that even mean, you fucking idiot?" Mallory challenged.

"I am a nice guy, but I am vindictive when someone takes something away from me or hurts someone or something that I have feelings for. I have feelings for you, I have feelings for my work, I have feelings for my family. I care about each of them, with you being my top priority. For someone to take me out completely from the work and family I love so much though, I would then turn into a vindictive person, a nightmare to live with, a nightmare to call your husband, a nightmare to call the father of our kid. This is where I have the solution. Let me marry you. Let me be the best father to our child. Believe in me to beat my brothers and to rightfully become the next Chairman of the Maska Triad, where I shall rule with an iron fist, with my wife and child beside me." Dan-Li said.

A few seconds passed by, and then Mallory responded. "I believe in you, iron fist. Although what you just said sounded like something you would hear in one of those lame and corny medieval war movies."

The seeming to be happy couple finish their delightful first courses, with their second courses now approaching them. Both of their plates included a perfectly cooked codfish, served with buttery potatoes and the freshest green vegetables, all locally sourced. The intense lighting made the conversation more intimate for the two and the pianist playing classic Korean romance music from the old-fashioned movies was also a bonus.

With no more ground-breaking news to report, the two decided to make small talk regarding their plans on the closely approaching wedding, their future child, and how delicious the food quality was in the restaurant, making him a tad jealous. After ordering a dessert to share and scoffing it down as quick as possible, they leave the fascinating eatery and go their separate ways back home.

The last of the three to leave the family house for their date night was Jing-Lee, meeting his girlfriend Zara.

Indeed the second of the triplet's partners was also a foreigner, and also just as intelligent. She had graduated out of one of the finest American institutions, taking home a degree in Liberal Arts. She was a stunning figure to look at too, with her supermodel like body, long black hair, addicting green eyes and a smile that could kill.

Before moving to Korea, her family was the most precious thing to her life. Tragedy struck when her mother passed away in an accident, so all remaining members decided to move to Korea to forget about the sadness that haunted them all, and to try and find happiness in a different place without the constant reminders of a mother being gone. Her father quickly managed to find work with the Maska Triad, with her old man being undefeated in his legal cases back home. Even though she has acknowledged each member of the triad and has visited the house, she didn't want any involvement with them, until she discovered that one member was the handsome man who she gave her phone number at the airport to. That man was now her boyfriend, Jing-Lee.

The young-in-love couple met each other at a local steakhouse that converted into a food cart in a densely popular area filled with masses of people and narrow roads. Being a food cart and many other people in the tight area, they had no choice but to enjoy their food standing in the cool breeze outside, which wasn't a problem for either one.

"Two waters, two mid-rare steak bowls with rice and special sauce, two napkins, please." Jing-Lee requested to the man behind the cart.

"You didn't let me choose." Zara replied.

"You trust me, don't you?" Jing-Lee grinned.

After several minutes of waiting for their incredible food, they received it, smiling with glee in an instant. They both tucked into their meals straight away, making sure they get forkfuls that contained the flavours of the steak and rice to complement each other's taste. Both of them were speechless for many minutes, just focusing on the tenderness and feel-good feeling of the amazing food in their mouths.

After finishing their meals and drinking their water, the couple begin to walk all around Gangnam, specifically in less occupied spaces for the two to converse better. They enter a massive-scale park and sit in a well-lit area with wooden benches, with no other person in a far-sighted radius. Even though the food they had just experienced was breath-taking, something seemed off with Zara.

“Is everything alright?” Jing-Lee asked.

“Yeah, it’s just.” Zara replied, taking in a deep sigh. “Nothing actually. Forget about it.”

“If I tell you something, will you tell me what’s bothering you?” Jing-Lee questioned.

“Seems like a fair deal.” Zara responded.

“My father is dying from terminal cancer. Although it’s not confirmed yet, I’m most likely going to be the new Chairman.” Jing-Lee admitted.

“I’m so sorry to hear about that, it’s truly horrible when a family member gets taken away from you so soon.” Zara cried in reply, “I remember when my mother died in front of my very eyes. Some Asian looking man shot her in broad daylight. I did nothing to stop the attack. I was so scared.”

“Princess, I’m so sorry that happened to you. Was that the incident which has been on your mind today? Does it feel better now that you’ve released some inner tension?” Jing-Lee asked.

“No, that wasn’t even what has been bothering me. Ever since my family moved to Korea to make a new life without my mother, trying to find a new place for new joy, I thought life with my family would return back to the good state it used to be. Instead, my dad is working so hard nowadays that I only get to see him every morning for breakfast and my brother too, he hasn't even returned home last night. I just hope he is okay." Zara worried.

"Firstly, I want to say sorry on my father's behalf, concerning your father's late hours. I'll promise him to stop forcing your dad to work so many hours each day, it's not ever okay to be overworked like that. With your brother, where does he work?" Jing-Lee replied.

"I can't remember, he's at some big company being one of the newly-trained up engineers to help them fix their machines." Zara answered.

"An engineer, correct?" Jing-Lee clarified.

"Correct. I just hope everything is fine. I just worry so much because I'm his big sister, it's our jobs to worry about family, especially younger brothers. He means the world to me." Zara replied.

"You definitely do sound like a great big sister. I wish my brothers were like that with me all the time. Then again, I'm the most handsome out of all of them, so I'll make that the reason why they hate my guts some days." Jing-Lee chuckled to try and lighten the mood a little.

"I remember the place my brother works." Zara interrupted.

"Where?" Jing-Lee asked.

"It's a place called PlaciCorp." Zara answered.

CHAPTER SIX:
FISTS AND PERSUASION

The next day arose, with all three brothers ready to make an impact in one way or another. Yung-Ko Jang was in his usual office workspace, inviting the three to discuss the best strategy to land the PlaciCorp deal. His detailed intel regarding the PlaciCorp company was five folders full, containing a good few several hundreds of pages, regarding former presidents, projects, surgeries, clients, profits etc.

PlaciCorp was one of the main companies in Korea that increased the amount of Gangnam beauties in the city (a euphemism for a girl who looks completely plastic) in the past recent years. They offer surgeries such as: breast enhancement, facial contouring, facial rejuvenation, skin rejuvenation and body contouring, alongside many experimental surgeries on other parts of the body. Upon reading this, Dan-Li was incredibly shocked into discovering so many different procedures a person can go through, thinking twice about the pretty girls that he takes a glimpse upon when commuting.

Analysing the profits section was completely mind-blowing, with the company earning over 500 billion won each year, which was greater than all of the combined family owned nightclubs yearly profits – a truly remarkable feat. All three brothers and Yung-Ko started to wonder why a company in this industry was never bought in the first place by the triad.

Going through the client's information, it was calculated that over two-thirds of women returned for at least another two surgeries, with an almost perfect satisfaction rating. The majority of clients were girls aged 18-24, with the most popular surgeries being breast enhancements and facial contouring. Whilst being amazed at the stats and return rate, each brother was still unsure how this would help them in anyway. Perhaps to calculate a business value price?

A darker tone was set when the information was released regarding the failed project list of PlaciCorp, intriguing everyone, with a definite addition of disgust, too. The list included: rib cage removal, spinal shortage, spinal growth and nipple extraction. Jing-Lee was trying not to gag, thinking about if those surgeries led to any deaths or injuries. Then a lightbulb moment came to him. He could perhaps blackmail the Takani Triad to sell their business to him, and if they declined, he would leak the experimental horrors to the national media outlets. It was definitely the greatest idea he could think of currently, and he was exuberant in confidence that his other two brothers hadn't thought of it.

The last of the PlaciCorp intel concerned former Presidents of the company. To be honest, everyone in the family business thought that it was government owned, like the Korean Investigation Unit. Turning to the second page, there it said on the A4 sized paper: 'PlaciCorp is a government owned business.'

Flicking through each of the pages, there was a recurring theme. Each President of the government owned facility was a previous Director at a university or private hospital, at least 50 years of age and had half of their lifetime or more dedicated to medicine. Each page was exactly the same as this, until the very last page of them all, it read: 'undisclosed new owner, no longer a government operated facility.'

"You have got to be kidding me." The three brothers mumbled at exactly the same time.

"Look at the date of the announcement of new ownership in small print; it looks like the date was only a week ago. If the deal wasn't already impossible to begin with, now it's completely laughable." Tarawa-Li said.

The three brothers spent the next few hours with Yung-Ko Jang devising their game-plan. The Chinaman announced that he was able to fill three business meetings with the PlaciCorp CEO tomorrow, meaning each brother could individually have a chance to secure a deal for themselves, leading them to be the new Chairman. Unfortunately, the PlaciCorp CEO wasn't the Takani Triad Chairman, but that may just increase the likelihood regarding a successful business deal.

The morning meeting slot was agreed to be for Tarawa-Li, not to pursue for the announced vacancy, but to cause the carnage he is most famous for. He decided that he didn't want to become the next Chairman. The role just wasn't right for him. But he still wanted to take part in some sort of fashion. His evil scheme was to impersonate as a surgeon at PlaciCorp, which in fairness wasn't his worst idea of all time, considering he is an actual surgeon. The plan was to kill patients currently undergoing surgery at the company, to help his two other brothers secure a deal, attempting to further blackmail the Takani Triad. He was to arrive with a suitcase which constituted of his favourite weapons, including his beloved electric drill, bloody axe and samurai sword.

He was more than thrilled when the other three accepted his murderous idea that included killing innocent girls who just wanted to be prettier.

The noon meeting slot was agreed for Dan-Li, who decided that his fists would do the talking to anyone who disagreed with anything the desperate man had to say. He knew this meeting would change his life if he failed or succeeded, so he prayed for the morning meeting to go in his favour. He would be able to blackmail the CEO on the legal terms of human torture and inhumane surgical experimentation, as he would have physical evidence via Tarawa-Li's destruction and intel given to him by Yung-Ko Jang. His heart began to race expeditiously, just thinking about life without his fiancé, not being able to be the best father, failing a promise to the only person he promised eternal happiness. He had to become the next Chairman, otherwise his life would be over, knowing Mallory would badger him about not keeping a promise for the rest of their lives. He couldn't imagine a positive life without her being involved in it.

The afternoon meeting was pencilled in for Jing-Lee, who thought long and hard about his eventual strategy, knowing his two weaker brothers wouldn't be able to get the job done by themselves. He remembers the two words his father said about being a true gangster, only needing fists and persuasion. He knew physical violence wouldn't secure a successful agreement, genuinely believing that in business deals, persuasion is the only weapon that can garner a lucrative result. Jing-Lee would blackmail the CEO with his words, not actions, threatening leaking pictures of human torture by PlaciCorp to national media outlets and exposing documents confirming inhumane surgical experimentation. He knew that was the exact same method his brother Dan-Li would be attempting earlier in the very same day. But he also knew that his brother would fail, due to his insistent focusing on the method of his deal being based around fists instead of persuasion.

After several hours of scheming up their actions for tomorrow, Yung-Ko Jang left for home and the three brothers gather up around their dining room table to eat their last meal for the day. The meal for today was an exquisite serving of grilled chicken breast and egg noodles. The three sat around the food and exchanged some small talk.

"My wife is pregnant." Dan-Li announced.

"Congratulations!" Tarawa-Li congratulated with a mouthful of noodles in his mouth, "How far along is she?"

"I have no clue. I'm assuming pretty far though, she hasn't been drinking alcohol for a while and she told me that she attempted to give me subtle hints to realise. She might give birth before our wedding." Dan-Li remarked.

"Well, we're both happy for you. No matter what the hell happens tomorrow, let's promise to be by each other's sides until our last breaths." Tarawa-Li exclaimed.

"Are you hoping for a boy or girl?" Jing-Lee asked.

"I just want my wife and child to be healthy, that's all I ask. That's why tomorrow means so much to me." Dan-Li replied.

After an awkward silence, all three finally finished their big helpings of chicken and noodles and headed to their bedrooms. Atheno-Li requested no child to see him until the rightful next Chairman was officially confirmed.

Whilst sleeping, Tarawa-Li began to experience another flashback of his troubled past. Seeming so real, he was fully immersed into the vision, he truly felt like he had time travelled. The specific day and time, however, was of an experience the poor man would like to have forgotten on the day receiving the horrid news. It was many years ago, Atheno-Li had gathered him and his two other brothers, sitting his children down for a serious conversation. Even as a child, he intuitively knew something atrocious had transpired.

“Kids… while me and your Mamma had visited Hong Kong, a terrible, terrible accident happened.” Atheno-Li cried.

“What happened, father?” Jing-Lee asked.

“Our last night before coming back to Korea, me and your Mamma decided to eat in a luxurious restaurant, right next to the coast.” Atheno-Li answered.

“That doesn’t sound bad at all.” Jing-Lee replied.

“I know, son.” Atheno-Li reassured.

“Then what happened?” Dan-Li asked.

“The night was getting extremely late and we both got very drunk, since we wanted to celebrate our anniversary holiday. Anyways, we were both walking by the harbour after finishing our meal, walking back to the hotel we were staying in. Then, we got lost. I went by myself to ask locals to help for directions for us to go back to the hotel. Ten minutes later, walking back to the harbour, I catch a glimpse of Mamma in the far distance. She managed to trip over something, and she fell into the harbour. She had never learned to swim. It was dark, and she hit the side of her head on one of the boats. I ran as fast as I could to try and help, diving straight into the harbour to try and find her, to no success. I yelled and begged for anyone to help. After many minutes which felt like an eternity to me, the Hong Kong Rescue Team tried to rescue her life." Atheno-Li cried, trying to remain as calm as possible, "They managed to somehow locate her in the dark water, but it was too late. She was pronounced dead at the scene. I'm sorry, boys. Mamma is gone."

Tarawa-Li began to cry real tears whilst he was sleeping in his bed. He missed his mother so much, knowing his mental state would be in such a better stable condition, had she not passed.

The day of the three meetings finally came, with Tarawa-Li the first to wake up for his big opportunity to make a long-lasting impact, albeit a different impact compared to his brothers. He quickly scans the game-plan he had drawn up the day before to be certain and confident everything was as perfect as it could be. He goes into his wardrobe and changes into his surgeon outfit that he typically wears for his Oculoplastic torture jobs each morning, hoping the PlaciCorp Surgeon outfits were either identical or majorly similar in comparison. Since his father had banished the three from using weapons, he knew he would be automatically disqualified from being the next Chairman, which he didn't care for anyway. For extra mockery from his father's speech, he even decides to steal the family car for good measure. After driving for a few minutes, Tarawa-Li eventually reaches his destination, PlaciCorp.

The PlaciCorp structure was an architectural feast for the eyes. Comprised of 100 floors and being over 1,200 feet tall, it stood one of the largest buildings in not only Korea, but the entire continent of Asia. Each floor held home to different shaded colours of tinted windows and looked like something so surreal that you would only find in a CGI-heavy film. Upon gazing this beautiful sight, he knew it would be practically impossible for one of his brothers to cut a deal in their favour, but he wouldn't cancel on what his focus of the day was: to kill.

After entering the building, he quickly talks to the first-floor receptionist, who herself appeared to have had many surgeries completed, lips especially.

"Hello, I'm one of the surgeons. It's my first day, what floor do I need to be on?" Tarawa-Li asked.

"Did you not check your e-mail?" The receptionist growled.

"I'm the Emergency Surgeon, my agency just sent me here today due to short staff on your side." Tarawa-Li answered back in a quick and calm state.

"Oh, sorry, sir. You may be transferred to a different floor, but it's most likely the forty-fourth floor. Shall I let the manager know you're on your way?" The Receptionist said.

"No, thank you. I know him personally, so I want to give him a nice surprise." Tarawa-Li replied.

After nearly ending before it even began, he enters the elevator, hoping the forty-fourth floor doesn't contain security. The Surgeon knew he could easily kill them if they happened to be there, but he wanted a stealthier approach, in order for his brothers to be able to blackmail the CEO later in the day. After many floors, stopping-starting with other PlaciCorp employees going to their respective destinations, finally, the forty-fourth floor arose.

He took a silent approach, even making sure the footsteps leaving the elevator to the floor wouldn't be too loud. Now on the floor, he started to locate his easiest victim or victims to kill. To the left of him, ongoing surgeries. To the right of him, waiting room. He knew the easiest victims were the ones currently being surgically performed on, meaning a few surgeons to kill, but nothing major considering his past. Avoiding attracting any audio attention, he quietly sets his suitcase onto the floor and opens it. Luckily with the hallways being completely empty, the sociopath grabs his electric drill and quickly tests that it's still working as normal. With the demonic look in his evil eyes and the devilish grin he wears, mayhem awaited those Surgeons and clients nearest to him. Tarawa-Li silently speeds to the closest room and opens the door, holding his electric drill and crazed look. Without any time to talk, he slams the door behind him shut, appreciating the carnage he's about to cause in this soundproofed room. In front of him lay the innocent girl, perhaps 18 years of age, and two male surgeons. He instantly drills into the first surgeon, targeting his left eyeball, drilling until the tip penetrated completely through the man's skull. The second surgeon, who tries to desperately escape from the crazed lunatic, gets a visit from the electric drill too. This time it goes completely through the throat. Gasping for breath, the second surgeon quickly meets his fate of death alongside his eyeless colleague.

He quickly approached the teenage girl, who was hoping to have woken up after her surgery with a nicer face or breasts. Instead, she will never wake up from the surgery she had been looking forward to for many months, due to Tarawa-Li. He places the beloved drill in the centre of her skull, piercing the weapon until death met her, leaving the girl side by side with the deceased surgeons. He quickly takes a photograph of the crime scene he created, sharing it with his brothers later in the day, when he returned home.

He exited the room and realised a potential rookie mistake. The suitcase. He knew he couldn't risk infiltrating another room until he returned to the place where he left the bag with his other weapons, which was beside the elevator door. Quickly sprinting like an Olympic athlete, pleading to god that his suitcase was still there, was a PlaciCorp surgeon who stumbled upon the unclaimed baggage mere seconds ago. He had no choice but to act fast, sneaking behind the man and drilling a hole through his wrinkled neck. The PlaciCorp surgeon instantly dropped dead, causing a loud thud on the hard floor.

Knowing that the sound would grab attention, he picked the dead man up and went on his way to dump him in the room already filled with other dead surgeons, predicting the waiting room staff were more likely to check out the noise first. After dumping the surgeon with the drilled neck, he decided to call it a day. His personality disorder came into strong effect, making the man to become very forgetful regarding his locational presence, and his social disorder making him extremely paranoid, believing he was being watched by a thousand security cameras.

He exits the room of death for the very last time, checking to both his left and right side to confirm that the coast was clear. Quickly rushing to the elevator, he makes sure all of his weapons are back into his suitcase properly and presses the button to go down. Luckily, no staff member from either side decided to check up on the mysterious sound in the hallway, making Tarawa-Li's plan a mild success. He manages to successfully leave the gigantic PlaciCorp building untouched and with evidence for blackmail for his two brothers, sending the crime scene to each of their phones on his drive home.

The second of three meetings finally approached, with Dan-Li hoping that his brothers' effort earlier this morning and Yung-Ko Jang's effort were not to be inefficacious. If all went accordingly, he was to go to PlaciCorp and return home as the next-in-line Chairman. For the special occasion, he decided to dress himself charmingly, wearing a designer suit which contained the rarest diamond on the planet.

He had more riding on this compared to his other brothers. He knew that his love life counted on this, his promise he made to his future wife, the promise he made to his future child. Not only was his love life up for high stakes, his happiness was too.

Noon was here and Dan-Li just finished the long walk from the family home to see the PlaciCorp building for the first time himself, acknowledging that he's probably seen the building before, just not realising what the purpose of PlaciCorp was. He started to comprehend how many girls in Korea have had a surgery from this company, due to its sheer size in architecture. Every street he had walked on in the big city, he had seen many pretty girls that look freakishly similar. Have they all had plastic surgery?

He was astonished by the appearance not only from the exterior, but also of the interior of the building. It was as big as a stadium. He made his way to meet the PlaciCorp CEO, which was on the highest floor of all, the hundredth floor.

After the elevator journey, which took an astonishing twenty minutes or so, Dan-Li finally reached the top of the bewildering structure. He was amazed about how humanity had created such an impressive place, how much it must have cost to build, how many construction workers must there have been to complete the job.

Reaching the hundredth floor, he was met by two guards, who were obviously part of the CEO's private security. The two men were at least 6 feet 10 inches tall, looking down at Dan-Li like he's a fresh piece of undevoured meat. The guard to his left opens his part of the door, gesturing for him to go inside. He strolls inside, wonderfully amazed to see what's inside the hundredth floor.

The marvellously crafted room had a built-in swimming pool with adjustable temperature, almost like a 2-in-1 swimming pool/hot-tub. Not too far along from that was the sports arena, with mini tennis and basketball courts, alongside a gymnasium area. To the opposite side of those impressive features was a home theatre, with a screen size that spanned over 200" dimensions with over ten comfy red lounge chairs to relax on. The hundredth floor was a literal paradise for any man or woman who had lived. After seeing this, Dan-Li was in love, almost to the same level as he is in love with his fiancé. Straight in front of the door, however, was a long red carpet, perhaps 400-metres long. After the 400-metre walk, there lay the CEO in his red leather chair, and his black wooden desk.

The CEO went by the name "Mouse," with no wonder why. His eyes were nearly pure black, with the size of his iris taking up nearly the whole space of his eyeballs. He was also accompanied by a small nose that constantly looked like it was sniffing. The beady looking man had a noticeable scar, too, spanning from the top of his right eyebrow straight down to his right ear lobe.

“First off, I want to apologise for my lateness.” Dan-Li said.

“No worries, I want to apologise for none of our three leaders being here today. We’re even. Rest assured though, if it’s a deal you want, I can still accept or decline for the Takani Triad.” Mouse replied.

“I’m going to purchase PlaciCorp for 30 trillion won. Failure to agree to this deal will result in the leak of inhumane surgical experimentation and human torture regarding this company to the national media outlets.” Dan-Li joked, although the intent was serious.

“You are one funny man. I thought the Maska Triad ran the Korean underworld? Is that really the best you’ve got? Seriously? One of you punks didn’t even show up to the morning meeting.” Mouse snickered.

“Listen here, punk. I’m not going to repeat myself. If you think I’m crazy, lets fight.” Dan-Li declared.

“Security!” Mouse shouted.

Storming through the door were the two giants, now armed with assault rifles with extended scopes. Dan-Li miserably failed in his attempt at the sole opportunity that would either make or break his life from this day onward. His attempt lasted only seconds. He was too depressed to even move, realising that his tactic wouldn't have ever worked. He was just too desperate for everything to go right in his life.

After being escorted by the two guys, the weepy mess got chucked into the elevator and was returned to the first floor to leave PlaciCorp immediately. He was unable to gather his thoughts, unsure on anything and everything in the present situation he had got himself in. Is the marriage going to be called off? Is my fiancé going to get an abortion? Is Tarawa-Li going to kill me because of his great efforts earlier today?

After some time, the third meeting was about to begin, with Jing-Lee being the only hope to score success for the triad, and for himself. The man was beaming with confidence.

After walking the undemanding journey, he finally arrived at his destination. PlaciCorp. He couldn't be cared about the appearance of the building, or what it represented. He just had to persuade the CEO to take the business out of the Takani's hands and into the Maska's, also making sure they flew back to Taiwan never to lay a foot back in Korea ever again. Yes, that sounds impossible, but that's what he does.

He arrived at the hundredth floor, being motioned to proceed by one of the giants. It was the same situation where Dan-Li had been previously. Remarkably, Jing-Lee wasn't impressed by the layout of the place, always taking in his fathers' footsteps regarding being simple instead of sticking out. That's how the family business has been able to shine all of these years, by never revealing any identity to the public eye or dressing up or acting like an important person. To succeed in crime, you cannot look like someone who does it.

Finally, after the long walk on the red carpet, he was in front of the most important person in his life at this specific moment in time, Mouse.

"Hello, nice to meet you, Jing-Lee, is it? Just call me Mouse." Mouse welcomed.

"Hi Mouse, nice office you have here." Jing-Lee said, not really wanting to engage in too much small talk.

"Thanks. It's a shame the three leaders never get to come here. It's awesome." Mouse replied.

"It could be a blessing if you think about it. They won't have front row seats of the leaked information I have on the company. Human torture and inhumane surgical experimentation." Jing-Lee bragged.

"Come on, punk. I thought we were saving the best meeting until last. Is that all that you've got? If so, let me have my turn." Mouse replied.

"Your turn in what, blackmail?" Jing-Lee asked.

"Yeah." Mouse provoked.

"Try me." Jing-Lee joked.

"You're a funny guy, so you know what? I changed my mind. You can own PlaciCorp, on one condition." Mouse declared.

"What's the condition?" Jing-Lee replied.

"The Takani Triad will take all of your non-affiliated triad businesses which break the sacred rule of your triad. If you don't want the Takani Triad to expose you to your family, you must also give up your micro islands located around the coasts of Taiwan and New Zealand." Mouse asserted.

"If you tell me the source of the information, I'll even pay you money to kill the fucking snake." Jing-Lee shouted, instantly enraged to find out that Mouse knows something so secretive – he knows that his family has no idea about it.

"I can't do that, I'm afraid. Do we have a deal or not?" Mouse asked.

“Fucking punk. Fine. At least tell me if it was our new lawyer that blabbed to you guys?” Jing-Lee said.

“I’m surprised. I thought you would be more concerned about that Jason Holland kid. You know, your girlfriends’ little brother?” Mouse chuckled, his nose sniffing non-stop.

“Where the fuck have you guys put him?” Jing-Lee shouted.

“He’s six feet deep in the ground now. If you want to know the real killer, you’ll have to ask Pigbreath.” Mouse murmured, “Only thing is, he’s in the Takani Triad over in the Taiwan safehouse, guarded by twenty or more punks like yourself.”

“I own PlaciCorp now, get yourself and all of your lackeys out of here by tonight.” Jing-Lee demanded.

He rushed out of the hundredth floor, filled with many overpowering emotions. He is fulfilling his life-long destiny of becoming the next Chairman, taking over the family business. Dampening the amazing mood is the fact that some punk in the Maska Triad is either helping or working with the Takani Triad, with the most likely option being Derrick Holland, the newbie lawyer, he thought. The tattoos that the foreigner had made him so untrustworthy – making him look like he was capable of anything dark and disturbing. He just could never trust the man from the moment they met. Filling his heart with sadness is having to break the news to his girlfriend about the passing of her younger brother. Who could perform such a cruel act to someone so young and innocent. The boy was an intern engineer with no social life, he had no enemies.

After running back home, he decides to take a quick nap in his bedroom before revealing different pieces of huge news to his father, brothers and girlfriend. An hour later, Jing-Lee wakes up and decides his plan to relay the news. He was to visit his father first, then his brothers, then his girlfriend. Without knocking on Atheno-Li's door, he immediately enters his fathers' room to announce his successful (although with worrying undertones) deal in acquiring PlaciCorp.

"Son, I told you not for anyone to see me until the next Chairman was decided." Atheno-Li said, with the man looking as poorly as ever.

"I know. I'm going to be the next Chairman." Jing-Lee exclaimed.

"I knew it would have been you to follow my footsteps, Jing-Lee! I'm so proud of you, son." Atheno-Li congratulated.

"Thank you. Do you know what I used?" Jing-Lee added.

"Persuasion?" Atheno-Li guessed.

"Persuasion." Jing-Lee answered.

"That's my boy. Now tell the others." Atheno-Li replied.

After telling his father the wonderful news of the official next Chairman, Jing-Lee was on his way to gather his brothers to share the news with them. He knew Tarawa-Li would be as happy as a clam, with Dan-Li most likely being his usual jealous self. Unfortunately, neither man was spotted around the house, so Jing-Lee decided on telling them both the news at a later time. Instead, he started focusing his energy completely on his girlfriend, getting the courage of telling her the bad news. The two decided to meet outside, only a few minutes' walk from the family home.

"So, what's up?" Zara asked.

"I have good news and I have bad news. I strongly suggest you hear the good news first this time." Jing-Lee replied.

"Okay, sure. What's the good news then?" Zara asked.

"I'm going to be the new Chairman." Jing-Lee said.

"That is such good news." Zara beamed, giving him a hug. "I'm so happy for you!"

"Even though it is good news, that's not the important news right now." Jing-Lee interrupted. "I have something even more important to tell you right now."

"What is it?" Zara responded.

"Jason..." Jing-Lee said, his eyes starting to water up at the girl he loved, "Your brother... he's dead."

Being unresponsive, she falls to the street floor, collapsing right in front of his eyes. Unable to react, he puts her into the recovery position and takes off his coat for his girl to use as a pillow. After many minutes, he was able to not fear as much, as she managed to return to consciousness. Instantaneously, she starts to bawl her eyes out, shocked to realise the surreal events that she has just heard.

"How do you know he's dead?" Zara cried.

"I don't know officially, but I know someone who does." Jing-Lee lamented.

"What's his name and where is he from?" Zara interrupted.

"Pigbreath. Taiwan." Jing-Lee answered.

"Looks like me and you are going to have to get some answers out of that fucker. We're going to Taiwan, tomorrow morning." Zara cried.

"What if this Pigbreath guy doesn't give any answers?" Jing-Lee asked.

"Then I'll be the one with pig blood all over my hands, looking for his other pig friends until I do get fucking answers!" Zara yelled.

CHAPTER SEVEN: LILAC

Jing-Lee and Zara head to the airport for the earliest Taiwan flight, knowing well this is a complete suicide mission, but a mission needed to be completed for a greater cause.

The flight was majorly uneventful and by a near three hours, they were in the oppositions' ground, the home of the Takani Triad. They were in Taiwan. He had done his research, knowing their rival triad had over at least fifteen safehouses in the country, with their wanted man in the most central one. The plan he had devised for him and his girlfriend was to visit his former house on the island off the coast of Taiwan, (although now owned by the Takani Triad, Jing-Lee knew it was very unlikely for anyone to be living there, due to its isolation with the rest of mankind). Upon arrival, they were to prepare for their plan on how to capture Pigbreath, and what to do to him if he failed to comply with their request.

After getting into a cab from the airport, the couple reach the south coast of Taiwan, right beside the docks. Jing-Lee managed to purchase a speedboat for rental from one of the security workers for himself and Zara to visit the isolating island they would be staying at, which contained more than enough weapons to kill. The speedboat journey was tougher than expected, with the ocean waves crashing heavy every few seconds or so. After a rough and unsteady ten minutes, they arrived at the micro island that Jing-Lee used to own. He didn't spend many days here, as it was majorly used for accommodating the rich and wealthy who were either his business partners or future business partners. Nonetheless, it was a hard sight to see, considering it was now official property owned by his main rivals, due to someone disclosing top secret information to the opposition. He would get to the bottom of that too, but at a later date.

After parking the speedboat, the two enter the house. It was surrounded by pure ocean and isolation. The house wasn't at all big, only containing two bedrooms, one bathroom, one kitchen diner and one living room, all on the same floor. Jing-Lee always kept stocks of tinned food that had an expiring date of many years to come, always paranoid of an emergency or a pandemic, always wanting to be prepared. In the wardrobes of both bedrooms is the location of the weapon storing, with one wardrobe being completely full of pistols, assault rifles and machine guns, all with silencers and removable sights. The second wardrobe respectively was full of so many gadgets and grenades that the Korean Military would be jealous of. Frag, Illumination, Chemical and Smoke were the frontrunners for being the most useful on the grenade half, whilst Drone Track, Bug Track and Invisible GPS for the gadget.

The couple unanimously agreed for their capture plan of Pigbreath to arise at late night, meaning a greater chance of success due to darkness and strategy. The journey from the island to the capital of Taiwan, Taipei, would be for an hour maximum, with the suggested number of members of the triad being present roughly twenty, give or take a few, depending on if Mouse told any of the leaders.

With Zara being a complete novice in the field of crime, Jing-Lee made sure she was competent with the handling of serious weaponry, stealth, reaction time, and reflexes, making her perform serious routines that his father taught him and his brothers at an early age. She completed the gruelling training practice, knowing she had to be prepared for anything for the night approaching.

After being crime and murder-oriented for several hours, doing the various exercises in harsh conditions, it was time to rest a little. He thought that talking about the situation they were in could help her open up a little. He tried to do it in a nonchalant way though.

"What's your crime name going to be then?" Jing-Lee asked jokingly, trying to lighten the mood just a little. "What's your alias?"

"Lilac." Zara replied, wiping the sweat off from her fatigued face.

"Why? Is it because it's your favourite flower? Flowers aren't dangerous, but suit yourself." Jing-Lee chuckled, trying to make his girlfriend crack a smile.

"My brother gave me lilacs each year for my birthday." Zara said.

After a brief silence, with Zara starting to cry ever so slightly, Jing-Lee consoles her with a comforting hug, knowing he dug himself into a hole with that attempt at a conversation.

"I wasn't going to do this until after tonight, depending on the result, but I think I need to do it now." Jing-Lee whispered, looking into Zara's tearful eyes.

"Do what?" Zara replied, looking straight back at him.

He finished the comforting hug and left the couch that both had been resting on, and went away to his bedroom. He quickly returned to see her being even more confused, a teary mess on the leather two-seater couch in the living room. He knew that the timing of this was clearly wrong, but he also knew he had to do it, not knowing of their future tonight. He approaches Zara, gets down on one knee, revealing the most gorgeous looking engagement ring, costing the man over 100 million won.

"I know this isn't perfect timing, at all, so I'll keep it short and sweet. Will you marry me?" Jing-Lee asked, with a smile on his face.

"Yes." Zara cried, trying to hold back her tears. He puts the engagement ring on her finger, and she continues speaking. "Let's leave early, I don't want the entire night of my engagement to be killing these bastards."

After a quick kiss of the life-changing moment, the two quickly equip themselves high of the weapons they want for this adventure, mainly assault rifles and smoke grenades. After stocking themselves, they set sail on their rental speedboat, daring to play with the ocean waves. Both had so much adrenaline that they believed they could just knock on the Takani Triad safehouse front door and shoot each member dead.

The hour-long journey from the private island to the destination was mainly silent, full of compassion, and eagerness to kill. They were the new 'Bonnie and Clyde'. Both were cuddling up to each other on the cab which would take them to about a mile from the safehouse, allowing the two to scan and plan their chronological order of deaths. Both wished that the proposal had been done in a different way but knew it could potentially be their last day together, which subtracted the almost "lacklustre" method Jing-Lee used to ask the question.

After leaving the cab, both started to walk to the Takani Triad safehouse, with their guns strapped to their backs and grenades placed in their pockets. The mile walk for the two was uneasy. Whichever street the two walked on, they knew they were being watched. The newly engaged couple just wished for it to be locals of the surrounding area, not anyone affiliated with the people they were about to kill. Walking through several streets, the population density started to dramatically decrease. That's when they found the safehouse right in front of them, with their very own eyes.

Guarded by two armed men, the safehouse was not an impressive sight to see, appearing to look like a rusty hundred-year-old building with many bullet holes, smashed windows and a leaking roof. Jing-Lee and Zara felt brazen, about to kill so many people on the outskirts of Taipei, on one of the busiest places in the world.

"I got the guy on the left; you get the guy on the right." Jing-Lee said.

The two guards were hit straight between the eyes by the silenced guns, falling to the floor immediately. One of the dead guards' guns fired bullets that were aimed to the floor beside him and his other dead associate. The two were pouring with blood, with the couple hoping that the other eighteen or so members would go down and drop dead that easily. Rushing down the stairs, another member checks to see what the gunfire was regarding. Running to the door, he detects his dead colleagues, with Jing-Lee shooting the man in the testicles first, bursting his genitals open, and then a few silenced bullets through the man's skull. A cocky move indeed, considering the stakes, but the third man somehow didn't produce a decibel of sound.

"Seventeen or so left. Let's go in there." Jing-Lee declared, signalling to Zara to watch his back.

The two quickly rush into the measly building, identifying no one on the first floor, meaning there was a boatload of enemies on the two floors above them. The mission would be an instant fail if they kill Pigbreath, meaning they would have to act stealthy from now on to avoid the possible game-breaker.

Jing-Lee, in front of his now-fiancé, slowly walks up the stairs to the middle level of the safehouse. With a tad of luck being on their side, as the stairwell was situated completely to the right side of the building, he was more likely to identify Pigbreath without getting shot from all angles. Glancing the dull, unlit room, there were no signs of a hacker, just gunmen. He knew it would be a death wish to speak using words, so the couple used sign language to communicate with one another on their strategy.

“On the count of five, I shoot the right side, you shoot the left side.” Jing-Lee signed slowly, making sure Zara understood. The girl responds with a simple nod.

He threw one of his smoke grenades, bouncing to the far-left side of the building, making his next kills easier than taking candy from a baby. The vicious but silent annihilation occurred, with every gunmen instantly dying from being shot in their backs and in the back of their skulls, causing an instant pool of contaminated blood. He counted seven total deaths on this floor, meaning the estimated number of people left in the building were ten.

The two quickly head up to the highest floor of the building, hoping the final floor was just as easy. The couple noticed this floor was substantially louder however, hearable multiple conversations. Entering a prone position, they began to analyse their strategy, considering the number of gunmen in the building and if they could spot Pigbreath. Just about to decide on an approach, they both hear a ground-breaking revelation.

"Pigbreath is on the roof, he told us that he wanted to be left alone." A Takani-gunman said, "I was more than happy to, the fucking loser."

The simple nod to each other indicated the same plan as the floor before, total obliteration for the men. Quickly standing to their feet, Jing-Lee threw another smoke grenade to the opposite side of the building. The two then proceed to run-and-gun every man in the room, with multiple bullets sprayed in extra for good measure. Running to the roof, Zara gets captured by a gunman who faked his death, strangling the girl's neck with his scrawny left arm, with his right arm holding a pistol, pointing it at Jing-Lee.

"Do you want me to kill your girl, punk?" The Gunman yelled, about to fire a bullet to the face of Jing-Lee.

Instantly jumping to his left, Jing-Lee fires his silenced assault rifle straight towards the skull of the gunman, mere centimetres next to the face of his perturbed fiancé. The man instantly dies, letting go of his grip on Zara. Seconds later, Pigbreath enters the room.

"What's with all the noise?" Pigbreath said, instantly observing that all of his triad members were dead on the floor, bathing in their own blood.

Pigbreath was exactly as what you would think he looked like: 5 feet 4 inches tall, obese, buzzcut black hair, rotten teeth, and breath that smelt like a manure-filled pig sty, which he claims is a disease from drinking too many energy drinks and cheese dip.

"Who are you? Why haven't you killed me? What do you want?" Pigbreath blurted, looking paranoid to the bone.

"Mouse said you know who killed my fiancé's brother. Get talking." Jing-Lee demanded.

Pigbreath motioned the two to join him on the hole-filled roof, which was overlooking the outskirts of the otherwise beautiful place known as Taipei. He logs onto his computer to find out any and all information he can to help Jing-Lee and Zara, knowing quite well if he failed to work with them, he would see the same fate as the others.

"What's his name?" Pigbreath asked, slurping heavily on an energy drink.

"Jason Holland." Zara replied, giving herself the chills every time she realises her brother is dead.

"Oh, I remember him. One of the leaders told me to request specific services on the kid, meaning an external company did the dirty work." Pigbreath replied, typing heavily on his keyboard.

"Who the fuck killed my brother?" Zara yelled in frustration, anger and sadness.

"Hang on. It's loading." Pigbreath whispered, hopefully not angering Zara any further.

"Tell us exactly who they are and where they live. I know you won't ever reveal the identities of your three leaders." Jing-Lee demanded. "It's the least you could do for the poor kid."

"I finally got the information." Pigbreath replied, "The guy who killed him lives in Korea. His name is Dan-Li Maska."

CHAPTER EIGHT: START AND FINISH

Two days later...

Jing-Lee and Zara had eventually returned back to Korea, agreeing that she alone would deal with the death of her brother in the revenge act she most deemed appropriate. Jing-Lee indicated that killing Dan-Li would not be the solution, as all contract killings are first sanctioned by their father. He was now on his deathbed, about to die any day or so. He implied to his fiancé that she should take away something of equal value to what she had with herself and her late brother, whatever that equivalent may be.

After being unable to talk to his two brothers after the successful PlaciCorp deal and then sorting business out in Taiwan, Jing-Lee and Zara entered the family home again to announce the good news in person, even though the two have most likely heard it already by Atheno-Li at this point. Becoming increasingly curious, both brothers were not seen in the house yet again. Very unlikely to be returning to the surgery or restaurant, as Jing-Lee would be declaring new triad rules after his father's soon-coming passing, he wondered where they both could possibly be. He decided to call both of his brothers to see where the hell they were, calling Tarawa-Li first. Straight to voicemail. Second attempt. Voicemail again.

"Surgeon must be either sleeping on a park bench or causing grief in the local strip club." Jing-Lee joked, even though he knew it was more than plausible for that to be happening right now.

Calling Dan-Li, this brother answers the phone. The phone call was exceedingly difficult to comprehend, due to a bad signal or what-not, but Jing-Lee heard the words 'hospital' and 'Mallory'. The couple got into one of the family vehicles and dashed off to the nearest hospital, hoping Dan-Li and Mallory were there and not transferred to another place. Driving like a lunatic and speeding triple the legal speed limit, they arrive at the hospital in a record time. Even if he were to have been pulled over for speeding, he would never have to face any criminal charges.

Dashing into the main reception, the helpful receptionist located Mallory to be staying on the third floor, with both subconsciously pleading that nothing terrible had happened to her. The two enter the floor with the first sight being Tarawa-Li in a deep sleep, laying on three armless hospital chairs. Knowing not to ever wake the lunatic up, they head to the room where they were told Mallory would be staying in. They were then welcomed in by Dan-Li and Mallory herself – who was resting on the uncomfortable hospital bed.

She found difficulty to talk for extended periods of time, so Dan-Li explained the situation into why his fiancé was sitting on the hospital bed, with various medical machines and drips placed either on or in her body. She has an underlying condition of diabetes, which took a turn for the worse when she suffered a traumatic episode whilst the Jing-Lee-PlaciCorp meeting was taking place, the reasoning to why which both brothers were not seen at the family home that day. On the day, the hospital nurses decided that because she was pregnant and severely ill, they had to perform an emergency caesarean delivery, in any hope to protect the lives of each vulnerable party.

A few hours later, the couple had their child introduced to the world, a daughter, naming her Aria

Maska. Due to the premature birth, the baby is still being carefully surveyed by nurses at all times, to prevent any mishaps. Mallory was to stay overnight until her condition improved, which unfortunately hadn't happened yet.

The newly arrived couple congratulated the other couple on their birth, revealing their engagement and the new Chairman of the family business, too.

"Really? You couldn't just say congratulations for our child, huh? You really are a little punk sometimes, aren't you?" Dan-Li chuckled, "Congratulations, though."

"Thank you. I know for certain you have a special connection with your new-born already, don't you?" Zara asked, in a surprisingly positive manner.

"Of course I do. I'm engaged to the most perfect girl in the world. I'm now a father which I've looked forward to ever since Mallory announced her pregnancy, albeit hardly that long ago. Most importantly, Tarawa-Li isn't going to be our Chairman. I'm so thankful for everyone in my life." Dan-Li replied, "What took you so long to get here though? It's been days."

"We just had to do some private business. Did you already forget we're engaged? Take the hint." Jing-Lee chuckled, looking at Dan-Li straight in the eyes.

“How did he propose, Zara?” Mallory asked, trying to gasp for her breath and attempting to relax on the stiff surface, with her condition worsening every time she either talked or changed positions in her hospital bed.

“Well, we flew to Spain, as apparently Jing-Lee and his brothers used to visit when they were children. He took me to a very romantic dinner, went back to the hotel room and went down on one knee.” Zara replied, knowing to create a fake story about the engagement, realising the true story would be too suspicious. Just hopefully they wouldn’t take into consideration the flight times from Seoul to Barcelona.

Mallory started to close her eyes due to her extreme pain and fatigue taking a toll on her for the past few days, signalling for herself to be left in peace and quiet. Her fiancé motioned for his brother and Zara to leave with him and to follow him to see the new-born Aria for the first time. The three were able to observe the baby from a far distance through clear see-through glass.

Dan-Li finally felt he had purpose in his life, a fire he hadn’t legitimately had for as long as he could remember. He tried and tried to have that fire back a few days ago in attempting to become next-in-line Chairman, which only resulted in him being a laughingstock compared to his two other brothers on the PlaciCorp day. Now however, he was looking into his daughters' pretty little eyes, with a small tear dropping down from his right eye onto his cheek, now knowing he is the luckiest man he could ever be. He wanted to marry Mallory as soon as she recovered, knowing as long as his future wife and beautiful child were with him, that's all that mattered.

Jing-Lee realised that he was an uncle for the first time in his life, knowing that Aria would see him for the first time with her two eyes as Chairman Jing-Lee, not Uncle Jing-Lee. That resulted in mixed feelings for the man. Bittersweet. He wouldn't be family oriented to any juniors in the family, not even his own children - if he had any in the future. He knew how much the family business needed to evolve with the times, meaning no time to get sentimental over things that didn't concern themselves in the real everyday world. As Chairman, his job will purely focus around business, money, laws, crimes. He knew that he can be just as good of a Chairman compared to his father, but his heart sank just a little, realising that he won't have any strong sentimental relationships with the next generation of the Maska Triad.

Zara had a sinister look to her face, not thinking about the poor vulnerable baby, but instead thinking about the revenge plot on Dan-Li, who treated her exactly the same before and after Jason's death. The monster. She just had to devise a cunning yet sophisticated plan to hurt him even more than the family death she so recently experienced. She decided to act on the matter as soon as possible, taking precautionary methods to prevent anyone knowing about her future actions she may cause to the new father. Every single day in her life up until a few days ago, she was a model citizen. Now, she was thirsty for some blood. The night in Taiwan woke the devil inside her. She was thirsty to avenge her little brother.

Jing-Lee and Zara decided to leave Mallory and Dan-Li to themselves for the rest of the day, hoping the diabetes condition improved at a significant pace. The couple attempted to look at the condition of Tarawa-Li, who seemed to be positively startled in whatever crazy dream or nightmare the Surgeon was having. Not wanting to accidentally be eaten alive for waking him up, the couple leave him be and return to the family home.

Before entering the family house, Zara had decided to not enter and instead return to her own house, to announce to her father about the death (still not knowing the news). Both agreed not to disclose any information on what they discovered in Taiwan a couple of days ago.

He entered the family house by himself, appreciating that this property will soon be his majority of rights. Appreciating the scenery, he acknowledged everything, by living in the present, widening his eyes and taking a full, deep breath of clean fresh air. The afternoon clear sky, with the sun in the distance preparing for a spectacular sunset, the singing of Chestnut-winged cuckoo's together in perfect harmony resting in a distant tree, and the perfect cool breeze gushing through his hair.

In the amazing greenery besides the physical home was Yung-Ko Jang, standing next to the pretty sight of traditional Korean flowers and plants. The beloved loyal man was on his phone and likely smoking his tenth cigar of the day, noticing Jing-Lee in his peripheral vision.

The relationship between Yung-Ko and Atheno-Li spanned forever in the mind of Jing-Lee. The future Chairman couldn't remember a time in his life without them two running operations together, or in honest terms, couldn't remember a time in his life without Yung-Ko being his fathers' yes-man. Regarding relationships, Jing-Lee and Yung-Ko weren't as close as they should be, considering the future that awaited them one day. They both heavily respected one another, but they hardly had anything in common to talk about, making the majority of conversations slightly awkward between the two. The man in discussion, Yung-Ko Jang, was a former Detective of the Korean Police Department, the only person in the planet's existence to trace the Maska Triad and their acquisition of Korean services - excluding the Korean Investigation Unit, which was the only service too impossible to buy for Atheno-Li. The detective was in his third year at the job when he reported the case in his department. It resulted in getting the job he had today, truly being every pennyworth for the family over the years. The Chairman could've just killed him for finding out about his illegal activities – but he didn't. It's as clear as day now, the Chinaman is not only one-of-a-kind in intelligence, but he's also one-of-a-kind in loyalty.

He approaches Yung-Ko, with the Chinaman ending his current call and finishing his cigar, blowing the second-hand smoke pretty much straight in Jing-Lee's face, looking to be as grumpy as can be. The aging man appeared to be physically drained, with the bags of tiredness span from his under-eye straight to the bottom of his nose. He most likely had been looking after Atheno-Li for the past few days, as Dan-Li and Tarawa-Li were in the hospital due to the recent birth. Not only drained physically, but mentally a wreck too, Atheno-Li was well known to be a nuisance to look after even without his illness, most likely causing Yung-Ko to have lost his mind in the past days, being isolated with his boss, being his carer every single second. The two signalled to go inside and relax in the living room, with both sitting in comfy chairs above the luxury chandelier.

"How is he?" Jing-Lee asked, looking above him at the chandelier.

"Well, he's finally sleeping for the first time in forever. I know that because he's been shouting from his deathbed before then." Yung-Ko replied, "I don't know why you keep looking at that stupid chandelier when there are more serious things to deal with, like preparing for your life as Chairman."

Even though Yung-Ko wasn't giving him the usual affable approach, he knew he was absolutely correct. He had been caught up on so many other things that being the next-in-line Chairman - his life's dream - was already being overshadowed instead of being top priority. Every decision was soon to be made by Jing-Lee, the increase or decrease of staff numbers, expenses, profits, properties. The Maska Triad was to become his sole responsibility, it was a proving ground if he cared at all about the life he had been living until now.

“You look tired. Go home to your wife or girlfriend or whoever you have at home. I’ll take care of my father until one of my brothers or fiancé gets here.” Jing-Lee stated, glancing at his fatigued look.

Yung-Ko nodded and made his way out of the living room, leaving the family home to return back to his house, presumably to sleep an entire two or three days due to the dire stress placed on him.

Jing-Lee continued to glare at the opulent chandelier, considering his first cause of action he will decide to take. He knew if he made life more lenient for the family, it would be displayed as an unenthusiastic move. If he decided to do absolutely no changes in his role of power, then that would indicate that he’s a non-confident Chairman who received such a high position in pure luck and coincidence. He wondered if becoming a more violent triad would be a possible route for him to take. Owning literally nearly everything in Korea could be the biggest blessing of all. Perhaps he could take the step further by owning the Government of Korea or the Korean Investigation Unit. The violent part of that proposition being using their masses of weaponry as their plan to get their own way. Jing-Lee quickly concluded the idea was too idiotic to go with. He wanted to make a statement the right way, the way in which the members felt enlightened in his presence.

While sketching up numerous ideas about the future in his head, there was a loud thump to be heard in the house, with the source of the sound directed in the area of his father's bedroom. Jing-Lee instantly reacted, heavily sprinting into his father's room to see the damage of impact. There the old man lay, unable to move a singular muscle and looking as gravely ill as ever. He knew that these moments in his life would be some of the last moments in the life of his father. He and Atheno-Li always had a special type of relationship, he always gave this particular son bounds of favouritism. Atheno-Li always knew that Jing-Lee would be the next Chairman, considering his intelligence, arrogance, logic and looks. The old man was never concerned in the slightest of his favourite son failing him.

After picking the old, frail man up off the cold wooden floor back into his bed, both knew it was time. Atheno-Li was about to pass. Crying at what his father's health had become, his father smiled ever so slightly and gestured the next Chairman to take a seat right next to him for one last conversation.

"Son...there's something I need to tell you before I pass." Atheno-Li barely said, with his voice becoming ever so quiet in volume.

"Don't say things like that. You're a fighter. You're the only reason our family is in the position it is now." Jing-Lee shouted, crying with masses of tears, wiping them from his face.

"Well, you make sure you get your generation and the generation after into an even greater position." Atheno-Li replied, looking at his crying son.

"Yes, Chairman." Jing-Lee said, hoping for this conversation to last forever.

"Me and your mother. We had another child. She was many years before you three were even thought of. We named her Wera-Li Maska, although she's most likely to have changed her name by now. From an incredibly young age, she had shown signs of psychotic behaviour, so we tried to discipline her. The discipline techniques failed, and in fair time she turned fully evil. There's only a matter of time until she hears about my death, so I'm warning you now Jing-Lee, be prepared for her attack. She will ask for a battle to determine the 'real' next Chairman of the Maska Triad, claiming the first one to be exempt as one family member was not involved in the decision-making process. She was banished from the Maska Triad as a child. She was abandoned and sent away to Taiwan. Do anything and everything in your power to make sure you stay alive and she dies. She is going to make your life a living hell if you let her win."

Atheno-Li said barely, fighting to stay alive, with his eyes closing slowly second by second.

He had closed his eyes for the very last time in his life, with Jing-Lee desperately trying to re-open them, not wanting to let go and also wanting more details on Wera-Li. But the time had struck, and his father was now gone from this world. The Chairman had passed.

An abandoned older sister? Attempting to become Maska Triad Chairman? Wanting revenge?

He observed his now-dead role model father for several more minutes, spending the time in his bedroom thinking about all the good memories he and his father enjoyed over the years. Jing-Lee didn't want to disappoint him from the heavens. He didn't want to disappoint any of his previous ancestors, he didn't want to disappoint any current members, but most importantly, he didn't want to disappoint himself. The new Chairman then sat on the cold wooden floor, cross-legged, reminiscing on everything he learned because of the man.

In the evening, Zara entered the hospital after a very emotional few hours with her father. Derrick shed bundles of tears, becoming an emotional wreck. With his wife passing and now his son passing in the same very year, the man was becoming a depressed mess. Derrick asked his beloved daughter to tell him any information she can get her hands on regarding the death of Jason, which was too much for her to handle, knowing the grim truth that occurred. She promised him, despite knowing that she couldn't tell anyone about the night in Taiwan.

Approaching the entrance of the third-floor hospital, she saw that Tarawa-Li was still in his peculiar looking sleep. Apart from the lunatic, no one else was to be seen, with the ward's hallways containing an eerie presence around them.

Zara entered the room that Mallory had been staying in. She was welcomed by a surprised-looking Dan-Li and Mallory, with the latter still suffering pretty badly from her underlying condition, looking the most stressed a new mother could be. Dan-Li and Zara sat on opposite directions, centring themselves around the poorly mother. She had a significant increase of medication and testing, which made it most likely that she wasn't fully aware of her surroundings.

Dan-Li also looked abysmal, attempting to keep his eyes open for the unexpected guest, constantly sipping his energy drink that he purchased at the near-enough vending machine. He was quite astonished by the fact that Zara came alone to visit them both once again, especially without her new fiancé. He didn't mind at all that she came by herself. The surprise almost felt heart-warming for him, considering that someone would visit Mallory more than one occasion in a single day (Tarawa-Li hasn't really "helped" the couple much, except startling and spooking out anyone who came to visit the third-floor).

Nebulous on her reason for visiting, she asked the couple if there was anything, anything at all, that she could do for them both. By this point, Mallory was already becoming extremely fatigued once more, almost fully asleep. The energy drink that was once grabbed in the hand of Dan-Li was transferred into the trash, and he too was on the verge of falling into sleep-state. Zara walked over to the other side of the bed and prodded the right arm of Dan-Li and indicated him to sleep. Zara herself would be on overnight watch to accommodate his ill bride-to-be. He nodded and made himself scarce. He scans the place he would be sleeping for the night, as far away from his lunatic brother as possible.

After he had found a place to lay his exhausted head for the night, she was alone in the room with an almost sleeping Mallory, who could barely open her eyes. Zara silently approached the door of the room, glancing to her left and right. Still, with barely anyone in the near radius, she had her revenge act all to herself. The murder of Mallory Reece.

Mallory, who was at this point only seconds away from sleeping, sensed Zara's presence. Zara removed one pillow that was below the head of her soon victim, and Mallory knew for definite something wasn't right.

She started to position the pillow in front of the lifeless woman, knowing that suffocation would be the quietest and safest option she could think of. She then decided to apply force to the already breathless new mother.

"Your fiancé, your special Dan-Li, took my little brother's life! Your future husband killed my brother!" Zara whispered, with tears pouring down her face.

Mallory was non-respondent, attempting to survive the current situation, with only her brain recognising the strong accusations that she barely heard due to the force of the pillow. She knew what her fiancé did for a living, but she never knew that he would kill so close to the family circle. Zara wouldn't have made such extreme allegations if she knew there were any plot holes whatsoever.

Increasing the force, Zara cried ever so more, knowing whatever she would do would never bring her little brother back into the world. But she had to avenge his death. She had to. Mallory now drew blood, pouring out of her mouth downwards from the pillow.

She began to shake with every bone and muscle in her body, hoping that Dan-Li wouldn't return for an unbeknown reason. She missed her younger brother so much, she had to take something of equal value away from him. She couldn't do anything so cruel to the baby, so Mallory was the only relevant person she could truly target.

"I can never see my brother again because of your fucking fiancé! Do you realise that?" Zara said, with more of Mallory's blood pouring out of her lifeless body.

Before applying any more of the brute force, she stopped applying the pressure to the bleeding and hardly breathing girl. She realised that even if she did kill her, even more family tension would occur. The killing wouldn't stop until only one person was left. She knew she couldn't live with those thoughts. If she killed Mallory, she would die next. No amount of killing could ever bring her brother back. The new-born baby would have to start her life with only her father, who would be the sole reason why her mother wouldn't be alive. She did this for Aria Maska. She stopped the killing for the baby.

Zara ran out of the room for emergency help, knowing well that the events that occurred with herself and Mallory would never be mentioned in any future of theirs.

Emergency aid responded to Mallory's bleeding and breathing problem within a heartbeat, with the new mother recovering well within an hour. Zara decided not to wake Dan-Li up, knowing that he would question her on the bleeding of his fiancé, perhaps even killing her - like he did her brother.

She decided not to even question his actions regarding the day he killed her brother. The event had occurred and there was nothing to do about it. Zara was the bigger person eventually, deciding not to continue the war. She would always be upset about her brother, but she wouldn't continue the act of violence.

After recovering from the recent incident, Mallory eventually fell back to sleep, too tired to talk. Zara left her once again and was on her way out of the third floor to return home. Shockingly, Tarawa-Li shot out of the three armless chairs for the first time since his sleep perhaps almost a full day ago.

"Need a ride?" Zara asked, still with a few tears on her sad face.

“Yes, please.” Tarawa-Li replied, perspiring rapidly, speaking in an uneven tone.

“Let’s go then.” Zara said, wiping the remaining tears off her face.

CHAPTER NINE:
LUCID DREAMING

"I've been awake for the past couple of days to make sure you two are managing well, so I'm going for a quick sleep." Tarawa-Li yawned, "Don't wake me up unless it's an emergency. Jing-Lee coming is not an emergency; a true brother would've been here by now."

Tarawa-Li left Dan-Li and Mallory, citing three armless hospital chairs to sleep on, as the location was prime considering it was only a few footsteps from the room that Mallory was staying in, and it smelt odourless in comparison to his other sleeping options. He was effervescent of becoming an uncle for the first time - for baby Aria Maska. But being awake for days on end resulted in him nearly collapsing due to unbearable fatigue due to the no rest.

The Surgeon approached the three lifeless chairs and laid down. His head hurt not only from the rushes of adrenaline he had been receiving, but now hurting for a second reason, with non-existent head support to comfort and guide his sleeping. This didn't bother the man for long, though. He was too tired to care about a first-world issue. He had been assisting to Dan-Li and Mallory's everyday needs on hospital grounds without any help. He was due to crash and burn at some point.

After a mere minute or two, Tarawa-Li fell asleep. He started to experience a dream similar to a few other dreams he had been receiving recently, but this one in particular felt even more extraordinary. He had full control in this dream, and he knew he was definitely dreaming this time, without a sense of doubt in his mind. The man gained almost full control of the dream, including the characters, narrative and environment. This was truly a fascinating spectacle for Tarawa-Li, who couldn't barely even control his feelings or actions in his everyday life anymore.

The first part of his elusive dreaming included a sandy beach, specifically, a beach on the coast of Korea. Standing in front of him was his mother, who always had been his role model. Besides the woman was Dae, his former dog. The feeling felt surreal, and he believed he may have legitimately died and ended up in the after world. His mother and his dog smile in unison, almost as if both could see him in front of their eyes, too.

All of a sudden, in his right hand was a tennis ball - which he always used to carry around with him as a child, with many several hours dedicated to playing catch with his dog. He threw the ball as far as he physically could, almost falling over into the sand in the process. The ball went flying into the air, with Dae desperately sprinting to catch the airborne ball into his saliva-filled mouth.

“How have you been, cutie pie?” started to repeat and multiply in Tarawa-Li’s head over and over in the same soothing voice his mother used to ask him as a child. The voice kept on replaying and replaying in his shaking head until he started to produce tears.

“Mamma, can you hear me?” Tarawa-Li asked, “Can you hear your son?”

No response. Perhaps this was just a lucid dream after all. The great thing about a lucid dream is that you can bring back the dead into the imaginary world of dreamland. The worst thing about a lucid dream is when you realise the dead don’t live in the real world anymore. It hurt Tarawa-Li even more, seeing his mother in lucid flesh, knowing he can’t communicate with the one person he admired for years ever again. He just didn't want to give up that easily on the one person who always supported him.

"Mamma. Please. It's Tarawa-Li. I miss you. Please tell me that you can sense my presence." Tarawa-Li yelled, wanting to hear the voice of his mother one last time.

The woman approached Tarawa-Li with two footsteps forward on the sandy beach. She brushed through his longish hair, caressed his cheek, and gazed into his confused eyes. Tarawa-Li was more than confused. He didn't know whether she was a hallucination of his mind anymore. Maybe she was real. Maybe his mother knows about his psychotic actions since her death and doesn't want any acknowledgement of the two together. He became paranoid, became worried, became upset.

"Play with Dae. I'm going now." started to repeat and multiply now into his broken mind, with the identical repetition and soothing voice as before. He physically started to shake, toss and turn.

The perfect imagery of his happiness in life vanished in front of his very eyes once more. She was gone once again. The lucid dream he was encountering wasn't strong enough to hold all the good thoughts and ideas simultaneously. The Surgeon had major control, yes, but not complete control.

Dae finally approached once again, this time returning with the tennis ball covered in his slippery saliva. The beloved dog releases the ball out of his mouth and starts his usual panting that he did back in the day. Tarawa-Li picks the soggy tennis ball up and clutches it in his right hand for extra grip, making sure this throw was even further for the dog to catch.

"Fetch boy! Go get it, Dae!" Tarawa-Li yelled, throwing the ball as far as he physically could, this time resulting in him falling onto the soft sand.

Dae ran as fast as he could; the throw Tarawa-Li gave was an impressive feat for him to run. The warm sand felt great for his four paws, and Dae would have known it too, if he wasn't being portrayed in a figment of his former owner's sleeping hallucinations.

Finally after a good minute or so, Dae returned to give him the even sloppier green tennis ball. Identical to the old times the two would spend their company together. For a brief moment, both paused and took a valuable good look at each other, reminiscing on their past. Dae could have never caused any carnage, he never showed any signs of aggressive behaviour or any negative characteristics or attributes at all. Atheno-Li must've just hated animals with a passion and wanted a good excuse for them not to be near him.

After three or four more times playing catch with Dae, the fifth time was different. The lucid dream almost felt crashed or disturbed. When Tarawa-Li threw the tennis ball into the distance for his dog to chase, the dog stood stationary and unresponsive, like he was staring at nothing.

The pleasant lucid dream he was having started to decline rapidly at an alarming pace, beginning to create isolated, abused and worthless undertones. The surrounding heavenly yellow background blur transformed into a demonic red colour and the imagery he was seeing in front of him regarding the setting and characters was less clear and instead more blurred. The second part of his lucid dream was by the entrance to the family house. This time the dream involved Atheno-Li, a few of his security members, and Dae.

He attempted to run to Dae, who was besides Atheno-Li, casually resting on the patio floor. Before making a successful first footstep into the direction of his loved dog, he was unable to. He was static in position. The Surgeon was met by security, who were now rushing at him like an escaped fugitive who had just robbed another bank. There were two of them restraining him on each of his arms.

His father greeted him with a sadistic smile and a sarcastic wink. He started to rub his hands together, almost like he was an evil monster. Which was wrong. He wasn't "like" an evil monster, he definitely was an evil monster. Before speaking a singular word, he taunted his son, gesturing for him to move forward if he wanted to save his dog. By this point, Tarawa-Li was physically moving so much that he began to tussle and turn heavily in the real world – he would do anything to save Dae once more, no matter if it were a hallucination or not.

Nothing positive occurred, and he had to stay stationary with whatever malevolence his father decided to do with the poor animal. He couldn't believe he was about to see Dae die twice in one life. The beloved dog was still sleeping, which, unfortunately, will be the last peaceful experience for the friendly companion.

Atheno-Li woke up Dae, turned to his side and showed the dog whatever he was hiding in his pocket. The dog looked mildly startled, unsure of whatever was shown to him. Atheno-Li continued with his sadistic smile, knowing whatever he was going to do would cause his son to erupt in tears once more. He turned fully forward to Tarawa-Li and revealed what was in his pocket from the beginning. It was a knife. The wicked man laughed out loudly this time, with saliva forming at the corner of his mouth.

"You don't need any stupid animal in your life, punk!" Atheno-Li yelled, with a crazed look in his eye.

He began to stab the dog, with the first slashing to be on the helpless animals' rear-left paw, too deep a wound for Dae to move for aid and to survive this attack. The second slashing was received in Dae's front-left paw, resulting in the dog to lay and rest on his unharmed side, crying in the process and howling for help.

Tarawa-Li once again attempted to come to the aid of Dae, only resulting in the identical animation of him being static and the same security members restraining him, two for each arm. The Surgeon pleaded for his father to stop the torture. He pleaded for him not to kill his pet.

"To be a success in your life, you need to be the hunter and not the prey. You need to kill and not to die. You need to hurt and not to bruise. The only way I will ever be proud of you and hopefully one day call you my child is if you make me proud." Atheno-Li shouted, whilst slashing the dog's two previously unaffected paws.

Tarawa-Li was drowning in his own tears, both in the lucid dream and in the real world. All the hatred and anger, all the negative energy and suicidal thoughts was all because of this man. The day he would find out his father's passing would be the day he could finally let go of the man his father forced him to become. The sadistic Oculoplastic Surgeon, Tarawa-Li Maska – those days being that person were numbered.

The third part of the dream came into fruition, with this portion having more of a bizarre twist. The setting was still the same, being in the family house, but the characters involved were different, making Tarawa-Li insecure. He turned to his left and saw a mirror in the hallway. In his reflection was Tarawa-Li, but a version of himself as a child.

He was located not too far from some normally quiet rooms, but he could distinctly hear a conversation in the near background. This time, managing to move again, he deciphered where the noise he could hear was coming from. The living room. He silently made his way to the room, sneaking up until he met with the cracked door. Taking a slight peak inside the room, he could see his two brothers, Jing-Lee and Dan-Li, who were also children.

Tarawa-Li didn't want to interrupt the conversation, not knowing the repercussions of intruding moments in a lucid dream. He just stay put, staring at how wonderful his brothers were.

“Tarawa-Li is a lunatic.” Jing-Lee whispered, trying to snigger as quietly as possible.

“Be quiet. The lunatic may hear you.” Dan-Li replied, looking out at the door entrance, unable to identify Tarawa-Li.

His heart sunk. Did his brothers always hate him? Was this just a stupid lucid dream? Did this really happen when he was a child? The first two sections of this lucid dream had some truth to it, so maybe this did too. He was shocked to hear those sentences coming out of their mouths.

“How can a dog be his best friend? What a loser. Animals can’t talk.” Jing-Lee said, unable to contain his laughter.

“He’s definitely the last one to get a girlfriend out of us three. He might not even get a girlfriend in his entire life!” Dan-Li replied, trying to contain his laughter.

The third part of the lucid dream came to a quick conclusion, with the fourth part putting itself into play. This time, however, was even stranger than before. This fourth part of Tarawa-Li’s lucid dream was something no one could have ever drawn up.

A completely dark background, with an almost blinding bright light displaying two people ahead of him. The two people were Tarawa-Li. They were completely identical, excluding one major detail.

The first Tarawa-Li, to the left side, held a sign which displayed:

Option One

- The Surgeon
- The Psychopath
- The Killer
- The man that your father always wanted you to become

This in particular version of Tarawa-Li was the current day version. He had become everything he hated, which made it worse knowing he may not ever change back to what he used to be as a child.

The second Tarawa-Li, to the right side, held a sign which displayed:

Option Two

- The Sweetheart
- Animal Enthusiast
- The Healer
- The man your mother always thought you would end up being in life

He began to cry again. No matter how hard he could try now, he knew his brain was programmed to always hurt, not heal. But he still attempts to choose the version to his right, but selecting it was impossible, with his finger touching an untouchable, holographic Tarawa-Li. He then attempts to choose the version to his left this time, which was an instant success.

Upon touching the left version of himself, the Tarawa-Li that he saw in front of his very eyes changed into the face of Atheno-Li. His father would always be in his mind until the day both of them died. He profusely screamed, which was when he finally woke up from his lucid dream.

Tarawa-Li shot out of the three armless chairs for the first time since his sleep, perhaps almost a full day ago now.

"Need a ride?" Zara asked, with a few tears on her face, seeming upset.

"Yes, please." Tarawa-Li replied, perspiring rapidly, speaking in an uneven tone.

"Let's go then." Zara said, wiping the few tears off her face.

CHAPTER TEN: LAW AND ORDER

It was once again a beautiful sunrise in the background of the family home, with an important day ahead. Today would mark the first official day of work for Jing-Lee as the Chairman of the Maska Triad, as his lifelong desire came true. Jing-Lee knew he couldn't mourn his father passing for one day longer. He needed to set his intentions into the future. He needed to decide what changes he's going to make, changes to improve their advantageous position even further ahead from the criminal and business field. The two main targets/rivals he now considered were the Takani Triad, and his newly revealed older sister, Wera-Li.

Jing-Lee woke up earlier than usual this morning, as he knew for himself to become a valuable and well-respected Chairman, he must prove displays of being competent at his job - instead of being a standstill leader with no clue on how to lead. He left his bedroom in a glowing golden robe, making his way into the beautiful gardens that surrounded the house. He took time to appreciate the scenery, appreciate what his father gave him, appreciate his powerful status, now that he had become leader. One day he thought that his fiancé could even become his professional companion, believing Aero and Lilac had a catchy vibrance together. He returned to his bedroom, getting prepared for the busy day about to approach him.

The first of his meetings was with Lawyer Derrick Holland. Their main topic of conversation regarded the legal work now that he had become Chairman, but both knew they had many several other topics to discuss before their meeting came to an end. Both sat at the dining room table, with Jing-Lee taking more of a casual approach to this meeting, considering he was still talking to his future father-in-law.

"Congratulations on becoming the Maska Triad Chairman, Jing-Lee!" Derrick congratulated sincerely, "The legal work in actually altering who's the Chairman isn't that difficult. It's the things you want to change, such as investments and other malarkey."

"Let's stop the contract killings. We don't need it. We have enough money to not ever need a full-time or part-time job ever again." Jing-Lee stated, clenching his right fist.

“Anything else?” Derrick replied, attempting a casual smile whilst writing scruffily in his notebook.

“Investigate whether we can transfer our main headquarters from here to PlaciCorp. If so, see if there’s potential for a helipad on one of the higher floors. Obviously not on the actual floor - side extension.” Jing-Lee replied, refraining from any eye-contact.

“I’ll look into it myself. Anything else you would like to immediately change?” Derrick asked, hoping for a friendlier tone of voice from the Chairman and future son-in-law to be.

“No matter if we can or cannot move to PlaciCorp for new headquarters. Let’s build an underground bunker nonetheless, with space to allow vehicles, weapons and military-level equipment. PlaciCorp is our key to success.” Jing-Lee replied, this time making eye-contact with Derrick, with a small grin, “Oh, and I almost forgot. Fire all of our security guards and working girls. We don’t need them.”

“Discontinuation of the contract killings, adjustment of headquarters location, construction of bunker. Got it.” Derrick replied swiftly, checking if his sweat was visible. “And no more security or working girls.”

“Do you like me?” Jing-Lee interjected, this time looking at him straight in the eye.

“Of course I do, why would you ask me that?” Derrick replied, with his perspiration levels increasing by the second.

“There’s a snake somewhere close to the route of the centre. I need to defang it before it poisons and kills everyone.” Jing-Lee stated, insinuating that the snake is the person in front of him.

“Do you think I’m the poison? I’m the snake?” Derrick asked nervously.

“All I’m saying is loyalty is what makes businesses thrive. Cheats die.” Jing-Lee replied, wanting to wrap up this in particular topic of conversation, rapidly changed the subject, he asked, “How are you coping with Jason’s death? Zara told me.”

“It’s difficult, for both of us. Thanks for asking. It’s still going to take a while for it to evade being so surreal.” Derrick slowly said, trying not for his emotions to get the better of him once more.

“Don’t mention it. I know how important Jason was to both of you. I wouldn’t be the same person if something of similar nature occurred to me.” Jing-Lee said – even though he couldn’t stop to stereotype the man with tattoos.

"Do you think you could find out who killed my son?" Derrick asked, "Is it possible for you to track down his or her information?"

"Sorry for not asking for your blessing." Jing-Lee interrupted once more.

"What? What are you on about?" Derrick said.

"I'm sorry for not asking for your blessing before proposing to your daughter." Jing-Lee repeated.

"This is Korea, isn't it? So many different cultural aspects, I presumed perhaps you didn't even need to ask for my blessing. It's absolutely fine. You mean a lot to her." Derrick smiled, realising Jing-Lee didn't always come off as an arrogant jerk.

Derrick left the dining room table with no signs of animosity between the two anymore, after the tilt towards a sentimental conversation. The lawyer returned home and would return as soon as he had all the relevant news concerning all of Jing-Lee's new directive regulations for the Maska Triad. Jing-Lee remained seated for a brief amount of time, hoping Atheno-Li was already proud watching him from heaven, with the strong and lawful decisions he had already made. He already knew what impact he was going to make in the criminal world now that he was leader of the most influential triad in Korea. He wanted to make the whole country his recreational playground – no matter how daft that sounded to some people.

After a few more minutes, his second meeting was about to begin, with this meeting being with Yung-Ko Jang. The quintessential triad right hand man had guided his late father for years, turning them into an indestructible empire. He hoped for the same relationship with him, knowing that if the pair bonded and talked business, surely it will be the exact same relationship. Both sat in the office, taking the formal serious approach, in comparison to the experience with his future father-in-law less than an hour ago.

Yung-Ko lit one of his traditional cigars in the room, with Jing-Lee allowing a plethora of habits the Chinaman had to be more than allowed. He was known to be somewhat annoying on off days, so Jing-Lee knew this type of behaviour would be happening on common occasion. The smoke filled the small office, even resulting in a concern for visual distraction by a few minutes later – and lots of coughing by the new Chairman's part. Yung-Ko wasn't impressed by the waiting, so he decided to initiate the meeting to speed the process up.

"What did you tell Derrick to change?" Yung-Ko asked, puffing away at his cigar.

“Contract killings are being stopped. I also want to transform PlaciCorp into an even bigger company than what it already is. No more security guards or working girls, either.” Jing-Lee replied, in a friendly but firm approach.

“Should’ve told me first. Now, if any backlash occurs due to those three things, you’ll be getting all the blame, not me. Your father used me as a shield, and I don’t expect you to be any different.” Yung-Ko stated in an almost derivative effect.

“I guess I’ll know next time. Are you feeling less tired from before?” Jing-Lee asked, trying to clear the cigar smoke from his eyes.

“Yes. Thanks.” Yung-Ko replied, puffing on his cigar even more.

“I’m glad we’re working together. You and my father had a great working relationship, so I’m hoping our working relationship will be the same.” Jing-Lee said.

“What’s your plan for the future?” Yung-Ko asked, curious to find out about the Chairman’s answer.

“Well, it would be nice if we could own Korea.” Jing-Lee joked, although he was actually considering the possibility by now.

“Let me know on anything you want to do. As I said before, run everything through me first; I can advise and take blame. That's pretty much my job role." Yung-Ko stated, finishing his cigar.

The Chinaman left the office in a hurry, most likely to visit a local shop to buy more cigars. The meeting definitely wasn't what Jing-Lee had pictured or hoped for, but he realised the relationship may take a considerable duration to truly form. He could trust Yung-Ko with his life. Like he had said in the meeting, the job role he enforces is to be the shield, protecting the Chairman for any bullets that would be shot in his direction. The shield he had was the most respected he could equip himself with, he was invincible.

The third meeting the Chairman had scheduled for the day would be with his two brothers, but it didn't start until evening, meaning he still had some free time. He went outside for a breath of fresh air, when he realised Tarawa-Li just entered the house with an unfamiliar guest. He had brought home a Nureongi breed dog, who was sitting by the side of the Surgeon. He saw his brother elated with emotion. It seemed as though he bought himself a pet, the first since their father had barred animals from entering the family house, also the very first full day since his death. Jing-Lee slowly approached the laidback dog and glanced upon his collar. The dog's name was

Kwan - which its name represents strength in Korean culture and heritage.

“What do you think of my new dog?” Tarawa-Li cheerfully asked, who couldn’t contain his excitement.

“Nice dog. It’s just a little embarrassing you brought the little guy here even though I haven’t lifted the animal ban on this house.” Jing-Lee replied. “I don’t know what has gotten into you lately, but I miss the sadistic version of you. I hate the new laidback gimmick you’re trying to pull. No pets. A dog can’t be your best friend, lunatic.”

Flashbacks of Tarawa-Li’s lucid dreaming re-emerge in his mind. He became paranoid. His two brothers may have thought he was a lunatic ever since he was a child. He knew he could never replace Dae, but bringing in Kwan could give the guy some aid towards his mental health. He still couldn’t believe that his family thought that there was no benefit in owning an animal, especially for companionship in regard to people who may need emotional and mental support in their everyday life. All he wanted was to bring in Kwan as his personal pet to give him some positivity in his life, to turn over a new chapter, to becoming a more laidback person. Instead, he was still seen no different than usual, no different than being a psychotic monstrosity that would drill, axe or saw through any person who did the family wrong. Tarawa-Li didn't want to continue living in that way, but it would take strong convincing into Jing-Lee changing his beliefs.

"What would change your mind in order for me to keep Kwan as my dog?" Tarawa-Li asked, with his hands shaking.

"Continue to be a helpful part of the Maska Triad and perhaps I'll let you keep your Kwan, or whatever his name is." Jing-Lee replied, looking at the distressed Surgeon.

"I made you become Chairman." Tarawa-Li interjected, with now a slight tone of anger in his voice.

"No you didn't, you gave the chance to me and Dan-Li, because you knew father wouldn't have allowed you to become Chairman in any circumstance." Jing-Lee replied, walking away from Tarawa-Li and Kwan.

Jing-Lee discontinued the conversation regarding pets, just in the possibility of an argument, which wouldn't have helped his later announcements regarding the evening meeting with the triplets together. He walks into his bedroom, knowing now that being Chairman is only going to get tougher from this day forward. The only way to reduce his schedule would be to acquire more staff on payroll, but he couldn't trust anyone in Korea anymore. Plus, the Maska Triad owned nearly every damn thing in the country, meaning he could free up his schedule to the bone if he really so desired. He was about to lay on his bed when his phone rang. He opened his pockets, finding out that Derrick was calling him, hopefully regarding good news about the alterations he wants to commit to in an immediate fashion. He answers his phone.

"I'm hoping for some good news, Derrick." Jing-Lee said, now laying on his bed.

"Contract killings are discontinued immediately. Security and working girls have been dismissed. The underground bunker you want to build below the PlaciCorp building is achievable but will take a long time to complete. The helipad is almost physically impossible to structure due to how high you want it and how tall the tower is." Derrick responded, hoping Jing-Lee wouldn't go ballistic hearing the not-so positive results.

"Bribe them to make it happen. If those changes are not made in my desired frame of time, you won't have a job anymore. And that's me being nice, since you'll soon be my father-in-law. Get it done. Remember. Are you a snake or tiger?" Jing-Lee demanded, hanging up the call immediately after speaking his last words.

He continued to proceed staring into space, daydreaming for a while, thinking about what he said earlier. Perhaps owning Korea could actually be achievable from all the power the Maska Triad already owned in the country. The family managed to even purchase the god-damn military, meaning owning a country wasn't an unviable hypothesis. The point of focus for gathering his two brothers for a private meeting wasn't regarding anything about this, but he pondered whether this topic of debate could become a legitimate discussion and turn into a feasible project in the future sometime. He continued to lay in his bed, until it was time for his final meeting of the day.

Evening began. With all three triplets in the living room, Dan-Li and Tarawa-Li were paying respects to their new Chairman, kneeling on the floor. Jing-Lee stood, realising the true power he had over his two brothers now. Looking down at them kneeling, he knew he could make them do anything he wanted. Although he wouldn't, knowing dissention in a small family would ultimately lead to a failure in operations and most likely lead to all of their arrests or death. He had many topics to discuss, knowing this meeting out of the three would be the most complex, most detailed, and most likely to fall flat if he didn't have the answers to back up his beliefs.

"The first major decision I have made to do as Maska Triad Chairman is to discontinue the contract killings. We all will still use our alias originally given to use by the former Chairman, meaning no need to change from Aero, Chef and Surgeon, respectively." Jing-Lee stated rather arrogantly, with an almost fire in his eyes, knowing he was in charge of everyone now.

"Does that mean we can do whatever we want now?" Dan-Li asked, constantly worrying about every minute he was away from his ill fiancé and baby.

"No. We're not doing the contract killings because we're going to be targeting the kills ourselves, instead of killing specific people that others have paid for us to do. Father told us that we have an older sister who he abandoned. She's dangerous. We also have the Takani Triad on our tail too. We need to drastically increase the crime rate in Gangnam, more in the public eye this time. We own everything apart from the Korean Investigation Unit, meaning we can get away with anything as long as we are competent at killing, which I know we all are. Gangnam is Maska territory, Korea is Maska territory. We need to make that obviously clear to both the Takani Triad and Wera-Li." Jing-Lee lectured in a crazed tone, hoping his two brothers would comply instantly, without the need of any more questions.

"We have a sister? Are you sure? Her name is what? Wera-Li Maska?" Tarawa-Li asked, stumbling in his speech, almost frightened about what Chairman Jing-Lee just told himself and Dan-Li.

"We don't need to worry about our sudden older sister Wera-Li Maska, or whatever her punk last name or first name is now. We don't even need to worry about the Takani Triad. You two just need to do what I order." Jing-Lee replied, rubbing his fists together in an almost excitement.

"You just went from talking crazy and now you're an almost sadistically calm man. Are you sure you're not the one acting strange? I feel normal compared to seeing you at this moment, Jing-Lee." Tarawa-Li said.

"It's Chairman Jing-Lee now, that's how you both address me from now on. Most certainly in the business meetings we involve ourselves in. You'll only call me Aero when we're involving ourselves in crime." Jing-Lee snapped, outraged that his brother thinks the three of them are still on the same respect and status level as before.

"Get to the point, Chairman. What's your plan in regard to increasing the crime rate in Gangnam? How are the killings, or whatever you want us to do, going to make sure the Takani Triad think twice in regard to expanding their operations in Korea?" Dan-

Li asked, legitimately curious about what answer would be said.

“PlaciCorp. We now own PlaciCorp. It’s our golden ticket into the future. PlaciCorp is the highest earning plastic surgery company in Korea, the biggest money maker we already have, if you exclude the National Services. Plastic surgery is the biggest in Korea. Do you realise how many Gangnam beauties you see in the city now? It’s not even just in Gangnam, so many other districts and places in Korea have them!” Jing-Lee answered, almost enthusiastic about the situation he was going to put the three in.

“Yes, you are correct, there are many Gangnam beauties in Gangnam and other places in Korea... you still haven’t come to your point.” Dan-Li stated, now confused about what the conclusion of this meeting will be.

“Tonight, we’re going to attack three individual Takani Triad owned businesses in the heart of Gangnam. Two of them are nightclubs, the other being a karaoke bar.” Jing-Lee announced, with his pupils widening, sporting a sickening smile.

“Are you crazy? The first day as Chairman and you want us to go into the public eye and shoot up a place?" Dan-Li shouted, standing up to the Chairman.

"Sit down, you didn't let me finish. We're not killing anyone, that would be unhelpful. I guess a little unethical, too." Jing-Lee whispered, with his brother Dan-Li returning to his seated position.

"So, I'm assuming they're all individual jobs. Who is going where and once we get to the location, what exactly do you want us to do?" Tarawa-Li asked in an intimidated tone, almost as if he were speaking to his father once more.

"You two will be heading to the Takani nightclubs where you will be doing your first acid attacks. It's up to you if you decide to bring any other weaponry. The nightclubs they own hold home many girls and boys who most likely have already had surgery, which will make the result even more ironically funny. You will have the acid stored in versions such as bombs, guns and detonators, it's your choice. Once you have targeted the optimal zone to unleash the acid, this will cause not only Takani property to get shut down, but also result in a rapid decrease of their profit margin and reputation. Hundreds, hopefully thousands of young teenagers living in Gangnam will have their faces and bodies destroyed, which is where we come in. PlaciCorp. Sure, a few may not choose to get plastic surgery, and a few may go to competitors, but PlaciCorp is the most well-known and has the highest satisfaction rating. PlaciCorp will thrive even more in profit and reputation, Takani Triad will fall, and wherever our precious little Wera-Li is, she'll go back to wherever abandoned shelter she stayed in for the majority of her childhood." Jing-Lee declared, with an almost sadistic laugh to his two brothers.

"Gangsters kill people who are members of another gang. Isn't this just terrorism? Innocent people are going to get killed. Acid can easily kill instead of injure." Tarawa-Li replied, hoping the Chairman wouldn't get snappy on himself again.

"These people are on Takani property. No matter if they are actually in the Takani Triad or not is irrelevant, they can all be considered the enemy due to being on the turf of the enemy." Jing-Lee snapped, not wanting anymore negative backlash on what he thought was the idea of a lifetime.

"Is that what you'll be doing in the karaoke bar they own?" Dan-Li asked, looking straight in the eyes of the Chairman.

"No." Jing-Lee smirked.

"Then what will you be doing? Singing a little rock-n-roll with one of their leaders?" Dan-Li sarcastically responded.

"Perhaps. It depends if he attempts to kill me when he sees me with my pistol." Jing-Lee said.

"What are you on about now?" Dan-Li asked, perhaps realising the Chairman had found one of the Takani Triad leaders.

"You remember Mouse, right?" Jing-Lee smirked, with an almost foam bubbling in the corner of his mouth.

"What about Mouse? Is he one of the Takani Leaders?" Dan-Li rushed, quickly concluding in his mind.

"Apparently so. He recently got promoted. One of the original three have gone far abroad, so they needed a replacement. Mouse is the replacement. Hopefully, I can get him to confess some information about the identity of the other two before I have to kill him." Jing-Lee answered, knowing that both brothers were praising this idea more and more the longer the conversation went on for.

"If it's already evening, how are we prepared for three huge attacks if you want us to complete them tonight?" Tarawa-Li asked, speeding his speech in curiosity and concern.

"We are the three most feared in Gangnam. We are the three most feared in Korea. We even own the police for fuck’s sake! We have so much power in Korea, one day the Maska Triad will even own the whole country! Tarawa-Li, your nightclub is Club Aitken. Dan-Li, your nightclub is Club Beauty Passion. You two can’t let me down. I know you can’t let me down, because if you do, you’ll receive the same punishment everyone clubbing in those two places right now will feel. That’s how I’ll know you’ll complete the attack tonight, because we’re the fucking gangsters of Gangnam.” Jing-Lee interjected, knocking out the concern that filled Tarawa-Li’s conscience.

CHAPTER ELEVEN: AITKEN

After a few hours passed from their meeting together, the three decided to share dinner, mapping out each strategies, escape routes and weapons they would be bringing with them. The three attacks would all happen in the same night. They all unanimously agreed it was safer to perform each attack in a chronological order, in case of any errors to rectify, and to shake the Takani Triad off their game.

The first of the three brothers, Tarawa-Li, was planning his attack on Club Aitken, one of Gangnam's fastest rising nightclubs in Korea. He wanted to experiment with more of a laidback and confident approach to the attack, in comparison to his normal sadistic self. But even Tarawa-Li knew that his mind would transform him into the volatile monster he knows too well once he sees weapons in his hands and people vulnerable at his disposal.

Anyhow, he decided his approach for the night's acid attack on Club Aitken. He was to bring hydrochloric acid bombs, an acid squirt gun, a mask, and a silenced pistol - in case of any potential mishaps. He would go up to the Club DJ, impersonating a Club Aitken Intern DJ, remove him temporarily off his set, and perform a DJ set for himself. Once he gathered all of the vulnerable clubbers together to rave, he would throw the hydrochloric acid bombs, labelling them to the crowd as 'water bombs'. Instantly after being thrown, he would then use his acid squirt gun to spray any clubbers who were unaffected nearer to his side of the DJ booth. The silenced pistol would then be used for any unaffected clubbers who were looking to fight back, or any of the Takani Triad who were present at the time of the attack.

Club Aitken was on high ground, meaning no vehicles were able to block the entrance, as the entrance to the club was via detachable metal stairs. Although Tarawa-Li knew he could detach the stairs, that tactic would then make him become vulnerable. He was to leave as the others, acting like he was running for their life and trying not to die. That's where the mask became involved with his equipment, removing the possibility for the Surgeon to receive any acid or acid residue on his face.

The targeted amount of people to be present at Club Aitken was roughly one thousand. Although, as long as the attack was successful, the numbers wouldn't be the biggest factor. PlaciCorp would have a high influx of new customers, meaning, as a high reputable company, they would be allowed to increase their prices for customers. This would be the same case for Club Beauty Passion later in the evening too.

Tarawa-Li had to dress up chic, modish and fashionable for the occasion, sporting the classical and overused designer clothing, sparkling wristwatch, and colour-coated sunglasses. He was to carry his inventory in a trendy rucksack, which would contain the different items separately in different sections. He was intrigued to see if acid attacks were better than shootings, and if the plan the new Chairman drew up would really work in the effect that he thought. The emergency plan for them all was to contact the Chairman, (In Jing-Lee's case, his emergency contact would be Dan-Li) with him corresponding in what the most suitable cause of action would be, dependant on the scenario.

The next cause of action Tarawa-Li briskly and briefly took was the actual part of being a DJ. In order to garner the greatest number of teenagers to target, Tarawa-Li knew he actually had to educate himself on the basic principles of entertaining a crowd of drunken teenagers with trendy music and a novice skill of remixing. Without having a physical set for him to practice on, he used his brilliant yet wacky mind to envision himself having a physical set in front of his very eyes. The Surgeon spent the next quarter-hour educating himself on the premise, with him believing he figured out the beginner's level of the skill already.

He left the family house, ready to adventure on a new form of attack he had never performed before. It was surprising for him, considering he spent many years of his life being a complete and volatile lunatic. He thought to himself about the plan: *Wait in Line, Enter, DJ, Music, Bombs, Squirt Gun, Mask, Real Gun, Escape.*

The Surgeon had recently been separated into two distinct personalities: sadistic and laidback. Perhaps that was a good thing for him; during work he could be the sadistic monster his brother wants him to continue being, whilst out-of-work hours he could adapt to the new laidback lifestyle he had been finding comfort in. This way, all parties would be happy. Plus, this would hopefully tame his multiple personality disorder for a while longer. Instead of having several various personalities which contained different moods and emotions, having two distinct personalities could help him cope better mentally.

He had finally entered a walking distance to Club Aitken. The streets of Gangnam were as busy as ever, filled with Gangnam beauties with their slutty skirts, drunken students pretending not to be lightweights, wannabe rappers with fake chains, drug dealers with cocaine and independent food carts serving portions of meat, noodles and rice. The streets were overbearing, with hardly any space to walk, making it feel like everyone was stuck in a field like a bunch of sheep. Walking past the other numerous nightclubs, designer stores, and restaurants, (which some were owned by the Maska Triad) Tarawa-Li finally approached Club Aitken. The waiting line to enter the club was utterly ridiculous, with a line full of teenagers queuing from the top of the high detachable stairs right down until the front semi-window of a food cart that sold meat on the street corner. The waiting time was definitely going to be an incredibly long period, but knowing Jing-Lee, it didn't matter. What mattered was getting the attack done and people hurt.

The three brothers knew that in case there was a slight chance of the Takani Triad having any lead on the Maska Triad, they had to conceal their identity. The Takani Triad may know the names of members of the Maska Triad, especially due to the PlaciCorp deal with Mouse, but fabricating identification cards and concealing their natural looks meant that the Takani Triad would have a significantly less chance of identifying the triplets.

The waiting line that Tarawa-Li stood was moving closer to Club Aitken than he had expected. It was full of the stereotypical people previously mentioned, with a few foreigners who were most likely taking a Korean vacation. Eavesdropping indicated that everyone was going to this club due to the recent reviews and price for alcohol, just wanting a good time. This made the Surgeon chuckle, as he knew the future that awaited these teenagers. He himself was about to have a very pleasant time indeed. The innocent people he was about to attack however, they were most likely going to experience their next positive day when leaving the PlaciCorp operation room with their new plastic faces.

The waiting line to enter Club Aitken gradually became scarcer, with Tarawa-Li now one of the next people to enter. Finally, the time came, and he was next in line. He gave the security his fabricated ID, which was a valiant success, and headed to the nightclub floor. Before taking his first footstep inside, he was grabbed by his backpack by the security guard that checked his ID card.

“Backpacks aren’t allowed.” The security guard said.

“I’m one of the DJ’s.” Tarawa-Li swiftly replied, pleading to himself that there wasn’t an official list of the performers each night.

“Oh, sorry man. Staff room is immediately to your left when entering.” The security guard replied.

He quickly made his way to the staff room, not noticing the layout of the club, but instead keeping his head down and minding his own important business for the moment being.

He opened the staff room and went over his plans for the night. Luckily, the staff room was completely empty, with a dusty couch, and leather stools in front of a counter and dirty mirrors. There were traces of cocaine and other unidentifiable drugs which were scattered across the disgusting floor, sharing it with cracked bottles of alcohol.

The Surgeon made his way to plod his rucksack quickly on the counter, thinking of a method to allow him to bring his rucksack alongside him when performing. Thinking of the most ingenious way, Tarawa-Li just gambled with his limited options, deciding on his stage name to be DJ Bag, hoping he could get away with the situation as easy as that. Before running into a potential legitimate member of staff for Club Aitken, he put his rucksack back on.

He left the dull and disgusting staff room. The entrance is extremely near to his right side, and the DJ booth extremely far to his north-west. The nightclub was fully chaotic at this point in time, making the mission walking to the booth feel like an actual marathon race. Barging through hundreds of drunken people, luckily not being groped by any sick perverts or hassled bumping into anyone, he finally made it to his desired destination. Standing in direct view to the minimal height incline of stairs to the booth was the current DJ performing his set, known to the mainstream world as 'DJ Lunar'. With the smoke fog that filled the floor, and the rapidly heightened heat due to a mass of clubbers being packed together like a swarm of sardines, it became a little tricky to decipher on the guy's features. He knew that was mainly irrelevant anyway, he just hoped that the DJ would comply easily with what he was about to say to him. Tarawa-Li slowly made his way onto the second step of the stage, motioning for DJ Lunar to hear what he had to say.

"Hey man, what's up?" DJ Lunar shouted, due to how close the two of them were to the main speakers.

"Manager told me that you have to cut your set short, man. Sorry." Tarawa-Li shouted back.

"That's such bullshit! Am I still getting paid full?" DJ Lunar yelled back.

"You're going to have to check with the main man, sorry. Just let me take over your set for the meanwhile, at least?" Tarawa-Li shouted back, hoping he would just simply agree.

"Fine. Sorry to put the blame on you, man. What's your name anyways? I'm Lunar. Nice to meet you." DJ Lunar shouted in all his might to make sure he could be heard, mixing the DJ set with his left hand.

"I'm DJ Bag. Nice to meet you." Tarawa-Li yelled back, with all the power in his voice, as the music speakers were ever-increasing in volume.

"No, man. What's your real name?" DJ Lunar shouted back, still mixing his current song for the clubbers.

"Call me Surgeon." Tarawa-Li shouted, resulting in a second nature sadistic smile to DJ Lunar. Whenever Tarawa-Li introduced himself as the Surgeon, he would always end up with the same sadistic smile.

"Whatever, man. Just watch my set, get the clubbers hyped and I'll come back to finish in a few minutes. Don't get too comfortable." DJ Lunar shouted, almost losing his voice completely in the process of conversing this time.

He left the booth visibly outraged, budging in the way of Tarawa-Li on his descent downwards from the stage. With no visible DJ on the platform, he quickly walked up the remaining steps to replace the void. Once on, he saw the hundreds if not thousands of people in front of him, jumping upwards in unison – picture-perfect like the rave trailers you would see on a social media advertisement. There was a detachable silver microphone to the left, and Tarawa-Li knew he had to act sooner rather than later. He grabbed the microphone savagely and introduced himself to the raucous intoxicated crowd.

"What's up, Club Aitken? Let me hear some noise!" Tarawa-Li exclaimed excitingly, trying his hardest to hype the crowd up and gather them as close as possible, and more importantly, further away from the exit.

The crowd goes wild, screaming to the top of their lungs, with one hand to the side of their faces up in the air, and the other holding their bottle of alcohol. Many of them had bloodshot eyes already, some with slurred movement, and some kissing people they never met until a few minutes ago. This was perfect timing for Tarawa-Li to attack. To keep the high level of interest maintained, he continued.

"My name is DJ Bag, and once the beat drops for the new song I'm going to play for you all, I'm going to be throwing some water bombs to mark this prestigious night for you guys and myself. How does that sound? I'll also have my special squirt gun with me, so the closer you are to this booth, the more chance you'll get either hit by the water bomb or squirt gun! Who wants that? Let me hear some noise, Gangnam!" Tarawa-Li hyped, surprisingly with an overwhelmingly positive and enthusiastic crowd who came even closer to him, with everyone swarming together.

He began to play a typical club song, just with a fancy pre-recorded remix, meaning he just had to be a hype man until the perfect timing to release his cloaked weaponry struck. He took his rucksack off and opened it, taking the acid bombs and squirt gun out first. The music became louder and louder. Especially considering Tarawa-Li was sober, he could definitely feel the increase in volume, he perhaps flicked up a button accidentally. After a minute or so, it was time to attack. The beat dropped, a near thousand clubbers at his disposal, acid weaponry in his hands.

Tarawa-Li first rapidly threw the bombs as close to the entrance as possible, with four throws perfectly blocking a safe entrance/exit, with the acid dangerously dispersing into the already fogged air. No one from the inside could escape safely, no one from the outside could help. The Surgeon then throws a second batch of the acid bombs, this time scattering them in random places, chucking them at random horrified clubbers. The acid spilled onto many faces this time, with the splashes of the dangerous liquid going into people's skin and eyes.

Tarawa-Li then brings his acid squirt gun into play. He ravages the people nearest to him with the hydrochloric acid, with the people instantly losing their eyesight and parts of their faces. All of the teenagers begin to scream for mercy. Some were already dead from the effects of the acid, some had lost their eyesight instantly, some had traces of acid on their faces or in their tongues. Everyone had at least felt a harsh burn of the dangerous liquid already, in the space of a minute or two.

He put his mask on but continued his attack. He had multiple acid bombs to his disposal, and he wanted to make sure he did a good job. The room was already filled with burnt or dead clubbers, so he chuckled when he threw the remaining bombs into the faces of the strangers, and into the ceiling fan, which sprayed the acid like it was a sprinkler of death.

People who were drunk and having a good time were now either dead, extremely burnt or mildly burnt. Many tried running to the exit, only to see the biggest cloud of foggy acid scientifically possible. Even being intoxicated, the teenagers knew that if they ran, they would most likely die attempting to penetrate through it. Many friends cuddled up together, trying to help each other remove acid from themselves, trying to stop the horrific burns they were feeling. Their skin was crawling in horrific sensations. There were even a few who attempted fighting back at the attack Tarawa-Li just did, only to meet themselves with the acid too.

Tarawa-Li didn't have all the time in the world to stare at the barbaric force he had just caused, even though he loved looking at the sight of his creations. He grabbed his gun out of his rucksack, put his backpack on, and used his mask to help his face avoid the acid torture.

He jumps from the stage into the bloody mess of the crowd, instantly shooting the heads of anyone who tried to come near him and touch him. Running towards the exit, he realised the acid cloud that haunted it had vanished. There were now a few clubbers running out of Club Aitken, which was bittersweet news for Tarawa-Li (bitter - due to the fact he had to make sure he could run away from the situation as fast as possible without others detecting he had a mask, sweet - meaning it wouldn't look suspicious for him leaving the club running away from the situation as fast as possible). Tarawa-Li completely sprints out of the nightclub alongside wounded others, placing his mask into his rucksack as soon as he left the acid filled site.

Managing to somehow complete the task with no damage to himself and huge damage to approximately a thousand people, the first attack on the Takani Triad for the night resulted in a huge success for the Maska Triad.

Tarawa-Li was proud of the carnage he had caused. Sure, he was transforming into more of a laidback persona, but he still loved killing people with a passion at other times of the day. It made Tarawa-Li incredibly happy to know his killings were for a purposeful duty, helping his family make the competition weaker, and soon for their rivals to be begging them for mercy and peace.

His conscience did create a small underlying guilt for him, claiming he is now a terrorist, but he trusted his brother's words more than the ones in his twisted head. This act of crime was committed inside property owned by their main rivals, meaning that anyone who was inside associated themselves with the Takani Triad, knowingly or unknowingly. They were to be seen as enemies, no matter what.

He finally returned home, with both of his brothers waiting for the Surgeon at the entrance of the house. He was met by the both of them with a welcoming smile and a signal of respect in their eyes – which warmed his heart just a tad.

The night was not even half completed yet. The Maska Triad weren't taking this situation lightly. They wanted to invade their only triad competition on the same night in multiple stages to send the signal. To go back to Taiwan and never step another foot in Korea again. This night would also make the statement truly clear for their apparent older sister. To not fuck with the Maska Triad, or you'll die.

After the completion of Tarawa-Li's attack, Dan-Li's turn was next.

CHAPTER TWELVE:
BEAUTY PASSION

Dan-Li's plan of attack for his nightclub was more of an inventive and sneaky approach to the act of crime. Instead of concocting an elaborate strategy that involved entering the nightclub, he wanted to stay safe to minimise the chances of getting caught or killed. He was to impersonate a city engineer, (well, with the minimal time of preparation, the closet clothing he could find was a Hi Vis jacket and a hard hat) climb the reported scaffolding in the back alleys around the club, jump past the small gap from the heightened scaffolding to the club roof, and release the acid bombs through the club's air vents. After releasing the bombs, he would jump back to the scaffolding and safely return to road surface, again to return home unseen.

As Dan-Li was to wear a hard hat and to attack the innocent victims via the air vents, it would be irrelevant for him to use the acid squirt gun and mask. Instead, he would wear a surgical face mask, which luckily wouldn't be seen as suspicious in a country like Korea, and he would also be given double the supply of acid bombs.

He was surprised for his plan to be approved by the Chairman, considering it was more safe and less of a chance to harm the clubbers in comparison to Tarawa-Li's scheme. The Chairman believed two identical plans wouldn't work, with the Takani Triad now being extra protective of their businesses since that they knew Club Aitken was attacked. As long as the acid sprayed down like forest rainfall into the club, injuring the many hundreds of people expected to be there at the time, it didn't really matter on the specifics.

Club Beauty Passion, unlike the previous nightclub, wasn't situated on any high ground. It was placed on a street corner, next to a local dinery specialising in kimchi. The alley and alleys surrounding the backstreets that set the two buildings apart were known to be dark, dirty, and dangerous to the locals, which held home to the common drug dealer or wannabe street thugs assaulting a salaryman for his wallet. Though being a nightclub, Club Beauty Passion was more of an upscale and luxurious nightspot, for the young adults who hadn't fully committed to adulthood just yet. Sure, it was still a nightclub, but many of them were able to dress up with actual chains and jewellery instead of the knockoff versions, and the rappers there were the real deal in Korea.

The scaffolding that he would climb was to be a stair tread tower that seemed to be designed by children, and placed by children, believing the structure and location of it. The scaffolding was positioned straight in between the middle of the club and an abandoned warehouse that was behind its shadow. The disregarded warehouse unfortunately didn't have a ladder to climb onto, so he was to climb the shaky scaffolding structure of stairs, and to jump immediately onto the club roof to throw his acid bombs down the club air vent.

Dan-Li left the family house. Although ready to adventure on a new form of attack he had never performed before, he thought that this plan of action may bite the triad back one day. But, as he knew being a gangster, 'the only way to call the shots is to shoot first'. Travelling to Club Beauty Passion, Dan-Li kept his cool and meditated, repeating the impromptu task he had been given. The plan: *Alley, Climb Scaffolding Stairs, Jump, Air Vent – Throw Acid Bombs, Jump, Off Scaffolding, Run.* He equipped his minor disguise of the black surgical mask, Hi Vis jacket, and hard hat, and was almost ready to attack.

Before entering the alley, he went to the building next door, the kimchi restaurant. Every minute of the day where he had left his wife and child took an emotional toll on the fellow, wishing he could be there for every step of both of their recoveries. He had to follow the Chairman's orders, but believed that taking a few minutes before unleashing a surprise attack couldn't be that much of a risk. He missed his wife. It hurt him not being by her side at the hospital. Dan-Li ordered a small order of kimchi, and whilst eating it, called his wife to check up on her current condition.

"Hey, are you feeling any better since I was last there?" Dan-Li asked, feeding himself kimchi with his other hand.

"Nothing has really changed since this morning; I just need some rest." Mallory replied, with an obvious shortness of breath.

"I'm sorry, I just worry. How's our little Aria doing? Have the doctors said anything new regarding how she's coping?" Dan-Li asked, knowing he would have to keep the conversation shorter than expected, both for Jing-Lee and for Mallory.

"She's doing fine. Nothing different than this morning, again." Mallory said, coughing after her words.

“Just wanted to make sure. I’ll leave you to get some rest, love you.” Dan-Li said, hanging up the call so his wife wouldn’t have to struggle speaking any more words.

Dan-Li spent the remainder of the next few minutes chomping down on his kimchi before returning to the task in hand. The acid attack. He left the restaurant quickly to swiftly scan the front of the club. Surprisingly, it seemed as though the place either didn’t know about the attack on Club Aitken, were too drunk to respond, or the club was managed by a third-party with no members of the Takani Triad present in this point of time. There was only one security guard present, which made Dan-Li chuckle, considering the guy was barely touching 5 feet tall. Was the attack really going to be this easy for him?

He quickly turned left into the infamous dreaded and dangerous alley. The alley was indeed dark, dirty, and dangerous. Half used syringes, used condoms, splashed blood, rotten excrement, urine, ecstasy pills, cocaine, bullet shells, and more haunted these feared parts of Gangnam. Whilst walking to the scaffolding stairs, Dan-Li was approached by three street thugs who had just beaten up a local lawyer for some unearned pocket money. The three punks were amassed with dark clothing, concealing their identities, and were equipped with machetes in each of their dominant hand. The central positioned thug motioned for him to come closer, believing they were about to hunt on their next prey. Dan-Li stepped slowly, closer, and closer, to the three thugs, with a sarcastic chuckle meeting the armed men.

"What's so funny, punk? Did we just make your death wish come true?" The main thug chuckled, clenching his fist that held his machete even tighter.

"No, I'm just about to show you how good my fists are. I can kill the three of you without the need of weapons. Punk." Dan-Li replied, now motioning the three men to approach him to fight.

The main man who taunted Dan-Li approached first, swinging his machete wildly in his direction. He managed to evade the harsh weapon by going down onto his knees and jumping straight back up to his feet (luckily, his knees didn't inject himself with any half-unused syringes). Whilst the main thug had just swung and now had his back to Dan-Li, he stumbled back into his two partners, resulting them into falling on the disgusting ground. The main thug resulted in having black, rotten, disturbing faeces spread across his eyes and concealing clothing. Whilst making their way back to stand, Dan-Li grabs onto the shit-covered main thug's neck and rotates it until a loud snap was heard, killing him at that very second.

Two thugs remained now, crying at the situation, realising they were nothing but worthless low-tier criminals who only became intimidating with their clothing and their boss around them. They both froze, releasing their machetes to negotiate a sort of plea deal to keep their lives, not wanting to experience the same fate they had just witnessed. They got onto their knees and pled for forgiveness, crying their eyes out. Literal litres of tears must have been released to the dirt-ridden surface.

“Please don’t kill us.” The two thugs cried in unison, shaking, looking into the eyes of Dan-Li.

Dan-Li decided on a creative way to punish the two first, scanning for anything on the floor to aid his choice making decision. There, by the side of one of the thugs, he had found two remarkably interesting items that he was about to use on them. It was two practically unused syringes of heroin. Dan-Li crouched down to grab the two syringes, walked towards the path of the two begging thugs (although at this point, they could most definitely be declassified as thugs), and demanded them to stand. The two complied, teary-eyed, wondering what was about to happen to them two both. Dan-Li held a syringe in each hand and gave them one of the heroin dosages each. Without using any speech, he motioned them to inject themselves with the heroin, pointing at the neck for the place to inject.

The two took off their clothing that was concealing their identities, revealing themselves to Dan-Li. The two were young teenagers, most likely either attempting to start off in the world of crime or being forced into it due to a troubled childhood. They both had multiple tears rolling down their face, the bottom of their lips were trembling, and their hands were shaking excessively. Reluctantly, but obeying their command given, both took the syringe full of heroin and released the deadly addictive liquid into their necks. What the two didn't realise, however, was when Dan-Li had grabbed the two syringes, he also grabbed one of the machetes that belonged to the thugs. After instantly giving themselves an injection, Dan-Li had sliced the first thug straight in the skull. The second thug was almost unresponsive, even without Dan-Li laying a touch on the young kid, most definitely due to an allergic reaction or shock reaction to the dodgy syringe of heroin. The second thug laid down on the floor, besides his deceased comrades, with his eyes widened, foamed mouth, and twitching body. Dan-Li finished off the second thug by slicing the machete from the top of his skull until it reached the bottom of his neck. The three, especially the last killed, caused a tremendous blood scene. Luckily, the treacherous alley was most likely used to these events occurring on a daily basis, meaning no need to clean up after the deadly mess. He now had to re-focus on the actual task he needed to complete before the distraction.

He made his way to the scaffolding structure, up the wobbly, unstable, and untrustworthy stairs. It was a high view, when reaching upon the top of the structure. The gap between the high scaffolding stairs and the roof of Club Beauty Passion wasn't at all a large feat, it was the risk factors that were concerned with it. The highest risk factors included that the stair structure would bail and separate whilst either attempting to jump, once on the club roof, or on return.

Dan-Li, at the top of the stairs, took a deep breath in and closed his eyes. He meditated. The gap was small, and all he had to do was trust a semi-reliable structure placed in an alley of death, whilst performing an acid attack on a nightclub that was owned by his triad's greatest opposition. Nothing similar to what he has had to do in the past. He opened his eyes again, rejuvenated, and optimistic on his plan. He jumps the farthest he can from the high structure, and he awkwardly lands on the club roof with the side of his shoulder landing on the corner of an air vent.

Once he brushed the muck off his shoulder, he scans for any possibilities of a potential witness, to no avail. He puts on his surgical mask and takes all of his acid bombs out of his rucksack, and next to the ground besides the hole of the air vent, where he's going to release the liquid of damage and death onto the oblivious partygoers. Looking at the imagery of the air vent machinery, it visualised that the acid was indeed going to hit each area of the club, which was particularly good news indeed. He quickly grabs as many acid bombs as he physically could and releases them harshly down the air vent. Knowing he only had mere seconds before someone realised about the acid, Dan-Li throws the remaining acid bombs into the air vent and makes a run for it, jumping from the club roof almost reflex-like onto the stair structure. Not wanting to risk anything at this moment in time, Dan-Li walks half the amount of stairs, jumps again to impact himself onto a nearby brick wall for landing and makes a run for it, hoping no one from the club would look for the alley direction as their route for escape.

A swarm of people were heard screaming, leaving the nightclub in an instant, with many running to get any sort of help they could find. The acid seemed to have given a full-on rain effect this time, with many people seeming to have their hands covering or aiding their eyes and foreheads. Crying would make it worse for the innocent sufferers, as it would make them cry out literal tears of acid, making their torment even more of an unbearable experience.

He had no time to analyse how well his plan had worked. He just needed to make sure that no one saw him, which to his luck, worked out. The acid attack had been a triumph, meaning the first two attacks for the night were a complete success. He returned home, being met by the Chairman and Tarawa-Li at the front door with a welcoming smile. Dan-Li explained the situation regarding not being able to analyse how many were dead or hurt, but he was definitely certain that the acid was sprayed all over the nightclub floor, due to the instant pleas for help by masses of teenagers exiting Beauty Passion seconds after dropping the bombs into the air vent.

The time was now to focus on the main event for the night, Mouse. Both brothers knew that the Takani Triad must know about two of their biggest Gangnam properties being completely destroyed, so the two offer the Chairman some support. Mouse may not even be in the Takani-owned karaoke bar anymore.

“Chairman, want us to help?” Dan-Li asked, taking his surgical mask off his face and onto the kitchen counter.

“No, you two have both impressed me tonight. As your Chairman, I must now go above and beyond independently. I’ll only contact you if there’s an emergency like we had previously planned.” Jing-Lee replied.

CHAPTER THIRTEEN: MOUSE TRAP

Jing-Lee knew that the two acid attacks of the night were nothing in difficulty when compared to the task of capturing and killing a Takani Triad leader. There were bound to be perhaps even a hundred-or-so rival triad members in this karaoke bar, some intoxicated, some on security patrol. The best method he could think of was to run-and-gun. Anyone to exist in the karaoke bar was to be shot dead, no matter if they were just a member or a prostitute hired by them for the night. The structure of the place was believed to contain a various array of small karaoke rooms, meaning due to the sheer volume of the karaoke music, a good chance that Jing-Lee could easily eliminate everyone room by room as long as he used stealth to his side and silenced weaponry. No gimmicks, just the usual method of his kills.

Mouse may not even be at this karaoke bar anymore due to the earlier events, but Jing-Lee knew that he couldn't risk anything. He wanted the cold-cut truth about the two other leaders. The only way to complete his wish was to come face-to-face with the only person who he could threaten, that knew the sensitive and classified information, that knew the day-to-day operations, that knew his other two main rivals.

Ever since the PlaciCorp meeting that took place with Mouse and Jing-Lee, it was confirmed that there was a snake in the Maska Triad. In turn, perhaps the snake would be present in the karaoke bar on this very night, revealing their dastardly act to attempt to dissolve the most powerful triad in Korea, siding with the fresh new criminal blood in the country. The most likely candidate to undertake this measure would be Derrick, he thought, but in the world of crime, nothing can be considered a surprise.

Jing-Lee put on his favourite suit, diamond cufflinks, gelled and styled up his hair, brushed his teeth and flossed his gums. Finally, he was ready to embark on perhaps the biggest challenge of his criminal life. One man versus an estimated hundred. The Chairman has been familiar pulling off the impossible, so instead of feeling any sense of nervousness, he felt what he had always felt: confidence with a sprinkle of arrogance.

He had finally arrived to see the place in walking distance - stepping forwards slowly to glance the nearby buildings and attractions, just to check on any suspicious people either looking at he himself or the past-time criminal hideout. Looking straight ahead at the entrance to the karaoke bar, he realises this night is going to be one heck of a ride. Standing right at the front entrance were seven guards, all holding devastating crowbars, glancing in all directions, knowing that a greater force would be approaching them very soon. Mouse knew that he was expecting a visit from Jing-Lee. It was the Chairman's' duty to make sure his visit to Mouse wasn't by him being dragged by any of the Takani guards, because if that occurred, it would be his last day alive. Since the guards out the front who were currently visible were out in public, his beloved pistols would put him in great jeopardy, which in a way made it more fun for him. He was no slouch in occasional fistfights either.

Before taking another step further, Jing-Lee knew he had to be sensible. He was arrogant, yes, but he knew moments like the one happening right now could be deadly. He knew when it was the right decision to call for any backup. He quickly calls Dan-

Li on his burner phone, still looking in the direction of the seven guards.

"What's wrong, Aero?" Dan-Li asked, knowing to revert to his brothers' alias when engaging in criminal activity.

"Nothing right now, but I'll perhaps need you to accompany me soon, Chef. I might need a Surgeon too. There are many, many lobsters that seem to be needed out of the tank." Jing-Lee replied discreetly, hanging up after his last word.

Jing-Lee decided his best bet to attack the seven-armed guards was to be perceived as a drunk, holding his head down to the floor, and moving erratically. This way, passers-by would only suspect himself to be a casual drunk, with security trying to escort him off the Takani Property. This is when the security would grab him first, claiming self-defence as his means to fight back. Gangnam of all places was no stranger to fights outside karaoke bars and nightclubs, and it was the most relevant tactic he could think of.

Jing-Lee starts his approach to the karaoke bar, with his head swinging downward left to right, his constant slurred groaning, and his inability to walk in a straight line. He approaches the seven guards, and softly brazes one of the guard's arms, which then resulted in a strong push back. Jing-Lee immediately runs back to the guard in a perceived-drunken act and kicks him harshly, aimed straight at his testicles. The guard screams for mercy like a baby, and releases his crowbar, dropping to the ground and making a loud rattling noise. Instantly, Jing-Lee grabs the crowbar and retaliates before the second guard could whack the crowbar of his own onto him. Now, to his left was the entrance door. In front of him were six guards ready to attack, and one measly guard holding his testicles and crying mercilessly.

Two of the six uninjured guards come to attack next, with Jing-Lee swooping to the floor in a prone position, grabbing them by their calves and pulling them to himself forwards in an extreme fashion. This results in the two banging the back of their heads on the concrete road surface, releasing their crowbars. Jing-Lee uses the same weapon to smack both straight in the face, with one losing his entire nose and the other suffering a double fracture in his jaw. They also receive a harsh kick to their face for good measure, rendering them unable to fight for the rest of the night, perhaps for the rest of their lives. Four guards were left to fight, with the guard who previously had his private parts injured now bleeding from his mouth, focusing on trying to breathe.

Two of the now four remaining front entrance guards come to approach Jing-Lee next, rashly swinging their weapons at the Chairman. He reacts by eliminating the current crowbar that was held in his hand, and grabs each of the guard's crowbars with both of his hands, with the two crowbars millimetres from the skull of Jing-Lee. His pure strength and determination allows him to gain control of the two crowbars, with his first attack coming to the guard on his left side, swinging at his unprotected throat, causing carnage at the first strike, with litres of blood spewing out. With no time to fully witness the first strike, Jing-Lee immediately turns his attention onto the second guard, this time using the crowbar in his hand to crush the man's neck, hearing a loud crack and snap after the second quick hit.

Two front entrance guards remained, but this caused more unwanted attention by casual Korean citizens walking past, knowing the next two guards must be eliminated quick with no shenanigans if he wanted to get to Mouse. The entrance was filled with near-deceased or full-on dead guards at this point already, with castrated testicles, an exposed throat, and a fractured neck being the three main focal points.

The final two front entrance guards came to attack him with their game plan surprisingly working so far.

The guard managed to distract him so his security colleague could grab him by the back and strangle him. The guard in front of Jing-Lee swung his crowbar, with Jing-Lee ducking in perfect timing. The guard to knock his colleague out cold with his own actions. Jing-Lee used his crowbar to hit the final guard in the back of his neck, making that his final day on the job, too. With a bloody mess to begin the attack, and considering it occurred in the public eye, this was actually a win for Mouse. Yes, seven of his men were either killed or put on the hospital bed for years by Jing-Lee, but the kills were done in the exposed streets of Gangnam, and not in privacy. He knew that every single member of the Maska Triad hated to kill as publicly as this, even if the entire family did own almost everything in Korea. The Maska Triad hated to operate in front of potential witnesses who could blabber to the Korean Investigation Unit - the main service they just didn't have the chance to own.

Jing-Lee quickly opened the entrance door to the karaoke bar, where he was greeted by a compact lobby, leading to rooms in four different directions, two to the left, and two to the right of the check-in desk. The difference with this check-in desk, however, was the fact that Jing-Lee wasn't greeted by an overbearing receptionist, but instead with five of Mouse's giant henchmen. Four of them were holding machetes, and one holding an electric taser.

He tried to enter his inner left pocket, where he would always place his favourite pistol in a time like this. Unfortunately, he was too slow, as one of the henchmen was so close at striking his machete in Jing-Lee's face. Forgetting his beloved pistol for the moment being, he defies gravity by swooping his upper torso and head upside down, whilst completely having control of his feet placement and balance. He returned to his normal standing position, evading the first machete that was struck in his direction. Whilst all of this was happening, the man with the electric taser aimed at him. He charged up his taser to full power, meaning it's not only going to electrocute, but most likely kill, too. The henchman aimed his shot towards him. He pressed the trigger, but Jing-Lee ducked, and the metal prongs of the taser arrived at the throat of the first henchman who tried to attack Jing-Lee with his machete. There were so many bolts of electricity appearing at the henchman who had just been hit by the electrical weapon, it was almost like he had been turned into a physical lightning bolt. The taser was still stuck in the first man, so Jing-Lee took care of the next person who took charge at the Chairman, arrogantly knowing he could have some fun with this fight of death.

The next man to approach was using his machete in his left hand, which resulted in an excessive kick to the right hand of the henchman, snapping his weaker arm into three unfixable fractures. The devastating kick reflexed for the guard to release the weapon in his left hand, holding his right arm in agony. The triple fracture to his right arm was too much to bear. He couldn't even try and fight anymore, death was as equivalent to what he was experiencing in this point of time. Jing-Lee followed up by taking the dropped machete and slicing the man's unprotected throat. Three henchmen were left at this point. Specifically the taser user was still alive, and was ready to strike again after what had just happened a couple of minutes earlier.

The third and fourth henchman most likely to experience their deaths next teamed up, in which both were equipped with the devastating weapons. The two placed themselves right in front of the Chairman, looking to strike at any second. Something felt unusual however, as both weren't coming any closer to him, even though they had the mathematical edge. Then a distinct sound occurred. The two-henchman drifted apart instantly, and the taser filled with electricity appeared between the middle of were the two had been standing. The shot brushed the left cheek of the Chairman, who knew it was a miracle that he didn't get hit this time, with the taser hitting the entrance door, the physical line of electricity clearly visible. He quickly wall-ran to his right, which was met by denting the next henchman straight in the skull. He tripped and received the same experience as the first guard who was electrocuted to death. Two were left at this point, with two weapons. One machete, and one taser.

Looking ahead, the next henchman with the machete was trapped from experiencing the same destiny as his fallen comrades for the moment, as a shockwave line of electricity split the two for the minute. So, due to the spare time he had to recuperate stamina wise, he took a few seconds to finally release his most trusted weapon. The signature move. He retrieved his most trusted weapon out of his inner left pocket, his silenced pistol. It was the weapon that has caused the most kills in the criminal underworld of Korea.

Jing-Lee, who now held his pistol of trust in his hand, aimed it at the henchman who was nearly finishing the process to re-use his taser. The Chairman aimed his gun, and shot at the intestinal area, resulting in the man to collapse. The almost funniest result in triad shootings history happened next. As the injured henchman fell to the floor, with his beloved gun of electricity aiming at his face, he unknowingly pulled the trigger to his own death. He electrocuted himself, causing a huge explosion of his intestines scattering across the karaoke bar lobby.

The last remaining lobby henchman knew he was going to die now. It was completely guaranteed, so he decided on a deceiving tactic. The henchman dropped his machete onto the floor, crouched onto both knees, and held his hands together, praying for any forgiveness that Jing-Lee could give the man. He replied to the actions of the last remaining henchman, not using words, but using the best reply technique: actions. Jing-Lee aimed his gun, shooting at the solar-plexus, and causing the man to bow down, with blood immediately pouring from his stomach and mouth, causing him to vomit. He quickly followed up with a bullet to the skull, killing the last remaining man in the lobby. He walked up to the henchman he had just shot and being the cocky Chairman he always knew he would become, gives the middle finger and smiles. The lobby was finally completed, with four more rooms to try and find Mouse, hopefully with the first room he chose containing the wanted devil.

Jing-Lee decided to enter the rooms from left to right, hopefully with his brothers coming to his aid any minute now. Knowing once he was in one of these four rooms, Mouse could easily escape without his knowledge. Thankfully though, due to the place being a karaoke bar, no one had noticed any extraordinary sounds. The main game-breaker however is the lobby of death, with sever amounts of electricity burns, exposed intestines, vomit, and other bloody parts. The only schoolboy tactic Jing-Lee could employ to perhaps buy a few seconds of time until his brothers came was to put a chair on each of the rooms door handles, and to remove them once he was ready to enter. That simple plan may not even work, but he had to try it, nonetheless.

After placing the three small wooden chairs on the rooms he wouldn't be approaching for the time being, he was ready to continue his attack. The front entrance had seven guards; the lobby had five henchman, so he didn't know who or what was to be met when he opened the doors to the undisclosed four private karaoke rooms. All that he did know, however, was that time was of the essence. He needed to capture Mouse as soon as possible. He also knew that Mouse was expecting him, making this an extreme game of psychological torture for both parties.

He blasted into the far-left karaoke room, not knowing what to expect. There, he was met with four drunk gunmen (who appear to be taking a "break" from their work duty), two stoned henchmen, and a stripper who also seemed to be under the influence, but he was unable to decipher what. Luckily, they were all out of their minds. The entire seven didn't even acknowledge the presence of Jing-Lee, making these kills about to be a very fun and enjoyable experience for the Chairman. The targets were all having fun currently, especially one of the gunmen and the stripper, who were singing a classic Korean romance song together. They were all faced in the opposite direction of the door that Jing-Lee had opened, either laying down or groggily standing, seeming to all be unequipped, as the gunmen and henchmen had their weapons placed on the floor.

Jing-Lee started his attack on the first of four karaoke rooms by unleashing one bullet to the three drunkest, yet nearest to the weapons, gunmen. The shot was a miraculous masterpiece, with the singular bullet penetrating the skull of the three Takani men, killing them instantly, putting them on the floor in a sleeping position. As everyone was incredibly drunk and the bullet wound was invisible to the naked eye of a drunken person, the others didn't even notice much of a difference at all, still making Jing-Lee unrecognisable. He walked up to his next victims, the two gigantic henchmen who were smoking marijuana, attempting to blow hoops of smoke in an already foggy area. He imitated the two stoned men, patting them on their back and laughing outrageously. The two men didn't even notice who had joined them, as they were too busy having the most relaxing time of their lives. Whilst the two men were cracking up exponentially, causing them to drop their herbed cigarettes, Jing-Lee shot both of them in the skull. It was an instant halt to the funny situation.

The first karaoke room was now left with Jing-Lee, and a one-night stand couple consisting of a drunken Takani gunman and a stripper, most likely a Gangnam beauty, from the first glance of her structured face. The two were still loudly singing Korean romance songs, having the time of their life, intoxicated on alcohol and other various drugs. Jing-Lee was also having the time of his life, too, knowing that this could be the same fate he meets in the other three rooms. Jing-Lee aims and shoots two bullets at the back of the neck of the plastic stripper, causing her to drop dead and bleed out within a few moments of time. The last remaining Takani survivor was jumping up and down, crying at his girl for the night, who was no longer alive, with an exposed hole in the middle of her neck. He turned behind himself to meet Jing-Lee, who had his weapon raised at the man.

"Where's Mouse?" Jing-Lee asked, with his trigger finger holding steady as can be.

"What...I don't...have a...boss..." The gunman said, trying not to trip over the dead stripper, or himself for that matter.

He had heard enough, knowing truly well that he wouldn't be getting any valuable intel from this drunken mess. He pulled the trigger, with the harsh bullet meeting the man's heart, piercing straight at the centre of the vital organ. All seven targets were now dead, with only six bullets used, with the rationing going well for Jing-Lee. Sure, he could just steal a Takani weapon, but the Chairman never liked risking leaving his fingerprints on weapons just in case the KIU ever became involved with their crime-related business. He left the first karaoke room for the night, just hoping the next room he was about to visit to be that much of an easy ride. If so, he should have never been worried about asking his two brothers for aid with the capture and kill mission.

He went back to the lobby and removed the first small wooden chair that was pressured against the door to the second room he would infiltrate. He blasted inside and was met with a vastly different, disturbing, and challenging outcome of rivals. Three Takani gunmen, with two aiming straight in the sight of Jing-Lee and the other gunman assaulting a man. It was no ordinary man: it was Pigbreath. Mouse must have found about Pigbreath's antics, helping aid their triad (although the result of Dan-Li being the killer wasn't exactly a win for the Maska Triad). Pigbreath was being battered to death for being disloyal to the Takani Triad. Mouse knew the perfect timing for Pigbreath's punishment was for Jing-Lee to watch him die in front of his very eyes. Jing-Lee knew he had to save Pigbreath. It was because of him, he knew the devastating truth, no matter how disgusting the truth actually was. Pigbreath literally risked his life for him, so he knew he had to return the favour for the once foe, now hopeful ally.

Pigbreath was not even aware of his sadistic surroundings at this point, with blood gurgling out of his mouth, his eyes unable to open, and his arms and legs unresponsive. He was seconds away from dying. The lone gunman kept on kicking him, specifically targeting his head now, with his shoes covered in the blood of the man known as Pigbreath.

The two gunmen who had their target locked didn't remove their direction of sight away from Jing-Lee, now any second away from pulling the trigger of their weapon. But he knew the two weren't going to kill him, he was too valuable just to be killed by two lackeys. Jing-Lee knew that the two would shoot him in a body part that wouldn't cause instant death, meaning that he had a one or two second advantage when it came down to shooting – a crazy assumption to some, but it was still the truth. He saw the eyes of the two men who held their guns high, noticing a change in pupil dilation. Jing-Lee shot his gun, shooting both of them in quick succession with the silenced bullets of death.

The two men who once held an advantage on Jing-Lee were now on the floor with a bullet sized hole in their skulls. He knew it wasn't time to be arrogant or even celebrate two admirable kills. Pigbreath was in serious danger of dying, as he was now only one or two kicks away from his death. Jing-Lee shot the last remaining Takani gunman straight in the heart - who was only milliseconds away from issuing his last kick of death onto his ally. The man dropped to the floor, spasming, trying to grab as much oxygen he could to bring himself back to a normal state, but it was over for him too. Desperately fighting for breath, the gunman was met by Jing-Lee, who walked quickly to kick him straight where the bullet wound originated. He started to cough up blood, only moments later for him to be deceased.

Another person who was used to coughing up blood by now was the tortured Pigbreath, the now ex-Takani Triad member, who was fighting for his life. Jing-Lee rushed to his aid, checking for any bullet-hole shaped wounds, lashings, or any other external injuries by weapons. In a sense, miraculously, he was nor shot or stabbed, but instead, punched, kicked, and milled to an almost state of decease. He was vomiting, bleeding, and hallucinating, which made it become a serious deal for Jing-Lee, knowing he had to take care of the man.

He called Tarawa-Li, just begging and pleading that the two were on their way already. Especially now the fact that Pigbreath, a man who had put his safety and wellbeing on the line for him and his fiancé back in Taiwan, was about to die any second now.

"What's up? We're on our way. Have you completed everything, Aero?" Tarawa-Li asked.

"Surgeon, take care of the Pig in the central left karaoke room. Take him to get medical care. Chef will help Aero with the Mouse trap." Jing-Lee rushed and pleaded, hoping the two were only seconds away from entering the karaoke bar.

Pigbreath was in no state to even communicate or move at this point in time. The main focus he was initiating was the power to inhale and exhale, the power to fight, the power to continue on living. His eyes were closed, ever-so determined to not die in this way. He had so much to live for, so much unreleased potential. Jing-Lee heard the door behind him was opening, turning his attention to the people arriving in the room, aiming his gun at the unknown.

Thankfully, it was the rescue team of Tarawa-Li and Dan-Li, also holding their weapons in case of an enemy intruder. All parties lowered their weaponry and focused on their ex-rival.

"Aero, this is a job for two men. The loss of blood and vomit alone has signalled to me that I'm going to need more than one set of hands if there's any chance of him surviving." Tarawa-Li declared, examining Pigbreath's condition.

"Fine. You and Chef help him at all costs. Just keep him alive. He's useful. He's done more for me than you'll ever know." Jing-Lee replied.

"Aero, what about the Mouse trap?" Dan-Li asked.

"No questions. You two need to hurry and save his life. I can do the Mouse trap by myself." Jing-Lee declared, motioning for Tarawa-Li and Dan-Li to carry Pigbreath to their vehicle to drive off for medical support.

The two brothers carry their former rival out, rushing out of the karaoke bar to get medical assistance. Jing-Lee, before entering the next room, glances on the bullets remaining on his most trusted gun. Thirteen bullets left. Unlucky for some - too bad he never believed in silly superstitions like that. The Chairman leaves the second room and turns his attention to the room to his next right, the third karaoke room he would be infiltrating for the night. He releases the small wooden chair once again, and slowly opens the door once more.

In the third room, he was met by nine armed gunmen, all holding a gun in one hand and a leash in the other. Meeting the leash that the nine men were holding were Taiwanese bloodthirsty attack hounds, growling and drooling at the face of Jing-Lee. This was the first moment in his career where he had truly felt like an ultimate underdog.

“Drop your weapon now, punk!” One Takani-gunman shouted, with his spit received on the face of the Chairman.

He slowly lowered his weapon down, but didn’t release any grasp of carrying it whatsoever. The only plan of survival was to attack when the men and dogs didn’t notice it coming. Now approaching the floor, he raises and tilts his pistol, shooting the first three attack dogs straight in the side of their noses. The gunmen did exactly the same as what he thought. They did nothing. They needed him alive. He shoots the remaining six dogs in the same position, until their growling was non-existent, and their drooling was due to their fight to stay alive.

The nine dogs weren’t dead, but it did leave him alone with the nine gunmen. Although he was surprised - he thought he would have been shot in the arm or leg by now. Jinxing his own thoughts, one gunman shot Jing-Lee in his dominant hand, which barred his shooting. Attempting to throw the gun into his weaker hand, another gunman shot Jing-Lee in his other hand, meaning the Chairman was defenceless.

"You punks think that you're so great, huh? Let's all fight to the death. One versus nine." Jing-Lee shouted, kicking his right foot into the air, like some sort of karate sensei.

"You are so arrogant, punk. There were nearly a hundred of us earlier, but we thought that you decided not to show up tonight. If there was more of us, you wouldn't even be alive right now." A Takani gunman said.

"All of you put your guns down and talk with your fists." Jing-Lee demanded, with both of his hands becoming numb due to the bullet wounds.

The nine men complied, with Jing-Lee knowing they have all made the gullible decision to die at the hands (or in this case, feet) of the Chairman. This was going to be the biggest blood brawl of all time, because Jing-Lee wasn't going to finish until he prevailed in killing all nine of these punks until they couldn't even be resuscitated in all of their afterlives.

He smiled and motioned for the first man to visit his destiny: an eternal death.

The first man attempted to throw a punch with his right hand in the direction of his face, only for his fist to be met with the glass of the entrance door, slashing his right hand into separate pieces of bone and muscle. Jing-Lee responded with a devastating kick to the back of his skull, and a quick second kick to respond with the first attack, with this kick again attacking the skull. The man was unconscious. Jing-Lee finishes him with another kick, this time placed exactly in the middle of his nonresponding punk face.

The second man came swarming in with an impressive karate kick of his own, only mere centimetres away from locking onto the jaw of Jing-Lee. He responded with a karate kick as well, which too was avoided. Both then had the same game plan, attempting with a spinning kick to the back of each other's skull. However, only Jing-Lee was successful with the kick, with his foot meeting his opponent who instantly blacked out.

The third Takani-man tackled him to the floor using his brute force, placing him into some elaborate martial arts submission, attempting to place his devastating fists into the face of Jing-Lee. This only resulted in himself damaging his own fists for striking the floor too hard - fracturing his knuckles. Causing his own to hands to bleed profusely, he was unable to strike more, becoming numb and fatigued in a matter of seconds. Jing-Lee noticed this, and instead of blocking his face to counter the grating-looking punches, he managed to kick the man straight in the testicles, and then followed up with a jarring kick to the side of his head, which in turn made the man's eyes roll to the back of his head. His skull harshly met the rock solid floor.

The fourth and fifth men to approach Jing-Lee attempted to work in unison to tackle the Chairman onto the floor to feel the wrath of punishment. The first successfully swooped behind Aero, with the second charging at full throttle ahead of him. With a counter-technique that legitimately seemed like it was made for movie purposes, the man performed a long-reaching jumping karate kick. But Jing-Lee managed to lower himself to the floor in perfect timing, and the man's foot penetrated and cracked the cranium of his now once alive teammate. With the man looking at his fallen comrade, he turned quickly behind himself to see where Jing-Lee had ended after evading his kick, only for him to be kicked to death in his head a split second after.

The sixth man decided that time for playing games was over, revealing his pocketknife. One feature that

Jing-Lee deciphered about his rivals was that they too enjoyed an actual street fight experience on occasion, not having to rely on guns for good violence. The man brought out his knife, sarcastically jabbing the foggy air that contained both of them, smiling right in the face of Jing-Lee. He smiled back, although his emotion drastically changed seconds after, getting his already injured right hand stabbed by the pocketknife, losing any sensation of feeling on the entire right portion of his body now. The man continued using his pocketknife to pierce through the hand of Jing-Lee, until the handle was the only part visible from the attackers point-of-view. The Takani-man continued his wrath of attack by punching him square in the face twice, with a couple of blood-spits being revealed out of the mouth of Jing-Lee. The Takani-man strikes for the third time in the same facial position he had been attacking before, only for this attempt to fail. Jing-Lee swoops his head down, and reverses with a devastating rapid array of elbows to the attacker's neck. He promptly followed up by repeatedly kicking the previously attacked neck until he heard the distinct crack which guarantees a man's death.

The last three remaining men had enough of the carnage the Chairman had caused, knowing he was unbeatable when it came down to the old-fashioned fist fight. The three reveal their weapons once more and aim at the face of the bruised and battered Jing-Lee. The Chairman at this point had two lifeless hands, with one of them home to a pocketknife, masses of blood pouring onto the gory floor by the second. Not only were his two hands motionless and bleeding copiously, but so was his jaw, rendering him unable to speak clearly or able to move his mouth without any harsh discomfort. His legs became a threat to his survival too, due to the sheer amount of force he had to produce with them in the previous fights, making walking an extremely difficult task to proceed with. The Chairman was now in serious trouble if he wanted to survive. He wasn't strong enough to punch or kick his way to endure the situation that faced him.

The three Takani-men gather around the lifeless Jing-Lee, who was trying carefully not to fall onto the blood-filled floor at this point of time. One man went behind him, with the other two aiming at his skull to his left and right side. One Takani-man gestures for him to come closer, which resounded in a reply of bloody saliva rocketed in the direction of the man's face.

"Do you want to die, punk?" The Takani-man said, who wiped his face quickly, trying to remove all the blood-filled saliva that was squirted onto him.

Recuperated from the gross incident, the three nod to each other, only a half-second away from piercing Jing-Lee with three bullets to the skull. Then, a knock on the door was heard - startling everyone involved. Who could it be? They would have some serious level of confidence to barge into this room, especially with the situation at hand.

A knock again, this time louder.

"Who is it?" The Takani-man shouted, with all three releasing their trigger finger, not knowing who was at the door.

A loud knock, again. This time, whoever was knocking wasn't giving up on their hopes of wishing to piss these Takani-men off even more. The man who had his aimed sight on Jing-Lee behind him gestured for the two in front of Jing-Lee to open the door, not losing his focus on the target in-hand. The two walked to open the door, clueless on who would be knocking at a time like this. They opened it, with the two men instantly being shot in the head by a silenced pistol. The last remaining guard who had been behind Jing-Lee instantly turned around and met his fate with all of the other eight guards and nine dogs who were already dead in the room at this point. The mystery person who had been knocking on the door revealed themselves. It was Dan-Li.

“Thought you might have needed some help. Looked like a difficult situation, Aero.” Dan-Li chuckled, reloading his pistol - impressed with the number of killings the Chairman caused alone.

“Thanks, Chef. I’m assuming Surgeon is treating Pig?” Jing-Lee answered, focusing more on his own health now. His whole body was in tremendous pain, his legs and hands especially.

“Exactly. I’ll take care of the final room; looks like you need some medical assistance now, otherwise you’ll end up like your buddy earlier.” Dan-Li stated, starting to lift up the wounded Chairman, who was only minutes away from losing consciousness.

“No. I need to do my job by myself. Final orders.” Jing-Lee shouted, shaking his sore head in an attempt to wake himself up from the suffering condition he was currently in.

Dan-Li adhered, letting his brother finish off the mission by himself. Chef wouldn’t be leaving Aero, though. He managed to at least help the Chairman by being a lookout for any karaoke bar intruders, mostly guaranteed people of the Takani Triad. Jing-Lee was to enter the last room by himself, as groggy as he could possibly be, but Dan-Li would overwatch his brother from outside the room, protecting him in the only way he could without the Chairman becoming angry. After an amateur bandaging for his broken hands, Jing-Lee had gathered enough momentum and adrenaline for one last ride for the night, for one last fight in the final room of the karaoke bar, pleading either Mouse was to be met inside or at least someone of Takani Triad significance.

Dan-Li removed the last small wooden chair for the Chairman to enter. Without causing further damage to his already shattered hands, Dan-Li opened the door for his brother to enter, without taking a peek inside. Jing-Lee slowly walked into the room and was shocked with the result he had arrived upon. There, in the final karaoke room of the night, were no microphones or karaoke machines, no fog machines or strippers, no gunmen or attack dogs. Instead, the room held host to two chairs, one coffee table, and one very important person: Mouse.

"It's nice to see you again, Chairman!" Mouse chuckled, motioning for Jing-Lee to take a seat, pouring both a glass of finest whiskey.

"Have you seriously been in here this whole time?" Jing-Lee asked with his slurred speech, dragging his lifeless body into the chair opposite of Mouse.

"Well, considering you've recklessly set your minions to destroy our biggest properties in Gangnam, I thought I should've given you a punishment to make you sweat. Don't worry, those guys you fought in the other karaoke bar rooms tonight aren't our fully trained boys, otherwise you wouldn't have made it. So, what's the reason for attacking the Takani Triad tonight?" Mouse asked, taking a shot of whiskey afterwards, smiling in the face of his bruised and battered rival who was unable to even lift his shot glass.

"To make you talk. Who are the other two leaders of the Takani Triad? I know you're the most recently assigned leader, meaning you're the most irrelevant. Give me your bosses' names. I know you're not on an equal level to both of them." Jing-Lee slurred, trying to no-sell his injuries, focusing on his confident body language instead of the measly failure of attempting to pick up his shot glass for the last time.

"You should be full of gratitude; I even gave you Pigbreath instead of killing him on the spot after I found out he helped you out. You really must be delusional if you think I'm going to reveal the other two leaders." Mouse chuckled, taking another shot of finest whiskey down his throat.

"I know one of them is currently working with my triad but secretly the leader of your beloved Takani Triad bullshit. Who is it? Tell me now." Jing-Lee demanded slurring, widening his eyes, about to erupt into pure anger.

“Why don’t you tell me something, instead. Did you tell your brother Dan-Li that yourself and your fiancé, Zara, know that he killed her younger brother Jason?” Mouse asked, raising his volume, knowing exactly who was eavesdropping outside the far-right karaoke room, leaning on the door.

Dan-Li instantly stormed into the room, smashing the glass door in the process, luckily with the shards not reaching his brother. He aims his gun to the chest area of Mouse, shaking in anger and nervousness. He didn’t know whether to confess his crime, or to evade the potential deathly monstrous heat and easily deny what Mouse had just said. This was perhaps the only time he had a chance to confess to his murder, but he shouldn’t be the main person to blame for it. After all, when the contract killings were active, all orders were sough through their father Atheno-Li before being confirmed.

“I know you did it, Chef. So don’t pretend you didn’t kill him. If you feel any sorrow or remorse, talk to Zara, not me. After all, you killed her brother, not one of ours.” Jing-Lee whispered, glancing at him to remove his gun from the direction of Mouse, which he quickly did - returning outside to protect his brother from any potential intruders.

Outside the karaoke room, Dan-Li was flabbergasted, knowing that the murder he committed on Zara's younger brother had been exposed. Perhaps more shocking, however, was the way in which Jing-Lee reacted to him, almost in a casual and calm tone, like he had known for a long time. Perhaps Dan-Li thought that his brother blamed their father for the kill, as the contract killing orders were only confirmed by the Chairman at the time. Dan-Li never would have killed Jason if he knew who he was and how close he was to the Maska family, and Jing-Lee knew that. If Jing-Lee knew, that surely must have confirmed that Zara found out about the true perpetrator of her brother's killer. Dan-Li thought that Zara must have known about the killer only very recently, however, as he noticed no personality change when the two conversed in the hospital whilst she visited Mallory. He pondered about how she had reacted to the news and if Zara would take revenge on him - although he hoped that the two could talk about it, instead of hiding this situation forever between the two of them now.

"Just tell me who the other two leaders are for the Takani Triad, and I will spare your life for the moment. Who says this will be the only Takani-oriented attacks from the Maska Triad? It certainly won't be the last if you don't reveal the other leaders right now." Jing-Lee demanded, trying desperately to feel any sensation or strength in both of his hands, clenching forcefully to no success.

"I know the Maska Triad are the only notable Korean-triad left, but the Takani Triad will eventually own everything you have. How do I know this? It's because I know who my two prestigious colleagues are. You're supposed to be the smartest out of the three brothers; use some logic in that brain of yours, because once you do, you'll understand why we've chosen to attack." Mouse replied, without one blink of an eye, deadly serious about his last remark.

At the entrance to the dishevelled karaoke bar, Dan-Li heard a suspicious loud sound, noticing that someone was stepping foot inside. Raising his weapon, aiming towards the opening door, millimetres away from pulling the trigger of his gun, he instantly retreats from performing the action. The person who had entered the karaoke bar, once again, was Tarawa-Li. Surgeon entered the bar with an unsettling amount of blood on his hands, which displayed more concern on the face of Dan-Li, worrying if Pigbreath couldn't make it through his fight to survive. Tarawa-Li groggily walked to his brother, wiping the blood on his already tatted clothing.

"That Pigbreath guy, that Jing-Lee, I mean, uhm, Aero, told us to stay alive. Well, he's alive, although it's hard to say if he'll make it. I managed to get him into an ICU though, same hospital that Mallory and Aria are staying in currently. Let's just hope for the best." Tarawa-Li wheezed, seeming like he had ran a marathon for the state he was in himself.

"Good. Well, Aero is with Mouse in the room behind us. It's seeming to be getting more heated by the second. Let's only intrude if we think Aero is in danger." Dan-Li whispered, gesturing for his brother to keep his volume of speech down to a minimum so they could both hear the conversation in the compact karaoke room.

Both brothers walked closer to the door to eavesdrop. While walking, however, a jaded and aching Tarawa-Li stumbles on arrival, resulting in him planting his body through the door and knocking himself out, landing on the top-right portion of his head on the lower leg of Jing-Lee's chair, instantly drawing blood out of his head. With Jing-Lee evading his attention towards Mouse and Dan-Li not in the small karaoke room yet, Mouse unleashes a smoke grenade from his pocket. The smoke pellet completely fogs the entire room and bar, with all four immersing themselves in a scene of white smoke, unable to see a single thing. The smoke grenade also twisted the other senses, too, causing a 'tinnitus' audio effect, dizziness, and a hallucination of taste. A definite military-grade equipment grenade used by Mouse here, which was impressive for a triad who was still considered low-life in comparison to the Maska Triad.

Incompetent to see or hear anything, a couple of minutes passed by with Jing-Lee and Dan-Li motionless, focusing on surviving, quite frankly. The amateurish bandages that once held in Jing-Lee's hands fell, with the hand-holes ever present, the Chairman in no condition to fight. Dan-Li began to vomit, hoping the vomit wasn't landing on one of his brothers. The poor man couldn't see or feel anything. Dan-Li was even unsure about vomiting, perhaps he had already choked on his vomit by now and the white light he saw before him was to a heavenly place.

A few minutes later, and the small karaoke room became clearer. Somewhat identical to the visual state before the smoke grenade attack by Mouse, who, had managed to somehow escape the three brothers. What remained in the room, however, were a used smoke pellet, the two chairs, desk, finest whiskey bottle, a dying Tarawa-Li, an injured Jing-Lee, and a vomiting Dan-Li. The three triplets had a long night. It would be over soon, once they had all checked in the nearest hospital, which seemed to be the temporary family household.

Dan-Li finally seemed on the verge of recuperating, picking up both nonresponding brothers to escort them to the nearest hospital. Masses of blood drew from the head of Tarawa-Li, and the hands and now neck of Jing-Lee - most likely from a mischievous knockout-type blow via Mouse during his smoke-filled escape. Gradually limping out of the karaoke room and bar, which was now full of practically blue-turning corpses, he managed to carry both wounded brothers into his vehicle. Knowing he wasn't safe to drive but still speeding like a demon, he reached the hospital for the medical staff to heavily assist them for all of their injuries.

The hospital currently, but hopefully temporarily, held home to Pigbreath in the ICU, Mallory and Aria on the third-floor, Jing-Lee and Tarawa-Li in Accident & Emergency, and Dan-Li, safe from his checks he completed, but present to provide moral support to anyone who needed it, and most likely the messenger for the Chairman once he had recovered.

This night will always be remembered in both of the triads' histories. This night was both a huge victory and commiseration for the triplets when given reasoning. Successfully attacking the two biggest rival properties in the huge, complex district of Gangnam. Successfully performing the first acid attacks for a plastic surgery business purpose, not only causing harm for the enemy but also gain in profit for themselves. Even successfully killing multiple Takani-gunmen with ease, including saving the life of an ex-rival hacker who had previously helped Jing-Lee (although Pigbreath didn't have much choice back in that illustrious night of central Taiwan). Considering this was the first full day of Chairman Jing-Lee in power, there was definitely more action-packed days and nights to come for all three, just hopefully with significantly less pain.

That's where the commiseration comes into effect. The Maska Triad failed regarding their biggest objective of the night, which is where their rivals still had the biggest advantage. The identities in all of their leaders. The Takani Triad seemed to know each triplet extraordinarily well, but the Maska Triad had no clue who two of their main rivals even were!

CHAPTER FOURTEEN: HOSPITAL TALK

Approximately a half day later from the three biggest attacks that the triad had performed in recent history, nearly everyone in the family were at the hospital. Some due to their extreme wounds, some already being there, and the others visiting the previous two mentioned parties.

In the ICU next to each other were Pigbreath and Tarawa-Li - both who had oxygen breathalysers covered around their faces and were practically involved in a constant daze until their condition improved.

Unaffected by the recent change as they both were accommodated by the hospital before the actions of the night, Mallory and Aria were kept on the third floor.

Treated for his violent heaving, but now able to leave the hospital whenever, sat Dan-Li, who currently rested beside his fiancé, which he discovered was now recovering well from her recent health scare.

Treated for both of his fractured hands and ready to leave the hospital whenever, Chairman Jing-Lee sat near the entrance to wait for his fiancé and his new assistant - who apparently had some ground-breaking news he had to share. The Chairman also had to speak with all others that were involved with the triad, so he wouldn't be as patient with the two visitors if they didn't arrive at the hospital in time. Today, just like any other day, would be a busy one for the new Chairman.

Being impatient due to current circumstances, he quit waiting for his fiancé and assistant to show up at the hospital, knowing well that he had many other people to address regarding the results of last night and the next plan to move the business forward. Becoming more abrasive now that he had become Chairman, every second felt like an eternity. In business, wasted time equated to wasted money. He couldn't care less about his fractured hands, as the codeine painkillers the nurse had him take made him feel on ecstasy. His previously battered legs only felt sore and bruised, which Jing-Lee deemed immaterial currently. He stood up from the squeaky hospital seat near the entrance and made his way to the Intensive Care Unit, focusing himself on the two people that lay their heads on the hospital beds in the specific ward. His rampant footsteps echoed the silent hospital floor, gaining volume the harder he stomped on the cold and sparkling surface. The mid-day sun gleamed through the glass doors of the hospital, which hopefully would correlate to the type of day Jing-Lee would be experiencing.

Still on the same storey as the entrance, the Chairman zapped through the complex first floor, eventually finding the room that housed both his brother, Tarawa-Li, and former foe (possibly future comrade) Pigbreath. Both men were laid uncomfortably as can be on their stiff hospital beds, taking in as much essential oxygen, and gazed at Jing-Lee with their slumberous state. Both were not in the right mental or physical state to lift a finger, let alone converse. Jing-Lee placed a chair in between the end of both beds, straight in the middle, and sat, but with his legs and body in the direction to the man on his left, which was Pigbreath.

"I know when I first met you in Taiwan, you only revealed the killer because if you hadn't, I would have killed you. You're different, though. You're not the typical gangster, let alone the typical hacker. You didn't even snake me out to Mouse or your other leaders, did you? I can tell you hate the Takani Triad the same as us. Why not join the Maska Triad? It's an open offer. Think about it when you next get to sleep, which I think will be soon; you look seriously faded right now." Jing-Lee said, throwing down another codeine tablet straight down his throat.

An almost-smile was put across on his face, who, in an instant, fell asleep to Jing-Lee's accord. Jing-Lee knew that Pigbreath could be the answer to eliminating the biggest enemy right now. It was of high importance to keep Pigbreath not only safe, but on the side of the Maska Triad – if he wanted to find out about the two mystery rival leaders. He knew that Mouse would have probably left for Taiwan once again by now, most likely to report to them two mystery-people.

After watching Pigbreath fall asleep, he adverted his attention to Tarawa-Li, by moving his legs and body to his right. His brother, too, also looked in an outrageous state, with a clearly visible stitched up portion of his skull in full display. However, being in such a state would turn out to be the saving grace for the Surgeon because the Chairman could easily kill him for his actions last night. He was the reason into why their main mission of the night failed. Tarawa-Li was the singular reason why Mouse had escaped his grasp. Yes, he successfully attacked a nightclub with weapons of acidity, but the attack was nothing in comparison to the 'Mouse Trap'. Perhaps Tarawa-Li was the mischievous snake that was coinciding with the Takani Triad and tossing all forms of brotherhood loyalty out of the window.

"I thought you were a lunatic that I could trust, yet here I am, looking at you half-dead, realising that you're nothing more than a psychotic punk who would do anything to see me fail. No wonder why Father hated you and no one ever wanted to be around you. Do us all a favour and turn into this laidback person you wanted to be. I'll even do it for you, because then I know for good who you are. You are a fraud. You claim to have been a sadistic freak for years on end, but once father dies you become a mellow punk who begs for a stupid dog to stay with him. As punishment for jeopardising the Maska Triad, don't be surprised when you enter your bedroom to see your new dog companion with his eyes drilled out. Oh, and don't cry, otherwise I might as well drill your eyes out too, freak. Comprise yourself of gratitude that we're brothers, otherwise I would have killed you right here, right now. You know what? When you get out of this hospital, you have two choices. Either remain the sadistic freak everyone knows you for or kill yourself being the laidback fraud you're pretending to become. I've had enough of your bullshit. I am your Chairman. I am your master. The reason you live is because I have been so kind to have spared your life today. Prove to me that I haven't made a mistake on this very day." Jing-Lee blurted, clenching his fists extremely tight that his bandages ripped off, with his fractured bones popping out of both hands.

Jing-Lee didn't even believe that his brother deserved any attention on himself, looking down on the hospital floor after speaking. He left sitting on the uncomfortable hospital chair, returning the object to its original position. He stormed out of the room with the foulest facial expression he had ever shown.

Walking back to the entrance of the hospital after a couple of minutes once again finding his way back, Jing-Lee came face-to-face unexpectedly with Zara. Obviously, the two were meeting today; it was the fact that both were in a crazy rush to find one another and now suddenly they were both in each other's company. The two motioned to walk to the cafeteria, both starving for some good food in their system. Ordering a coffee, a sandwich, and a cake each, the two sat down to enjoy their average tasting meal, with the main focus of topic being about their soon-approaching wedding date.

"I would ask what happened last night considering you and your brothers were all checked into the hospital, but knowing you, you'll just say it's to do with business." Zara said, scarfing down her sandwich.

Even with Zara joining Jing-Lee once in undertaking criminal activity, he didn't want to push his fiancé into the triad business entirely. She was of great aid back in Taiwan as a bloodthirsty mercenary to avenge her brother, but Jing-Lee knew she would be in greater danger if she continued working alongside him. She, on the other hand, vastly enjoyed the night of crime in Taiwan, and was ready to strike whenever commanded to. Her desires were even questioned by her own conscience, as she never used to be the criminal type of person, but sickeningly, she craved more of the action-fuelled scenarios now more than ever.

"When do you want to get married? Obviously, we have the money, so we don't need to consider any financial restrictions." Jing-Lee murmured, sipping his hot coffee, with the ever-present foul expression on his face.

"You sound like my father, not my future husband. Tell me what's bothering you." Zara replied, stunned at how humdrum her fiancé spoke.

"Sorry. Just pissed off at Tarawa-Li. I shouldn't express any anger towards you when you haven't done anything wrong." Jing-Lee said, trying to lighten the mood between both of them.

"Do you want to talk about it?" Zara asked softly.

"Have you thought about a date?" Jing-Lee blurted, not wanting to focus about business when he was around her.

"As long as I get to marry you, I don't mind." Zara whispered, smiling at her future husband.

"How about if we do a double wedding? You and I, Dan-Li and Mallory. Could be some fun, huh?" Jing-Lee chuckled, sarcastically gazing back into his fiancé's sparkling eyes.

"You've had both hands broken so I'll allow you to use that tone with me. I would barely even want Dan-Li at our wedding considering what he's done to me and my dad." Zara murmured, unamused at Jing-Lee's sarcastic tone he had taken in a serious conversation.

"I was being serious. Dan-Li wants to talk to you. He's currently on the third floor with Mallory. She's getting a lot better by the way. I suggest you talk to him, it's pretty urgent." Jing-Lee declared, almost ordering with motions for his fiancé to leave him be for a couple of hours.

"I love you, but sometimes you're a real punk! That's me being nice by the way. Back where I'm from, there are many harsher words I could have used to describe how you just treated me." Zara said, jumping out her cafeteria chair, knocking the hot coffee onto the lap of Jing-Lee, who simply reacted with no emotion, too tired after the effects of last night to give a single damn.

She swiftly exited the presence of her fiancé and made her way to the third floor to visit Dan-Li and Mallory.

Whilst the conversation between Jing-Lee and Zara in the cafeteria was going on, the other happy couple of Dan-Li and Mallory were also discussing their wedding plans, now that her state of health was significantly improving and most likely making her able to leave the hospital in a day or two. The couple were talking in her hospital room, with Dan-Li standing instead of sitting - as standing could provoke his recent haul of vomiting sickness again.

"How about a double wedding? You and I, Jing-Lee and Zara, that could be fun, huh?" Dan-Li asked.

"Well, you do know that I hate being the centre of attention." Mallory said. "Is that what they want too?"

"Zara's the only one that needs the idea given to her." Dan-Li replied, hoping the three could guilt trip for a double wedding.

"Why do you and Jing-Lee want a double wedding?" Mallory asked, genuinely intrigued.

"Jing-Lee thought that due to our father passing, we should all get married to truly turn over a new leaf in the family generation. The two best brothers marrying the two best girls. It'll only be a small ceremony I believe, unless he tells us any different." Dan-Li replied, hoping that Mallory wouldn't notice the sly dig aimed at his other brother, who she was fond of.

"What about Tarawa-Li?" Mallory interjected, noticing that her fiancé took a dig towards his other brother.

"What about Tarawa-Li? He's not married, he doesn't have a girlfriend, quite frankly, he'll be lucky enough to get invited. I can't go into too many details, but we're mad at him, especially Jing-Lee. Tarawa-Li is just a lunatic who you feel sorry for because he had a difficult time growing up." Dan-Li interjected, making him almost angry at the fact that whenever Tarawa-Li's name popped up in negative connotations, Mallory would be there to defend him.

"I don't know what he's done to make you two boys so angry, but at the end of the day, he's your family. Family stick together. Make him a Marriage Officiant for our wedding if you don't want him to cause any shenanigans, that way you two will have a close eye on him at all times." Mallory snapped, not tolerating anymore rude remarks towards the third brother, who she always thought as one of the sweetest people she had ever met.

To avoid any heated argument of any sorts, he promptly exited the room to take a brief break from the animosity between them. She was shaking in disbelief that her fiancé left her just like that, thinking about what possible situation between the three had caused this explosion of anger. She concluded that the argument must have happened last night, as it was the first without Dan-Li's company. Dan-Li was now seated central in the three typical squeaky hospital chairs that once previously accompanied a sleeping Tarawa-Li for an almost day. This was not a time to reminisce, however, as he was greeted by the person that he needed to confess everything to: Zara. She took a seat next to him, both of them almost nervous, as they didn't know how the outcome of this conversation would turn out.

"Apparently you wanted to talk to me?" Zara asked.

"If I knew he was your younger brother, I wouldn't have done what I did. My father foolishly told me who Jason was after I killed him. I know it's the past, and I can't change the fact that he's dead, but I would have done something different if I knew who he was at the time. Sorry won't bring him back, but truly know I am sorry for your loss. I'll forever be in your debt to try and bring any happiness or peace into your life." Dan-Li said, ready to receive vicious punches, slaps, and scratches from Zara.

"Jing-Lee told me that your father made the decisions on who to kill. He knew who Jason was. It's his fault, not yours, and if he we're still alive and well, I would have killed him no matter what. I just miss him. I just miss my brother." Zara cried, still taking in the fact that her brother was indeed no longer with her.

She looked to her side at Dan-Li, but she didn't see his face - she saw the face of her dead brother, Jason. She saw her younger brother smiling at him with his gracious smile, handing her lilacs which was his tradition as a present. The illusion of seeing her brother once more reduced herself to a teary state, knowing he wasn't real, but instead a fixation of her imagination. Snapping out of perhaps showing a vulnerable side to Dan-Li and staying strong, she played off her tears and blamed her fake allergies.

"I'm surprised that you're not attacking me right now. Have you known this for a long time? Who told you? Why haven't you tried killing me for my actions? My father may have confirmed who I needed to kill, but I'm the one who actually killed him." Dan-Li fretted, concerned about the mellow reply Zara gave.

"Jing-Lee and I went to Taiwan whilst yourself, Tarawa-Li and Mallory rushed into hospital when your fiancé had her episode. We tracked down the only person who could tell us the killer of my brother. That's how we found Pigbreath. Also, don't be mad at Pigbreath, he put his life on the line by being unfaithful to his own triad. He could have just refused to log into his high-tech computer and let us shoot him. Anyways, once he revealed you to be the killer, I couldn't believe it. After hours of talking on our way back to Korea, we realised that your father was the true killer. You were just the puppet. I did want my vengeance, however. Honestly, I planned on killing your future wife. That evening when I visited you both and you left the room, I was strangling her to death. That's when I realised if I killed Mallory, the killing would continue until we all were dead. You have a child; I can't ruin your child's life. I haven't forgotten about the killing, but I have forgiven you." Zara cried, now screening her true emotional sorrow, wiping the tears that were sobering out her eyes.

“I haven’t even forgiven myself for what I did. Thank you.” Dan-Li blurted, truly grateful for Zara’s words, now giving her a consoling hug to calm her sad and stressed well-being.

“What’s this about a double wedding?” Zara asked, trying to hold in her whimpering and trying to give a small smile of forgiveness in the direction of Dan-Li.

Back to Chairman Jing-Lee – who was taking a cab home as he found that Yung-Ko needed him at the house, instead of the two conveniently meeting in the hospital - where practically everyone (except Derrick) would currently be. The condition of his two fists ameliorated, with him finally feeling sensation in both of them once again. He was in no condition to fight, but it made him smile knowing that his fists were already making an improvement. After the cab journey, he walked into the family house and wandered until he had found his new assistant and advisor. He entered and met Yung-Ko in his compact office - this time with Jing-Lee opening a close-by window, wanting to avoid the gushes of smoke from roughly the tenth cigar that his advisor would be devouring. The Chinaman emoted a serious expression from his face, with Jing-Lee hopefully pleading to himself for no more bad news to be delivered.

"I have some bad news, some average news, some good news, and some ground-breaking news. Which would you like to hear first?" Yung-Ko asked, inhaling his crusty cigar.

"In that order. From bad news to ground-breaking news." Jing-Lee answered, fanning the smoke away from himself.

"The bad news is the Takani Triad. I have no intel on how Mouse escaped, I still have no intel on who the other two leaders are, I have no intel on their next plans. They've automatically gone off the radar, completely. They're definitely devising something for payback to get back at us, that's for sure. I have no clue on any of that plan's information, though. When I do know, I'll let you know." Yung-Ko stated, almost double-inhaling his cigar like it was a stress coping mechanism for the Chinaman.

"I still don't understand how he escaped so easily? All three of us were practically in that room with Mouse when he let out that smoke grenade. It makes no sense. How do we still not know two of their leaders, too? This isn't the old-fashioned days with no cyber-tracking, I can't believe it honestly. It's infuriating." Jing-Lee fumed, knowing their rivals still had the edge in that regard over the two triads.

"From bad news to hopefully average news in comparison. Your older sister, Wera-Li Maska. Still no information on where she is, what she does, who she's with. Couldn't track her down either." Yung-Ko stated, avoiding eye-contact with the Chairman, hopeful for no violent punishment delivering two unproductive pieces of news to his boss.

"She's either dead or intelligent since day one. Let's hope we never find out which one it is. Atheno-Li told me she was abandoned, so she most likely died from being a starving homeless child. What's next?" Jing-Lee grumbled, hoping to hear some more positive news now.

"Good news is PlaciCorp. Remarkably, just from the two acid attacks, appointments are fully booked for the next five months, and that's including the sudden increase of allotting more surgery rooms. Profits are expected to triple for this year alone, with PlaciCorp further dominating the field of plastic surgery in Korea. Tarawa-Li and Dan-Li were never caught on camera, plus an innocent guy is being framed for the attack on Club Aitken. Some guy named DJ Lunar. Incredible." Yung-Ko chuckled, hoping to remove the grump expression off the face of the Chairman.

"Good. Maybe next time I'll let you know beforehand that me and my brothers are attacking some place. Thanks for following up on us after and not getting angry for not being included in the planning and briefing. I just needed for my first night of being the Chairman to be with my brothers at the thing we do best. Being gangsters." Jing-Lee stated.

"It's fine, boss. As your advisor, I can only advise you, if you have a plan of attack already set-up then no need for me to be included in the planning and preparation. You might need me to help you out with information in regard to the ground-breaking news I'm about to give you though." Yung-Ko stated, finishing his cigar and dropping the micro remains in his ash tray.

"What do you mean? Why do I need to do another attack?" Jing-Lee asked, becoming confused at what Yung-Ko just told him.

"There's a new Chief. A new Chief of the biggest service to Korea that you don't currently own, the one service even your father couldn't own. There's a new Chief of the Korean Investigation Unit. This is one step further into your dream of making Korea a country that you could own and rule with an iron fist." Yung-Ko announced, looking at how his boss would react - starting from instant confusion to instant desire.

“Tell me everything you know about the new Chief, where he lives, family members, house structure, any security, just anything and everything I need to know.” Jing-Lee blurted, unable to contain his potential excitement – the idea of him owning an actual country could become a possibility in his lifetime, maybe even sooner rather than later.

“His name is Chief Mok, he recently turned 58 years old before his promotion. The intel that I have gathered suggests that he’s more of a lenient character in comparison to the former Chief. His family members that will be in the house include his wife Jin and son Baul. The house is comprised of four floors, situated in the middle of a 6-acre plot of land, with no obstructions to help such as bushes or trees. Security changes by the number each night with no fixed number, so expect anywhere between five and twenty armed guards in and around the massive property. I also have reason to believe there is a sniper on the roof, but I can’t confirm the rumour unfortunately. There are masses of security cameras which I have managed to destroy, meaning I would suggest you attack as soon as possible. I have also placed a clear-coloured signal jammer, meaning you have the edge on the guards already. I’m obviously not the person to officially make the decisions, but I strongly advise you to be as quiet as possible when you’re inside, as Chief Mok is known to be awake nearly all the damn time of day, suffering from an extreme case of insomnia. Kill quietly if you want to have more of a chance securing the deal. That's all I know." Yung-Ko addressed, with Jing-Lee impressed with the data he gathered regarding the newly appointed KIU Chief.

"Thanks, I can take it from there. Have some sleep. You earned it." Jing-Lee replied, exiting his chair, and giving his advisor a small nod of gratitude.

"Wait, Chairman. Don't you want me to be with you discussing the strategy of how you want to enter the house, silently take out the security, and persuade Chief Mok to give the Maska Triad the ownership rights to the KIU?" Yung-Ko asked.

"I'm a grown man who has experience in hurting people, I can take it from here. Don't worry, I trust you; I just prefer mapping out the tactics to the people who are physically getting involved. Have a nice night, take care, I'll see you tomorrow." Jing-Lee interjected, somewhat offended that his new advisor was treating him like a child.

"Yes, sir." Yung-Ko replied, with both exiting from the compact office and going to different directions, Yung-Ko headed to his vehicle to return home, and Jing-Lee prepared for his next attack.

This was the second day of him as Chairman, yet he was planning his fourth major attack. The timing for this attack was awkward, but he knew this was an opportunity he had to grasp before it was too late. If he could successfully seal the deal, owning the Korean Investigation Unit, he would only be fingertips away from owning the country as a whole, with the thought making the Chairman's mouth water. He had to attack tonight. He had two broken hands, but he still had to attack tonight. Who could he bring along with him? He couldn't even bring any security guards that the triad owned or even the working girls, they were no longer under contract.

The crisp evening sky began to set around the family house, with Jing-Lee inviting the only two people who he deemed to be fit enough, competent enough, and trustworthy enough to help him in his attack against Chief Mok. He hoped he wouldn't even need to attack the man. Perhaps the home invasion and threatening elements would be enough for him to acquire the KIU. To talk through the plan, the two he invited eventually showed up, and walked into the living area to see what he wanted to talk about. The two people that were invited were Dan-Li and Zara. The conflict between the two invited could perhaps be described as an unpredictable one currently, but Jing-Lee believed they would work strongly together once they knew the purpose of why they were both here.

"You wanted to talk to us?" Dan-Li asked, gulping down Pepto-Bismol.

"We haven't got a lot of time and I need both of you tonight. We're attacking a guy named Chief Mok, he is the new KIU Chief. This may be the only chance we can get in order to buy the biggest service that father couldn't buy. We need to buy the Korean Investigation Unit, not just because it's my orders, but for father." Jing-Lee replied, opening his blueprint for success for the two to view on the floor.

"Why should I want to help your father? He's the one who killed my brother." Zara interjected.

"I thought you had forgiven." Dan-Li said.

"I've forgiven you, not him!" Zara snapped, almost changing her mind on forgiving Dan-Li.

"Calm down. Forget those last words, just do it because it's the order I've given. I know technically you're not part of the triad yet, as we're only engaged, but you're considered as a temporary replacement. Tarawa-Li is still in the ICU, rendering him unable to do anything tonight – although that may be a blessing. The three 'Gangsters of Gangnam' tonight are myself, my fiancé, and my non-lunatic brother. We have no time to argue, we only have time to go through the plan, and time to complete the crime." Jing-Lee said, calming down his aggravated fiancé.

"What's the plan, Chairman?" Zara asked, knowing she wouldn't get her way no matter how hard she tried.

"Our target is Chief Mok. I need him alive. You kill him, you're dead to me. He has a wife named Jin, and a son named Baul. The house is comprised of four floors, but no clue where their bedrooms are located. Situated just a little outside of Gangnam, near a place called Segok-Dong, the house has around a huge 6-acre plot of land, but there's no bushes or other obstructions to conceal our identity. Estimated five to twenty guards, presumably with laser sight assault rifles, with an unconfirmed sniper around the roof level of the house. Yung-Ko helped us out, we don't have to worry about security cameras or enemy signals. Chief Mok is believed to be an easy target, but he suffers a great deal via insomnia, so we're going to be as quiet as possible to remain undetected. You two are performing all the physical tasks such as shooting the guards and tying the wife and son with rope, my hands are too broken to handle any weaponry right now. When we find

Chief Mok, lay his wife and son all tied up in front of his very eyes, and that's where I'll begin the blackmail. I'll threaten to stop the operations of all services we own in this nation, and if he stalls or disagrees, we'll kill one of his loved ones. He stalls or disagrees again; we'll kill the other loved one. Stalls or disagrees again, we'll kill him and wait for another newly appointed KIU Chief." Jing-Lee declared, becoming the definition of 'ruling with an iron fist'.

"When are we leaving?" Dan-Li asked shyly, not confident about the attack - believing the Chairman was not only weak, but Zara was inexperienced, and he himself was not feeling so good.

"In a half-hour. Grab all the weapons you need; I suggest one of you uses stealth tactics such as a silenced sniper rifle and pistol, and the other to use a silenced assault rifle and combat knife. Equip yourself heavily. There's only two of you, I'll be walking in the shadows until the coast is clear." Jing-Lee replied, making his way to the vehicle to wait for the other two.

CHAPTER FIFTEEN: HOME INVASION

Ready to attack after thirty minutes of Dan-Li and Zara preparing themselves with the weapons they needed, the two set out to join Jing-Lee in the vehicle he was in. Both devised a 'divide and conquer' scheme, with Dan-Li shooting far-away with his silenced sniper rifle - and Zara getting closer to the action to finish off the guards with her silenced assault rifle. When the two had finished killing all of the guards outside the house, Dan-Li would promptly return back to his brother, giving the silent hand signal to reveal that it was indeed safe for him to get out and join himself and his fiancé. Jing-Lee didn't care if this made him look like a coward, he wasn't stupid. There was just no relevance in him holding any weapons, his hands were broken.

She volunteered to drive the three to the house of Chief Mok, setting the GPS navigational system in the vehicle to the place they needed to get to. However, she instantly realised that the vehicle they were about to drive didn't contain any electronical software. Instead, Jing-Lee nodded to a map which he attempted to latch onto with his broken hands. The Chairman didn't want to risk anything in this attack; thus he prohibited any electronical software or device to be used for this night, reverting themselves to the old-fashioned method of military signals. Some may seem this move as paranoid, but Jing-Lee saw this move as playing smart.

With no time to spare, she drove the vehicle out of the family house and proceeded to listen to her fiancé giving out the essential directions, which would eventually lead them to an alley which was close to the back-entrance of the 6-acre plot of land. The alley that they had entered only managed to fit the single vehicle by itself. The good news was that this was the outskirts of Gangnam, meaning the alley that they had parked themselves was beside two abandoned buildings and no civilians in sight. Dan-Li and Zara exited the alley by walking a few steps forward and turned to their right, and then with their target house in sight, mapping out how far the alley was to the back-entrance of the house of the KIU Chief. The journey would take them roughly a few minutes of running, and that was taking into consideration their rucksacks of weaponry.

The aforementioned few minutes of running passed, with Dan-Li and Zara now having both of their feet on KIU Chief property. Both were astounded that the back-entrance of the property contained only a jumpable gate, no guards, and no security cameras.

After jumping the gate, the two immediately began to scan for their enemies, to no avail so far. The coast was clear for them to go further to the house, which was their only source of lighting from this point, not wanting to use a flashlight to attract any unwanted attention onto themselves.

The gigantic and lavishing house from the outside looked simply immaculate from their rear viewpoint. A lush colour of whiteness, a large space of gorgeous patio outside flooring, even an array of flags that captioned the illustrious history of the KIU, the list could go on forever. The two could appreciate the view but knew it would only be wasting time.

Holding their sniper rifle and assault rifle, the two ran as quickly and as silently as possible, until they could find a flat vantage point that they could use to their advantage to kill as many guards as possible. After running half the 6-acre plot, the two stopped immediately in their tracks, falling to the floor in a prone position. Three guards had entered their vision, albeit a far distance from one another. The soul-crushing news, however, was that the guards had weapons which were extremely to their advantage. The weapons of the KIU Guards had a heat-sensor, meaning both of them were screwed unless they could eliminate the three in quick fashion. Dan-Li placed his silenced sniper rifle on the grass-surface and aimed his sights to the three enemies that were slowly approaching them.

“These guards seem inexperienced. I can tell from their body language. The three should be spreading wide, but instead they are close-by one another. I know you think it’s an arrogant move, but I’m going to wait until two are so close to one another that I can kill both with one bullet. What I need you to do is finish the other one off with your assault rifle if you can. I know the distance is very far for an assault rifle to do any damage, but it’s the only plan I can think of. Can you do that for me?” Dan-Li asked gently, staring completely in his sniper scope, waiting for the perfect opportunity, which he sensed was in only a few seconds from now.

“I’ll do it for you. I’m better with a gun than what you might think.” Zara replied softly, now with her assault rifle on the grass-surface, pleading that her weapon would be able to do enough damage from such a distance.

The three guards with their high-tech weapons had definitely detected an anomaly from their normally uneventful day-to-day life working as security for the KIU Chief - walking ever so closer to the two. The three guards started to swiftly walk ahead in the dark night, trying to scan for the potential hostiles that were shown on their weapons' sensors. About to run, two KIU Guards went in front of one another for some bizarre reason, with Dan-Li seizing the opportunity by shooting his sniper rifle bullet, which penetrated the two straight in the centre of the skull, resulting them in dropping dead immediately. Before the uninjured and alive KIU Guard could even shoot, Zara lived up to her competent promise, shooting an array of her silenced bullets which pierced the entire torso and skull, leaving the three dead in their tracks. The two managed to kill the first three guards of the night, but there was no telling into how many there were left outside. The unconfirmed sniper and inside-working KIU Guards were also a mystery for now.

Both of them moved from their prone position after reloading their current weapons, placing themselves hopefully in an advantageous position for their next attack. The two were now extremely close to the back door of the house, laying prone and to the left-side of the property, behind a hopeful distraction which was the array of flags. In their vision, were two KIU Guards seeming to be taking a break. Their weapons were placed neatly on the floor, loud laughs were heard, and some alcohol exchanged between the two. Dan-Li noticed something 'off' with these guards. He expected them to act more professional than this. The KIU Guards didn't even have any special clothing, the men he had seen were wearing regular day-to-day clothes, pissing about at work with some fancy weaponry by their side. This wasn't the time to nit-pick though, this was the time to kill.

He zoomed into his sniper scope again, motioning for Zara to pay serious attention to the two men.

"I'll shoot the guy on the right who has our face towards us. After I shoot, you kill the guy to our left. Three seconds." Dan-Li whispered, issuing a countdown of sorts with his right hand so Zara could see in her peripheral vision.

Three seconds passed and Dan-Li's sniper bullet infiltrated the face of the KIU Guard, with Zara quickly following up by giving the other guard an unwanted present of bullets that pierced his skull from top to bottom. The two men were dead in their seats, with their deceased bodies bleeding profusely, especially the guard shot by Zara now looking like the devil. Both of them contemplated whether they should hide the two dead bodies out of plain sight, but not knowing if they should go ahead with the plan - with a sense of doubt filling their minds. But, with the adrenaline they had, Zara dropped her assault rifle next to Dan-Li and ran to the patio area, where the two dead guards lay.

Angry, but knowing to keep quiet, Dan-Li held in his dissatisfaction and just made sure he could guard her safety. Sprinting to the two dead men, she used her outrageously great body strength to carry both guards, running back to the direction of Dan-Li to dispose the bodies in a darker and more secretive location. She had made it back incurring no harm, but two more guards had now made it to the patio area, with them spotting bullet shells and blood.

Dan-Li sniped the first guard in the chest, reloading immediately. Zara dumped the dead bodies behind the position where she had previously been, grasping her assault rifle once more to accompany. She shot the other guard in the centre of the stomach. Both men were still alive, which wasn't a good thing. The two KIU Guards both let out a howling scream of mercy. Dan-Li followed up his first shot by killing one of the two, and Zara killing the other guard after reloading her assault rifle. But their cover had to have been blown now.

What came next was indescribable, as there was an undetectable sound that appeared to be approaching closer and closer. After a few seconds, both saw where the sound was coming from. It seemed as though all unharmed KIU Guards had rallied together to stop them, running out of their KIU vehicle. Now stood next to their fallen comrades were ten remaining guards, pointing their weapons at the darkness, it seemed. In reality, the ten men were pointing straight in the direction of Dan-Li and Zara. Sure, they had weapons that detected heat signatures - but these guards were legitimately looking straight-in-the-eyes at both.

Dan-Li knew it was a fight or die situation, and so did Zara. The two looked at each other and nodded, knowing this could be their very last second on this planet. Dan-Li sniped the first guard to his left, killing him immediately. Zara leapt out of her prone position and used the distraction caused by Dan-Li to her advantage, knowing the guards wouldn't be checking their heat signatures for the time being. The KIU Guards aggressively shot towards the direction of the sniper bullet that they had heard, but in reality, they were in shock of the shot and had lost their focus. KIU Guards don't have much experience in actually having to shoot, this was the first attack on KIU property since Atheno-Li tried to bargain with the former Chief many years ago.

Using a flanking manoeuvre, she managed to get behind the KIU Guards, who were now watching their footing carefully, perhaps being the most cowardly guards protecting a nation's government service in history. Dan-Li blurrily saw Zara in the distance, so he shot his second bullet reaching his second KIU Guard skull to help her out in her flank attack. With the men now incompetent at doing their jobs – they froze-still in shock. Actual guards who were meant to be the forefront for the country of Korea were incompetent in their job title. Seriously baffling.

The remaining eight guards met their fate of their comrades, with Zara loading heavy fire from her assault rifle behind them all. Not all eight turned out to be dead, however, with one faking his death and taking Zara down onto the patio floor to brutalise before she could have reloaded her weapon. Tossing and turning with the enemy, it was a scrappy fight with all fists turning into a gory mess. After a few more swings, the last alive guard gained an advantage by turning out on top, punching her vigorously twice, before Dan-Li ended it with a sniper bullet to the man's chest. She quickly grabbed the combat knife she remembered to place in her pocket for an emergency and slit the throat of the guard, causing a spurt of the red liquid to spray across her face. Both of them now just had to quickly check around the front of the house to scan any other outside guards before one of them could return to Jing-Lee.

She removed most of the squirted blood that she had received from the cut-open throat of the KIU Guard. With Dan-Li still prone with his sniper, it made sense for her to be the one to quickly check the front side of the house for any extra possible hostiles. She swiftly departed from the patio flooring that held home to the already dead men to see if she needed to add any more to the list. Staying as much as in the shadows as possible, she strained her eyes extensively from her far left all the way to her far right, with no other guards in outside sight. The outside guards were dead, it was safe for her to sprint back to the alley to bring Jing-Lee. Making her path back to Dan-Li, a distinct noise could be heard from the roof of the four-floor house. It was the rooftop sniper, looking for them both, and she had just been found. Remarkably, in a high intelligence move, she ran and dived toward the house, being protected by a small portion of the roof which sheltered her, with the bullet the sniper shot going between her legs when she made the bold and daring leap of faith.

The rooftop sniper still had his eyes set on her, with Dan-Li leaving his respective sniper lonesome, spotting a ladder that spun up to the fourth floor, perhaps due to the sniper either leaving it there or for the occasional construction worker. He ran as fast as possible to the ladder, and started to climb, only for the ladder to cause the highest amount of noise a ladder could possibly make, being an unstable structure of shattered metal.

To distract the roof-sniper even further, Zara began to exaggerate her breaths and groans, which made the steps that she could hear high above to move in panic towards different directions. Taking the ultimate risk in order for the KIU rooftop-sniper to not be averted to focus on Dan-Li, she ran to the previous position which she believed to be safe to run to, which was the patio flooring. With an array of dead KIU Guards, she scatters around with the weaponry and grabs the high-tech assault rifle with heat sensors and runs straight back to the small portion of the house that covered her head where she previously distracted the sniper. She picks the weapon and places it as vertical as possible, which was now aimed for the roof above her head, and imprudently opens fire left to right. The lurid noise of the bullets gives Dan-Li leeway to finish the risk-worthy climb from the ground to the high roof of the illustrious house.

He was now on the roof, with the sniper who was previously distracted by Zara now turning his attention to the man who had now invaded his battlegrounds. Luckily, both couldn't use their snipers in a fight like this, with the victor having to coarsen the other to death with their bare hands. Well, that's what the sniper would have wanted to happen.

Due to his brother's earlier advice, whilst the sniper sprinted into the direction of Dan-Li, he whipped out his silenced pistol and shot the sniper in the chest, arms, throat, and head. Bleeding to death within seconds, he smiled at the man he had just killed, because without the advice from his brother, he would have had to fight the long way. Some other time, he would have - but in a night like this, time was limited.

With both now returning to each other in the position behind the collection of flags, the two decided on their different roles. He was to stay where the two were currently seated, in case of any new potential KIU Guards who happened to show up, with Zara sprinting the distance back to the Chairman, for him to join now that the coast was seemingly clear. The two would discuss their attacking tactics inside the house once all three members were present. So far, so good, the teaming of 'Chef' and 'Lilac' showed impressive strength and teamwork.

After running the whole distance of the gigantic backyard and jumping the small fence once more, Zara quickly made her way back to the alley to escort

Jing-Lee to the property, with the Chairman now looking as haggard as ever. The two broken hands didn't prosper enough strength to open the vehicle door, with Jing-Lee lacking awareness and capability. The Chairman needed rest, but he simply couldn't. Not tonight. Zara and a groggy Chairman made their way to the KIU property, with him even needing assistance to climb a small fence due to his status. Finally, after longer than expected, both met up with Dan-Li to determine the tactics once they were inside the four-floor property.

The order of offense would be Dan-Li, with Zara right by his side as the second attacker, and Jing-Lee practically being a ghost in the shadows until the floor was clear of enemies. Silenced bullets were a risk of being too loud, so the assault rifle that Zara had previously used was considered inapt. Dan-Li's silenced pistol was selected onto a setting where only one bullet could be fired every five seconds to limit any suspicions of intrusion on the KIU property. He opened the back door and all three entered the first floor of the home.

Darkness loomed from the get-go, silence filled the open-plan room. There were signs of a whole bunch of nothingness. Making their footsteps as silent as possible, the three snooped around the first floor to detect anything that would lead them to either a KIU Guard or Chief Mok, or anyone in between.

The three discovered this whole floor to be practically empty. The main attraction seemed to be a polar bear skinned rug, which was set below a clear glass coffee table, accompanied by a black leather couch and flat-screen television which was outlined by gold extract. That mentioned attraction was part of the open-plan room, also hosting an average kitchen-diner, which was nothing to write home about. Rooms that were separated individually included a miniscule bathroom, compacted study filled with law textbooks, and an empty bedroom, which was perhaps used for guests who came to visit the family or Chief Mok in particular.

After checking out the bedroom, with Dan-Li leading the three out, soft footsteps were coming louder and louder to their sensitive ears. Jing-Lee returned to remain hidden in identity, returning to the bedroom, with his right side leaning to the wall that was next to the bedroom door. In the distance, a KIU Guard was sluggishly walking down the stairs, scanning the floor for his presumably quarterly hour maintenance checks. Dan-Li and Zara returned to the bedroom, waiting for the KIU Guard to walk closer and closer until they could get their hands on him and kill the man in the guest bedroom, perhaps even humorously tucking him into the white and daisy fresh duvet. Walking closer and closer, with his footsteps becoming increasingly amplified, Dan-Li was poised to attack, aiming at the bedroom entrance for his next ingenuous victim.

The footsteps now sounded like an attack helicopter flying through a bed of marshmallows. The KIU Guard couldn't possibly get any closer to where he was now without spotting one of the three. Dan-Li couldn't wait forever, and with one more footstep from the guard, he slid and shot him in the chest. Preventing any backlash of noise that would jeopardise the mission, he quickly followed up by snapping the man's neck and quietly dumping his deceased body onto the sumptuous bed. The three moved up to the second floor of the property, hoping for the experience to be just as easy.

The second floor contained actual lighting, with an array of candles that lit the living room area. The living room area didn't show any proof of a working guard, however, as there was no one in sight. Chief Mok certainly had a sort of animal fetish, this was the second floor that contained a rug of a skinned animal, with this one being an exotic white tiger. The other rooms for the second floor included two mediocre sized bedrooms which were empty, one bathroom that for some reason had a piping hot radiator, a fitness area, and a small home theatre, which is where one KIU Guard was found to be spending his time. He wasn't alone compared to the other guard before - being accompanied with someone who was believed to either be his actual girlfriend - or his girlfriend for the night. Quibbling over semantics could be deemed as an irrelevant matter right now.

This was a two-person job, so Dan-Li and Zara decided to creep up on both unsuspecting victims. Luckily, with the loud background music of the movie, it would conceal their enemies' screams of mercy whilst they were to bleed to their death. This is exactly what happened, too. He shot the KIU Guard in the back of his skull, and she slashed the naked woman in her throat.

The screams only went on for a second or two before they met the same fate as all the other KIU Guards measly attempting to give security to Chief Mok on this night-watch. Jing-Lee observed the three killings that he was technically a part of, thinking to himself how easy this has been for them so far. He had expected skill, strength, professionalism, and all-round competency for these guards. Guards that were supposed to be the forefront of this nation – but instead it felt like the

Chairman was up against a disorganised gang of low-level thugs.

The third floor was fully lit, with actual legitimate lighting that filled the entire room. Unfortunately, the lighting enhanced all the features of this room - that the three perchance wouldn't have wanted to see - perhaps scarring them for life. Crowded with gut-wrenching disturbing artefacts that all in some way, shape, or form, resembled: 'the devil', including and not limited to: multiple nude devil statues created from various metals or materials, (the same statues that were previously housed in a Lithuanian museum before being stolen) a fresco detail from the Rila Monastery in which demons are depicted as having grotesque faces and bodies, and a traditional Polish 16th-century oil painting which outlines horns of a goat and ram, goat's fur and ears, nose and canines of a pig; which is a typical depiction of the devil especially in Christian art. Something about this whole night seemed very bizarre, even more so now.

Unlike the two previous floors, the guard on the third floor recognised the arrival of intruders almost immediately. The three were met by two KIU Guards this time, with the second now by his partner's side. The two were both holding experimental weaponry, with the pistol-looking guns in their scrawny hands having an almost electrical charge sound and look to them. Before being able to get the opportunity to shoot their spectacularly looking guns, out of instinct, Dan-Li shot the guard to his left - and Zara leaped to the guard on her right, slashing his testicles in half and then finishing the job by lodging her weapon completely in the man's throat. Holding his throat, part of which was now visually out of his body, the guard held the small percentage of touchable bone as close and as tight as possible in order for any chance to survive, but reality proved that he wouldn't last even one more minute. Before the guard came to his death, Jing-Lee needed to ask something that he was desperate to find out about.

"Why does Chief Mok have all of this shit in his house? Why does he need a bunch of disgusting and obscene artefacts that symbolise devilish characters? Has he gone insane?" Jing-Lee asked to the KIU Guard holding his severely shattered and gory throat.

"It's...funny...that you still haven't..." The KIU Guard replied, until he was unable to speak no more - dying from the substantial wounds brought upon him.

He knew he would get the answers anyway out of the mouth of the Chief, either fairly one-on-one, or using the harsh methods of blackmail and torture. One meagre KIU Guard dying was literally nothing to him. The three scan the third floor one more time due to the bizarre layout of devil-oriented relics scattered around, not even knowing what they would find anyways. Nothing else was found except for the blood-curdling detestation for the devil personification.

The fourth floor of the property, was to no surprise, equally arcane in presentation. Statues that represented Korean mythology regarding the 'angels of death' were kept next to each other. In this mythology, the male angel of death is depicted as a stern and ruthless bureaucrat who is in service for his partner who led the way. The lead angel, the female angel of death, is depicted as a psychopath who leads all people, from poor to rich, from underworld thugs to business tycoons, to a world filled with evil in which they must sacrifice their souls for a chance of survival in their reincarnated spirit. The fourth floor also had all of their individual rooms with the door shut, which would indicate actual people in them. Somewhat peculiar was that there was no guard to be seen walking around the floor. The three just suspected he was sleeping on the job, which considering the others, was more than possible to be happening.

Keeping the same tactic as before, Dan-Li would be the person to kick the door open and aim his weapon, with Zara quickly following after, and Jing-

Lee to do nothing until he had to confront Chief Mok. On the hand-count of three, he kicked the first door open and ran and aimed his weapon to wherever the target was. The first room was not a success, it was none other than the umpteenth bathroom that this extravagant place had. Zara did spot however a bandage that would aid the healing process of Jing-Lee's hands, covering him with the material from the bottom of his wrist to the tip of his fingers.

The second unopened room, and Dan-Li viciously charged in once more, slipping instantly when his first footstep landed in the room, almost shooting a bullet through the window ahead when falling and mildly hitting his head on the floor. Not taking any chances, Zara jumps onto the belly of Dan-Li and slightly ricochets off to capture whoever was in the room. It was a bedroom, with no one in the bed - with him now coming to the realisation that he slipped over a loose floorboard. Thankfully, the bump that he endured didn't cause any significant damage whatsoever, and all three were able to continue the invasion as planned.

The third room on the fourth floor and once again, no persons were occupying the space. Instead of a normal household room such as another bedroom or dining room, or even another bathroom, this room was an art room - but not the art you would want to associate yourself with if you were KIU Chief. Another oil-painting, this one lust filled associating an angel and devil inappropriately enjoying their time together in hell. The painting spanned the entire length of the room, paired next to two sculptures: Satan and Shinigami (spirit of death in Asian mythology). After browsing once more the disturbing pieces of so called 'art', the three re-concentrate on the invasion. Three unopened rooms left. Three targets not tortured or negotiated with yet, even though Jing-Lee felt so unwell now that if Chief Mok rejected the deal, he would just order a shot on his wife and son instantly for not complying with his request.

Now focusing on the other side of the fourth floor, the subsequent room that was first ahead was first attacked. Forcefully once again using his power, Dan-Li entered the next room with so much strength that actual parts of the door started to fall apart and hit the floor. Finally, a bedroom, with someone completely under the covers. Since the person was asleep, he tucked away his weapon and Zara followed his action, tucking her knife back into her pocket. They both needed whoever who was sleeping to be alive for the negotiation process. He crept to the right side of the bed, with Zara creeping to the left side. She motioned to initiate the removal of covers, and for Dan-Li to get his hands ready to shut whoever was sleeping up and then to tie them. She grabbed the covers firmly with both hands and yanked the cover speedily away from the person sleeping, with Dan-Li instantly moving toward the bed to shut the person up if awoken. The result was just as shocking as every other room that they had intruded, with Dan-Li putting his hands and then body on top a collection of pillows that were planted there to look like a person was sleeping in the bed. The three couldn't believe another empty room was what they found. There was still hope that inside the last two rooms their targets would be met, but it did damper the morale slightly knowing that if the next room had no one, the last room would most likely have no one either.

The second of the three unopened rooms was approached, but the door for this room seemed impossible to open or kick down, like an object perhaps jamming it from the inside. Zara joined Dan-Li in kicking the door down, making noise whilst doing so. Jing-Lee was in the background keeping his eyes locked to the other unopened door in chance of anyone deciding to check up on the source of noise. After several attempts, the door almost folded in half, and was ready to be completely destroyed, in which it was. Finally, and thankfully, the room was another bedroom. With no shock factor that not one person again was here, this room did show potential of an escape - the windows were open and television on. Sure, the television could have been on for a considerable amount of time - but it was showing an international boxing pay-per-view, which was live - and had only started twenty minutes ago. This had to have meant someone was in this room a very short time ago. Dan-Li rushed to the window to peer at the vision ahead of him, and he believed to have spotted someone far off in the distance. Considering it was so dark, he wasn't certain. He couldn't risk it and ordered Zara to run around the property to this area, knowing she was the faster of the two.

She ran past Jing-Lee and down the four long flights of stairs which seemed like an eternity going down, even though in reality she was as fast as a track-and-field athlete. Successfully not tripping down a single stair and going rocket-speed ahead, she opens the back door and then makes a run to the area that Dan-Li specifically spotted the potential person in the dark. Sprinting and sprinting more and more to the area and then ahead to where she believed the potential person could be now, Zara didn't give up, running the whole distance of the 6-acre property. She ran so fast the non-existent wind turned into a breeze that shook her cheeks. Her ears became so great and powerful that you would believe she had hyperacusis, her heartbeat pumped rapidly in perfect rhythmic flow.

Running the whole distance with no luck, but knowing she couldn't give up this easily, Zara ran the entire perimeter for any hints or clues at a potential escapee from the KIU property. She ran and ran, looking for literally anything that could be counted as peculiar, perhaps a piece of material or a dropped belonging. After an impressive display, her body started to take a toll on her from the brutal sprinting she put herself through. She began to pant, sweating at a great extent from her head to her toes, gasping for breath and her hamstrings cramping up. But she had to find something; she couldn't return empty-handed. Zara in a physical regard, however, was done for the night. She could barely walk now, and considering Jing-Lee had two broken hands, she couldn't be another physically damaged person out of the three. No matter what the relationship was between her and Dan-Li, this also involved her fiancé, she had to think about his safety too. She couldn't be in a poor physical state if she wanted to help an already broken Jing-Lee.

Whilst she was running the long distance all around the gigantic property, Dan-Li was with his brother - with the Chairman now trying not to heave from all the powerful and somewhat experimental medication he had been taking. He couldn't wait on her return though - he didn't know how long it would take her to come back, and no matter what this night had become, time was still of the essence - as said earlier on by Jing-Lee.

The final room of the four floor KIU property, the final unopened room of them all, the potential ticket to either a night wasted or a night that would change the Maska Triad forever, acquiring the one thing that eluded the previous Chairman. The KIU was the golden ticket into the vision Jing-Lee now had - a potential process of owning the entire country of Korea one day. And this was the day that could make-or-break this said vision for a very long time.

Dan-Li kicked the door, forcefully trying to kick it down, but to no avail, the same result as before in the previous room. Knowing he couldn't ask for his brother to help him in the task, he turned to using his whole-body weight into the door to get them into the room. After three loud attempts, waking up anyone who would be in that room, he finally managed, and entered the last room of the property. Finally, an actual person. Unfortunately, not one of the three that they had hoped for, but it was a person, nonetheless. There, sat in the bed, was a sleeping KIU Guard, with his weapon on the bedside cabinet next to him. He immediately grabbed him by the mouth to make him wake up and talk, but the guard was still sleeping. As the guard was sleeping on his side, Dan-Li decided to move and shake his head to wake him up, which is where he found the reason into him being so sleepy. The KIU Guard in fact wasn't sleeping, he was dead. From the far-left side to central portion of his neck, were a knife cut so deep that the wound turned black, purple, red, green, and yellow.

This night turned out to be one of the most worthless and perhaps embarrassing nights for the Maska Triad. A criminal organisation that had been ruthless and had a hundred percent success rate in the ruling of Atheno-Li - but only holding a fifty percent success rate in the ruling of Jing-Lee.

With both brothers now accompanied by Zara in the final room on the fourth floor, they stared at the dead guard, thinking about how such a promising night ended up so disastrous for them all.

"I bet they weren't even KIU guards." Jing-Lee stated.

CHAPTER SIXTEEN: ICU LUCID DREAMING

Several hours earlier...

After Jing-Lee's crazed-tempered speech that was aimed at Tarawa-Li had finished, and the Chairman went on his way to go about his business for the day, Tarawa-Li joined Pigbreath trying to ease all the pain in his system - by sleeping until he was in a better condition otherwise. The condition of both men had improved after being under intensive care and close monitoring. All that could be done to aid the treatment further was to sleep. Plus, him sleeping would help him forget about the nasty occurrence that felt like stone-cold bullets piercing his already fragile heart. After only a few seconds, with his head laid on the hospital pillow, he had fallen asleep - but not only had he fallen asleep, but once again he had total awareness that he was dreaming. It was his second ever lucid dream.

The first lucid dream he ever had occurred at the same location, the hospital, the time where he slept on the uncomfortable surface near Dan-Li and Mallory. In his first, he met his mother and dog in the first phase, his father and security guards in the second, his two brothers in the third, and in the last phase he thought he had met himself, until it turned out to be his father controlling him like he always had done. What phases of lucid dreaming would occur this time? All Tarawa-Li had hoped was that thls tlme, it wouldn't cause him to wake up with a bucket-load of sweat, making him shower for an almost hour.

Just like before, he was once again approached first by his mother. The setting was very peaceful, with them sitting down in a place that both had spent in each other's company back in the day, when his mother had taken him many times after the school day was over. This place was the smoothie bar, the exact one that he also had gone to after Atheno-Li had announced his terminal illness. The smoothie bar was always a place where he could express his thoughts and feelings without being judged. No matter how hard his day was, he could always relieve his stress when he was here.

The two were slurping down on their fruit smoothies, wishing they were real so he could feel the delightful taste once more. Both didn't say a word to begin with, enjoying their company like both were still alive in the real world. After a few more minutes, and both finishing their first smoothies, his mother started talking.

"Am I really supposed to believe that you have a multiple personality disorder, dear?" Mother asked.

"Mother, you can now talk? I thought I could only hear the people who were still alive in the real world talk to me." Tarawa-Li said, grabbing onto the possibility that she could somehow still be alive.

"This is a figment of your imagination, dear. Perhaps your lucid dream perceptions are getting even stronger, so that you think I'm really talking to you. I know you had some real flashbacks of me when you were in this smoothie bar the last time, but that was in the real world. This is still a dream of yours." Echoed around the edges of the lucid dream, with the words coming from the background, not the voice of his mother, even though the voice was the exact same as hers.

"Sorry, I just wanted you to be real. I just wanted you alive again." Tarawa-Li mumbled, looking at his late mother.

"Am I really supposed to believe that you have a multiple personality disorder, dear?" Mother asked, in the exact same fashion as she asked previously.

"Many things changed once you were gone, Mother. I'm not the same boy that you know and loved. Father changed me. I've managed to contain it though. I've successfully become into two states: the state of anger and the state of calm." Tarawa-Li answered, not knowing how she would react to this news.

"Do you really think I believe you? Dear, I know that I'm no longer with you, but I do know for certain that you can be the kindest, most caring individual that I know. Yes, your father did always prefer your other two brothers, but you're my favourite. Just don't tell them that. They might get jealous." Mother chuckled.

"He turned me into a monster. He turned me into a maniac. He turned me into a psychopath. When I get angry, there must be a drill or a gun or some brass knuckles by my side. It's like he made me lust for gore." Tarawa-Li gulped, realising the state he was in now.

"You are the only person who can decide your actions." Mother replied, "By the way, I know you have a social anxiety disorder too. Do you really want to live in fear your whole life?"

"No, Mother. Sorry for disappointing you." Tarawa-Li cried, with his actual self in his hospital bed shedding a real tear.

"You haven't disappointed me, dear. You have never disappointed me. You will never disappoint me. You need to stop being so hard on yourself. You can do anything you put your wonderful mind to, you can become the person you want to be. You don't ever have to be angry or do whatever it is you do with drills. It's never too late to change or revert to your past self." Mother lectured, "I love you."

Whilst his mother was expressing her love toward Tarawa-Li, the setting suddenly changed from the smoothie bar to the beach. The second phase of the lucid dream involved his two dogs, Dae and Kwan, with the latter of which had now passed - according to Jing-Lee's speech earlier. The two dogs were chasing each other in the sand, a sight which made his heart warm. The two might've even crossed paths in the real world, if it wasn't for their unnecessary and cruel deaths.

He started to playfully chase both of them on the sandy surface, running to Dae and Kwan, realising, besides his mother, that these two dogs were his favourite living things in the entire world at one point. He would take these two dogs over his two brothers in a heartbeat if he had the choice. He never wanted to leave this lucid dream right now. It was perfect, and surrounded by the people he truly loved and would do anything for.

Tarawa-Li finally caught up to Dae and Kwan, with the two dogs toppling their once owner onto the comforting sand, licking his face profusely. Unfortunately, without the sense of feeling, it wasn't quite the same as reality - but the real world right now was far worse. Though the realisation of giving his dogs a belly rub or a pat for catching a tennis ball, for them to not actually exist was a hard pill to swallow for him.

Tarawa-Li had now stood up from the beachy surface, wiping off the stuck sand in his best efforts, with Dae and Kwan ahead of him, the dogs sitting in perfect harmony. Two tennis balls, one in each hand, appeared when looking down. He throws the ball in his dominant hand first, with the ball in the weaker hand following, as it gave him leverage to throw the ball further. Both tennis balls impressively went into the air for longer than expected. He was getting better at throwing.

Dae returned first, with Kwan in the distance retrieving his tennis ball, running back. Tarawa-Li threw with all his might once again, throwing the tennis ball (which was now covered in saliva and sand) further than ever. Dae could be heard panting once the ball was in the air, almost like his eyes had lit up once his owner threw the tennis ball. After a few seconds, Kwan had returned back, dropping the green sphere into the hands of his owner. Even in his lucid dreams, he still couldn't believe he was dead already, due to Chairman Jing-Lee's actions.

Suddenly, after thinking about the Chairman once more, his third phase of the lucid dream commenced. The peaceful bliss turned into a lucid nightmare within seconds, with only his hotshot brother in his vision. The two were stood in front of one another, with the image of the Chairman staring into Tarawa-Li's eyes with a hint of condescension being an image that will forever haunt him, in his dream state or his living state.

"Tarawa-Li, do you know the meaning to the word sacrifice?" Jing-Lee asked, not changing his direction of eye-contact.

"Yes, Chairman." Tarawa-Li answered, talking in the most formal tone as possible - forgetting he was in his lucid dream for the time being. Looking at his brother gave him the chills right now.

"What does it mean, then? What does sacrifice mean?" Jing-Lee asked, still without a blink towards his questioned brother.

"Sacrifice means you give something up to the benefit of others, Chairman." Tarawa-Li answered, hoping he wouldn't even get scolded if his answer weren't precise enough for his brothers' liking.

"Sacrifice is the offering of food, objects or the lives of animals or humans to a higher purpose, in particular divine beings, as an act of propitiation or worship. That's the exact definition in the textbook of knowledge father gave to us all these years ago." Jing-Lee lectured, "So tell me. What have you sacrificed, brother?"

"Why are you asking me this? Is it because I haven't sacrificed something that is mine to the benefit of others?" Tarawa-Li asked, hoping this conversation would be over as quick as possible - becoming very agitated about what would come from Jing-Lee's mouth next.

"Another meaning of sacrifice could mean the sacrifice of people or a person upon the death of a king, high priest or great leader; the sacrificed were supposed to serve or accompany the deceased leader in the next life." Jing-Lee interrupted, "Atheno-Li has now died, and you were his least favourite son. He was the Chairman. I am now the new Chairman. You are my least favourite brother. Perhaps you should at least serve the already dead Chairman, he'll at least never attempt to kill you over and over in his head."

"You want me to...die? To sacrifice myself?" Tarawa-Li vacillated.

"Sacrifice, or self-sacrifice, is sometimes referred to as altruistic suicide or benevolent suicide. Altruistic suicide is sacrifice of one's life to save or benefit others, for the good of the group, or to preserve the traditions and honour of a society. It is always intentional. Benevolent suicide refers to the self-sacrifice of one's own life for the sake of the greater good." Jing-Lee answered, and powerfully so. Tarawa-Li was fully immersed in this conversation, genuinely believing he had woken up now and was talking in the real world.

Cancelling the immersion was the end of the third phase, but Tarawa-Li was still trying to wrap his mind around the words that Jing-Lee had told him. To make a sacrifice. After contemplating some more the fourth phase of his lucid dream finally appeared in front of his very eyes, with the same nightmare theme as before. Instead of Jing-Lee being involved again, it was the only man who could beat him in being more of a bastard. Atheno-Li was present.

This phase was almost a flashback instead of a lucid dream (in fact it was exactly that, Tarawa-Li didn't even think seeing flashbacks of his real life were possible whilst he was lucid dreaming), his mind took him to the exact same places and events that once happened in real life. It was a phase in his life that he hoped would never come back to him. Forced to become an Oculoplastic Surgeon.

The two were alone in the garden, staring at the rather beautiful sunset on a summer's day. The beautiful sunset did not however reflect the tone of the conversation that followed.

"Dan-Li has decided he wants to go to Culinary School, Jing-Lee is already working on his degree in Aviation Engineering. How am I a bad father if I chose your next path in life if you couldn't decide a career for yourself? The family business will always stay intact, I'm a great parent to all three of you, but I'm not leaving this world without giving you an extensive educational background first. You're going to study to become an Oculoplastic Surgeon. End of discussion." Atheno-Li snapped, tired of the back-and-forth arguing between the two on this topic.

"Father, I already told you my choice. Let me have my degree in Zoology. Please." Tarawa-Li begged.

"You wouldn't be living in the real world. You wouldn't have actual people as your clients, meaning you wouldn't make a profit. You would be even more of a freak than you are right now. Your mother was the reason you had a pet dog as a present for your sixth birthday. I knew I should've fought harder for my case, because now look at you. All you want to do is play with animals. Why can't you be like your two brothers? At least be a little materialistic now that you're getting older, punk." Atheno-Li raged.

"Father, I'm sorry I'm not the same as my two brothers, but I have no interest in whatever type of degree you choose for me if it's not Zoology." Tarawa-Li announced.

"I'm putting you on the fast-track course, the same as what I'm doing with both of your brothers. In order to become an Oculoplastic Surgeon, you first need to complete your pre-med course. I thought a half-semester of Biochemistry sounded the most fun and sophisticated, so you're welcome. If that doesn't sound fun, consider yourself lucky. If I hadn't put you on fast-track the Biochemistry pre-med course would be for the full semester. Normal people become a doctor after several years of education. You're far from normal, but for two reasons: the latter being that you're a Maska. Let's see you be a doctor in four years' time." Atheno-Li educated.

"How can Dan-Li choose Culinary School?" Tarawa-Li blurted.

"Are you questioning your father's reasoning?" Atheno-Li said.

"I have nothing else to lose. You always banish me, even if I wasn't the source of your anger." Tarawa-Li murmured.

From the flashbacks of the dreaded conversation that announced the next few years of Tarawa-Li's life, came flashbacks of a later time. This flashback still included Atheno-Li, but the setting had changed. The unwilling student was in his room, with heaps of textbooks by his side that had pieces of sticky-note attached to the outside of some pages. This was perhaps the most stressful period in the man's life. Not only was his course on fast-track, but the assignments and exams were highly burdensome. Flicking through the several hundreds of pages in one of the dozens of textbooks he had, to the far right of him, Atheno-Li was sitting in a chair which was in the corner of his son's bedroom, making sure he was using his time to study like his other two brothers had been.

"Let me test you on how well you're learning. What are the required preparations and precautions for any eye surgery?" Atheno-Li asked, prompting

Tarawa-Li to stop looking in his current medical textbook.

"Since the eye is heavily supplied by nerves, anaesthesia is essential. Topical anaesthesia using lidocaine topical gel is often used for quick procedures. Since topical anaesthesia requires cooperation from the patient, general anaesthesia is often used for children, traumatic eye injuries, and for apprehensive patients. The physician administering anaesthesia, or a nurse anaesthetist or anaesthetist assistant with expertise in anaesthesia of the eye, monitors the patient's cardiovascular status. Sterile precautions are taken to prepare the area for surgery and lower the risk of infection. These precautions include the use of antiseptics, such as povidone-iodine, and sterile drapes, gowns, and gloves." Tarawa-Li answered.

"Next time try and sound like you're not living the textbook. One day in your life you'll have to forget everything you have ever learned to make your personal decisions satisfy you, and only you. Life decisions aren't written in any textbook." Atheno-Li lectured.

"I don't have a life anymore, Father. You destroyed it. I'm simply going to live my life working in a career you chose for me and end up dying alone because no one will care for me or have any respect for me." Tarawa-Li bewailed.

"Shut it, punk! Keep speaking in that tone and I'll continue locking you in your room for more weeks in isolation with nothing but rotten water, wasted beans and these textbooks. Is that how you want to live the rest of your life?" Atheno-Li snapped.

"Do what you want. I don't care anymore. At least if I die, I'll get to be reunited with the only parent that ever cared for me." Tarawa-Li replied.

Atheno-Li rushed out of the chair in the corner of the room and grabbed one of the largest textbooks in his son's room. Holding it in his right hand, he smacks the object into Tarawa-Li's face as hard as possible, causing a loud noise which could be heard from any room of the property. Instantly drawing two droplets of blood from his nose, one in each nostril, slowly dropping onto the bedroom floor. Atheno-Li hits his son once more with the textbook in the exact same position. This abuse was habitual between the perpetrator and the victim, and not one thing could stop the acts from happening.

"Do you know why you're the insignificant triplet? Because you continue to live in the past, you stupid punk! Jing-Lee has already passed his exam in Aviation Engineering and is now training to become an Aviation Pilot. Think about it. You were born on the same day as him, and you're struggling to read a few facts on simple fucking textbooks. Dan-Li has even passed his school with flying colours. You three are brothers, you all had the same mother, yet you're the only one still grieving over her loss. No one can bring back the dead, so stop being so sorry for yourself! Stop being an illogical fool!" Atheno-Li shouted.

"Mother would have told me to follow my passions no matter how weird or wacky they sound. Like you said before, we're only doing these degrees to improve our education, it's not like we're actually doing the job for the rest of our lives. The future for me and my brothers is to one day take over from you as Chairman, so why can't I choose a field that I will enjoy for the time being? Zoology is a respective path in education, and you know it." Tarawa-Li asked.

"I must have hit you too hard again for you to speak nonsense like that." Atheno-Li said, "Oh, and let's get one thing clear now. No matter what happens, if you manage to pull a miracle or anything, you will never, and I mean never, ever, be the Chairman of the Maska Triad. Jing-Lee or Dan-Li will take over as Chairman when the day comes when I can do the job no more."

“I’d rather drown in Hong Kong than ever follow in your footsteps.” Tarawa-Li interjected, taking reference to the death of his mother.

“What the fuck did you just say, punk? You’re lucky I can’t murder you right here, right now!” Atheno-Li shouted.

The next days after this conversation were the most draining for Tarawa-Li, as his father made him endure a gruelling two-week hunger malnourishment. For these fourteen days, he was only given a small cup of water three times a day and was forced to study for sixteen hours a day with no breaks. To confirm that he would study for sixteen hours a day whilst only on water consumption, a security camera was installed in his room, with an electronic device attached to his ankle, where he would be electrocuted if he were believed to be off task.

The toughest days were split from the first five days to the last five days, for two different reasons. The first five days were the toughest for the physical and mental aspects. Without eating food, his blood-sugar levels dropped massively, resulting in himself becoming extremely lethargic, which made him suffer extreme electric shocks for many periods throughout the days. The thought of anything during these days turned into the thought of food, the poor man was so hungry. In fact, being so desperate for a taste of anything, he started to eat the small cups that once held the small serving of water. That wasn't the only thing he ate, he also chomped down a few of his clothing material just for something to be inside his stomach. What made matters worse was when the other members of his 'family' gathered around together in the evening for their supper, with the smell always creeping into his locked room. This is when Tarawa-Li realised that he is just his father's experiment. His father wanted his least favourite son to become a psychopath. The worst thing about this revelation, was that it was working. Being locked in isolation with nothing but an essential liquid and being forced to do something he didn't want to do. Tarawa-Li was slowly becoming a psychopath, or was it a sociopath? What was the difference anymore, he was so confused at this point his head hurt from thinking about it. He was too weak-minded to fend off his father. Constant belittlement finally got to him, and he just let himself give up. Tarawa-Li would become whatever Atheno-Li had decided him to be.

That's why the last five days were the toughest on an emotional standpoint. Malnutrition only added onto his effects, with his fatigue, insomnia and anxiety skyrocketing to unknown new highs. His skin had now fully transformed into a 'white smoke' colouring, his crow's feet so large it could attract a large flock of the mentioned bird, and his eyes were so bloodshot that only his pupil was the only non-red colour. Due to the extreme isolation, he even struggled speaking, signalling, communicating. His bones had become so brittle you could easily mistake him for a long-term patient suffering from osteoporosis.

After a serious amount of time, the flashback had finally run its course, with Tarawa-Li even forgetting himself that he was still in his lucid dream. It felt though like the dream was still not over, and it wasn't. But now that the flashbacks were over, he had gained more control over himself and his emotions and movements. Hopefully, this phase could return to the emotions of the first two phases. Now that Atheno-Li, the abuse, and the bedroom were now out of sight, the final phase began.

The last phase was in the exact same location as the first phase, with the exact same person, in the exact same context as before. Tarawa-Li and his beloved mother. The two had talked earlier during this lucid dream, so it was unclear what this could be about - perhaps it was just a continuation from earlier. He thought that this could be about how his father treated him since her tragic death, but his mother that he saw in front of him was only a figment of his imagination, and he had to remember that. Only if the abuse had happened during the time when they were both alive; the real world could perhaps be a completely different reality from what it was now.

"You realise now that your father has passed, you've already started to change into the man you always wanted to become. A few days ago you were drilling through eyeballs as a passion, but now you realise the passion was only inside of you because of the manipulation from him." Mother said, "You're not a sociopath anymore, you may never have truly been a sociopath. You were his experiment, and that is cruel to confess, but it is true. But he's dead now, dear."

"Ever since I was a teenager, I thought I had wanted to be violent and do unspeakable things to other people. I thought I enjoyed the criminal life of killing others under orders. But you're right, I've been controlled by him all these years. Ever since I was abused, I became brainwashed so I didn't have to tolerate the pain as much, at least the physical pain. I was never a lunatic until he made me one. I can't believe that I've turned into this." Tarawa-Li said.

"Turn into the man you now want to become. I'm sure your brothers would accept you doing what you're truly passionate about. Talk to them about it. Now that you've realised you've been a puppet all these years, live a little." Mother said.

"Jing-Lee most likely wants me gone from the triad, same as Dan-Li, but I can't leave them. I must stay loyal to them. It's not their fault that I became Atheno-Li's experiment." Tarawa-Li replied.

"Even after Jing-Lee killed your dog, you're still protecting him. Even after Jing-Lee called you a lunatic to your face, you're still protecting him. Even after both Jing-Lee and Dan-Li always talked behind your back, you're still loyal to them both." Mother said, "What you're doing is a good thing, dear. Just make sure it makes you happy. They can survive by themselves if needed be."

"It does make me happy. I know that I'm the least popular brother, but I feel rewarded when I help them. Perhaps that's the thinking and beliefs from the original and untampered me." Tarawa-Li chuckled.

"Don't hide it then. I believe in you. I love you." Mother said.

"I love you too, Mamma." Tarawa-Li replied.

Her presence started to fade away once more, and the smile that once directed towards him had now gone completely. His mother was once again gone. He wished he could have these lucid dreams every single time he fell asleep, if he knew he could see his favourite person in the world, no matter the nature of the nightmare. She wasn't real, but the feeling of it all was more than just real for Tarawa-Li. He knew he had the chance to change his ways and beliefs, and he would start right now.

The next phase was about to begin, but the transition to the next scene seemed a little strange, almost like it was being tampered with. No people in his way, no sounds to indicate the location, no lights to perhaps tell the mood. A few seconds later, a sickening thud to the right side. The lighting was non-existent, just pure pitch blackness. The sounds, frightening, almost as if someone were being bruised and battered. Still no people.

This was no longer a lucid dream; it had ended about a minute ago now. This wasn't even a regular dream, it wasn't possible, surely. The surroundings felt unlike a dream. Taking a few seconds to decipher, there was only one conclusion. The sounds were real, and he had his eyes shut. Without opening his eyes, he heard another horrible thud to his right side, and then he realised: Pigbreath. He dreaded to think what was happening, but he had to open his eyes now and save him. The new Tarawa-Li was a healer and not a hurter. He would deal with the situation presented to himself with the most amount of calmness as possible.

He finally opened his eyes, where he found himself looking at the ceiling of his ward floor. Slowly looking further to the right of him, he came to see the most frightening situation and event. He felt the most nauseated and vulnerable he had ever felt in his life, and that's even counting the abuse he suffered from Atheno-Li from all the past years.

To the right stood three masked men, attacking Pigbreath. Pigbreath was already dead now; the poor guy was slit about twenty times with some sort of knife or sharp weapon or object, with his neck oozing out masses of blood. Tarawa-Li knew he had to do something, even if the three mystery men were still there. He turned his attention to the bed situation.

The two beds were close, so perhaps he could intervene without having to remove any of his medical aids. Risking it, he sat up immediately and looked to his right. What he saw in his direction was one of the masked men approaching him. A second later, and Tarawa-Li was knocked out – he received a kick to his already-injured head.

Pigbreath was dead.

Was that the same fate Tarawa-Li would be receiving from these three mystery masked men?

CHAPTER SEVENTEEN: THE NOTE

"What do you mean, 'I bet they weren't even KIU guards?'" Dan-Li asked.

"They have to still be hiding somewhere, surely." Zara added.

"Think about it. The KIU would never hire these fools, they could hardly shoot their weapons properly, let alone kill any intruders." Jing-Lee replied, analysing the situation.

"Maybe we've forgotten how good a shot we are." Dan-Li chuckled, which was immediately shot down by a glaring Jing-Lee. "I think we should call it a night. You're looking way too rough to continue further, Chairman."

"Please, it's pretty much dawn now. I'm the Chairman. I call the shots." Jing-Lee declared, "Yung-Ko has to be the snake. Let's go to the family house and then the hospital, and if he's slithered away, it's proof that he was the backstabber all along."

"Chairman, with all due respect, Yung-Ko has been by our father's side all these years. Why would he turn on us now that he's passed?" Dan-Li asked.

"Let's go back to the car. I need to rest before I confront that disloyal bastard." Jing-Lee replied, simply ignoring his brother.

After stopping the staring at the dead guard In the final room that they had hoped contained either Chief Mok or at least one member of his close family, the three make their way out of the chaotic, dishevelled and unfastidious house. By this point in time, Jing-Lee was physically unable to walk unassisted, so Dan-Li was the one to carry him. To his surprise, Jing-Lee weighed less than what he had expected, which was a relief, considering his stamina also took a toll tonight. The three still had a long way to go just to reach their vehicle, with each acre of land seeming to be marathon distance away. Zara was just thankful that she didn't have to carry her fiancé, not just because it made her heart broken to see Jing-Lee in this condition, but she too was barely able to walk with her own two feet now. She prayed that she would never have to run again, it almost killed her.

After what felt a lifetime of walking, they had arrived back at the lonesome alley once again and came to the vehicle. Dan-Li rested Jing-Lee in the back of the vehicle, with the Chairman immediately taking a rest. He was categorically shattered, and even though he knew the three should take an actual break, he couldn't until he found out who betrayed him. Yung-Ko was about to feel the wrath of Jing-Lee when the three got to the family house, or the hospital. And if he weren't in either of those places, Jing-Lee would kill him as fast as he could - hitman style.

Dan-Li took the wheel, with Zara following her fiancé's method of taking a short nap in the car until they had met their destination. Since the property was in the outskirts of Gangnam - near Segok-Dong, the drive would take roughly a half-hour due to minimal traffic on the roads. The fact that there was minimal traffic also relaxed Dan-Li a little. Minimal traffic also meant minimal effort to drive, and he also needed to ease down as much as possible for a while. Also, this would mean there would be hardly any noise on the roads, which would allow for the Chairman and Zara to nap for as long as possible. Don't get him kidded, he wished he were in the same position as the other two, but he couldn't disagree with the fact that his brother was exhausted and perhaps needed more medical attention, and Zara had run eminently and exceptionally.

Moments like this actually made him feel minutes of bliss. Down the road in a few years from now, the scenario he faced right now would come to him again, but instead of Jing-Lee and Zara it would be the wedded Mallory and beautiful child Aria. Sure, he knew the next few years especially would be challenging and tough, balancing the life of a gangster and father, but he knew he could make it work. He was enthusiastic to his core when he pondered about all the various things and life lessons he wanted to teach his daughter through the years.

Everything from swimming lessons, martial arts, high-degree culinary skills, his cringeworthy dancing, how to ride a bike, mathematics, Korean culture and tradition: such as the family business. The list that came up in his excited head could be wrote for an eternity. Recently, 'Chef' had thought all his days would have been spent in the restaurant. Now, he was driving away from a home invasion in the middle of the night. How times change.

He liked the change, as he never genuinely believed that he was a proper gangster in the first place. He killed on the daily, but it always felt different when it was the contract killings. Being a gangster wasn't like that in the real world. The three were always protected too much by Atheno-Li. Being a real gangster involved occasions such as home invasions and acid attacks that the new Chairman had ordered. He welcomed the change with open arms.

The half-hour drive back to the family home had been completed, and he pulled up to the property. Both Jing-Lee and Zara were still fast asleep, with both of them snoring loud and stentorian. He must have been in a deep thought to cancel the loud noises he now heard. He knew he would get scolded for waking both of them up, especially by his brother, but it was obvious the scolding would be more if he let them both to sleep until the two woke up naturally. After a few seconds of enjoying the peaceful bliss, he exits the vehicle and opens the vehicle side door that Zara had been leaning on. After a few seconds of prods, she had woken up, looking the most fatigued he had ever seen her. Now that both were awake, their mission was to wake up the Chairman, causing the least kerfuffle as possible.

Jing-Lee was laid in the back, with Dan-Li taking the left side that met his feet, and Zara taking the right side that met his pale and exhausted face. The Chairman was definitely in the land of dreams. The loud noise of both doors opening loudly didn't affect him in the slightest.

"Maybe we should just let him sleep." Zara said.

"He'll be mad either way, but if we wake him up now, he'll be thankful for it. Maybe the cold air will help him." Dan-Li replied.

Zara prodded Jing-Lee's shoulders, to no response. She was in fact paranoid that he had stopped breathing, but she checked his pulse and everything seemed normal. Dan-Li followed up by a light punch to Jing-Lee's somewhat injured leg, to no response yet again. Zara prodded his snoring face, no response. Dan-Li did have an idea that would be sure to wake him up, although it could be regarded as an unorthodox and unethical way. He went around to where Zara was and moved her to the side. Dan-Li, knowing this could backfire, didn't want Zara to get the blame for what he was about to do. He grabbed his brother's two broken hands, squeezed with all his might and then followed it up by punching the two broken hands viciously until Jing-Lee became awake. Taking longer than expected but succeeding, ten seconds after the punching and he eventually had woken up. Jing-Lee didn't even realise what his brother was doing, he was still completely out of it at this point.

"I'm not going to lie, I need a few more minutes." Jing-Lee said quietly and slowly, "Dan-Li needs to search the house for any sign of Yung-Ko. Zara, go to the house and see if you can find any pain relief medicine or any medicine at all. Anything will make me feel better compared to what I'm feeling right now."

Not wanting to cause any arguments, the two simply followed his request. Not getting too comfortable however, Jing-Lee sat up and closed his eyes for a few more minutes. He forced himself not to relax too much and to not lay down. It was axiomatic that he was suffering though.

Dan-Li and Zara made their way to the house, first checking the gardens for any sign of another person. The two stayed together instead of separating, as Zara had some general questions about the Maska Triad. She had always been intrigued, but whenever she asked her fiancé, he would change the topic of conversation quickly. Dan-Li was an opportunity to educate herself on the system.

"I'm not Korean so I wouldn't know, but why are you guys called a triad? I thought that meant you're a rookie or not "high up" in the crime world." Zara asked.

"I don't know, I guess it's because before my father took over the family business, we (the family) were a laughingstock all those many years ago. Anyways, if you want to get down to specifics - we are a triad. A triad is a family-run organised crime gang. Normal gangs can't declare themselves as a triad." Dan-Li replied. "I guess we could call ourselves a 'jo-pok' *(a Korean alternative for 'triad')*, they are family-run gangs, but why bother changing it now? Plus, a triad sounds cooler, don't you think?"

"So, you're from Korea but refer to the business as a triad? Even though the Korean term is a jo-pok?" Zara asked.

"I'll tell you the truth. When the business originated, there were no gangs at all that were in any way, shape, or form, notable. For a triad to thrive, the environment had to be democratic and neo-liberalistic, which South Korea wasn't at that time. The origin of the Maska Triad, although ethnically Korean, started in Hong Kong. Not because we didn't want to make a statement on our home turf, it was just due to the circumstances in those times. South Korea was in a continuous dictatorship which was set out to destroy all traces of gangs and criminals. If the general public didn't cooperate with the dictator, the government itself would hire internal mercenaries to kill anyone who was found guilty to conspire against the nation. Their efforts were successful, so whoever made the decision to start the triad and base it in Hong Kong can consider themselves a genius. We wouldn't be in the situation we are right now if we started in Korea under the watch of a dictator." Dan-

Li replied. “Don’t ask me anything else. That’s everything I know. That’s all that our father would tell us three. Oh, and by the way, not many people like to hear this, but – yakuza, mafia, triad – they all mean pretty much the exact same thing.”

“Thanks for telling me.” Zara replied. “But, if you’re a Korean triad, surely you wouldn’t accept anyone who wasn’t Korean in the triad, right? How is Yung-Ko involved? My father, even myself involved? How about Mallory?”

“Yung-Ko was the first non-Korean member to join. He joined because he was the only person smart enough to somehow find a single piece of evidence that supported the illegal activities of our triad. I don’t know what the evidence was, but my father was impressed, and he offered Yung-Ko a job as Head of Surveillance and Strategy at the triad, although he’s pretty much always been just a yes-man. Atheno-Li always said that anyone from any ethnicity can join our triad, as long as you can trust the person themselves like you could a family member.” Dan-Li said, finishing his search for Yung-Ko in the garden. “Feels ironic that we’re currently looking for him though. Let’s check inside. Remember to look for medicine for Jing-Lee.”

After one more walk through the gardens for any crack at a sign of Yung-Ko Jang, Dan-Li and Zara enter the family house. Sanguine at the situation, she quickly disembarks to find her fiancé any medicine that she could get her hands on. On the other hand, Dan-Li was scouting all rooms for the Chinaman. It was very unlikely he would be here if he were the backstabber or not. The time was still before the usual time he would come to the house to start his work.

After searching each and every room to be met by no one, Dan-Li returned to where Zara was, scanning for any medicine for the Chairman. She had found some very mild pain relief, but neither could complain about the medical strength during a time like this. Both were glad that Jing-Lee wanted to visit a hospital to look for Yung-Ko. Perhaps whilst they were there, he would be prescribed the medicine he was given on the night he broke both of his hands. Before the two returned to Jing-Lee, Dan-Li was curious to why he was asked those questions when both of them were back in the garden.

“Why did you ask me those questions earlier? Does my brother not tell you anything?” Dan-Li asked.

“Partly, I guess.” Zara replied, placing her fiancé’s medicine in her pocket, “Partly because I’m fascinated about Asian culture. I guess I’ve always been a little confused when you guys have called yourself a triad - when that word is mainly used for the Chinese."

"I guess now you know. Wish I could help you more though, but like I said. It's all I know. Sorry." Dan-Li said.

"Wait, back to what we were saying back in the gardens." Zara replied, "About your father only letting people join your triad as long as you could trust them like a family member. What about all the security guards and working girls he used to have? Could he trust them all?"

"That's different. All of those guys he hired as security were low-life thugs with no purpose in life. The working girls he hired were strippers or low-end prostitutes with nowhere to go. He knew none of them could stab him in the back with the salary he was paying them with." Dan-Li said.

"Do you think it could be one of them who stabbed us in the back then? Now that Jing-Lee has become Chairman and one of the first things he decided to do in his first day of power was to let them all go, make them go back to their lives before the triad and the big money. Maybe one of them were way more powerful than what we ever thought." Zara replied, thinking it could have nothing to do with Yung-Ko at all.

"That's true, maybe Yung-Ko wasn't the only one who received the information about the KIU. Someone could have played a trick on us." Dan-Li replied, "But let's think logically here. Yung-Ko is still on our watchlist. Plus, we won't hear the end of him from Jing-Lee until we find him to interrogate."

With the medicine in her pocket, both made their way out of the family house and to the vehicle which contained an awake, albeit inattentive Jing-Lee. The Chairman had now gone through spells of hot flushes, which were worrying symptoms considering only his hands were broken. It had to be from lack of rest and relaxation, but he was too stubborn to ever admit that. She took charge over the wheel, with Dan-Li in the seat next to her, passing the medicine backwards to Jing-Lee to take whilst on the way to the hospital. Hospital visits used to be rare as a gem for the triad, but they had spent more time in them compared to their own homes in the past few days.

The drive from the family home to the hospital was uneventful, with the three enjoying the peace and quiet for the time being. This day was going to be a long and rough one for Dan-Li and Zara especially, working on an empty fuel for energy. This would be the same for Jing-Lee, but his medicine was already proving a treat for the Chairman, although only a very slight improvement from his current morale.

The three finally came to their destination, looking for their target. Yung-Ko Jang. No matter the result however, the three would most likely be staying. Practically every single member was in the hospital right now. Well, that's what they had thought at the time being. Zara parked the vehicle and they were on their way to find any sign of Yung-Ko. No indication of past presence was needed, however. Walking out of the entrance hospital, meeting the three harsh expressions of anger, was Yung-Ko Jang, sweating like a pig.

"So, you're the snake." Jing-Lee accused, looking up and down at his supposed yes-man.

"Snake?" Yung-Ko asked, "What do you mean? What happened?"

"There was no KIU Chief. No wife. No son. I don't even think any of the guards killed were even KIU Guards. Explain now and I might spare your life. I don't care if we're by an entrance to a city hospital. Don't fuck with me." Jing-Lee exploded.

"What, you really think the first week your father dies, and I'll just switch sides to the opposition? I've worked in the triad more years than you've been alive, kid!" Yung-Ko defended, "Anyways, if I was the snake, don't you think I would have slithered by now?"

Jing-Lee couldn't help to think that perhaps he was too rash with his accusations. He seemed innocent with his body language. The night may have not been a set-up at all, but instead a dosage of bad luck. The 6-acre property did look exactly like how he would picture a KIU house. Perhaps Chief Mok was such an insomniac it caused him to become a paranoid wreck and wanted himself and his family to change locations for the night. Maybe there were hidden security cameras in the alley that they had parked in or by the gate they had jumped to trespass. There was a slight chance that he acted too harshly on the matter to Yung-Ko. After all, the Chinaman had been such a loyal man for the triad for decades.

"Who do you think is the snake then? Who is fucking with all of us?" Jing-Lee asked.

"Well, you did fire all the security guards and working girls on your first day. It could be one of them. Most of them have a low social status though, so it's pretty unlikely." Yung-Ko replied, "I think it's the only person involved with the triad that hasn't even visited the hospital once. Derrick. He must be plotting something."

"Tell me you did not just blame my fucking father for being the snake in all of this?!" Zara interjected, "The reason why he hasn't been around recently is actually because he's been working his ass off for this helipad extension, whatever that's supposed to freaking mean. He's been telling me that the notion was rejected twice already but he's continued trying for an overturn in their decision. He told me that his job was on the line for it, that's why he's not here. He's doing the job that he signed for. Being not only the greatest lawyer around, but the best businessman too, unlike you, fat piece of shit."

"You're his daughter. Of course you're going to defend him no matter what." Yung-Ko replied. "Chairman, please accept my deepest apologies that my intel was either non-exclusive or incorrect. My source is normally guaranteed in reliability. I need to leave right now to investigate why Chief Mok and his family weren't in their normal house last night. Excuse me." Yung-Ko rushed off in a hurry after bowing to Chairman Jing-Lee, the first time in which he was spotted speed walking in his life.

"Are you really just going to let him leave like that?" Zara asked in shock, looking behind her at a speedy and sweaty Yung-Ko Jang.

"Is that really the reason why your dad hasn't been seen these past few days? He should've called me if he's really having trouble with the helipad. It's not like it's an essential human need." Jing-Lee murmured.

“He likes to impress when it comes down to business deals. The finest art a lawyer can perform is negotiation, it’s a saying he has always stuck by all these years. If he were really having any trouble with it, he would have called you. It’s fine. He’s just a very industrious type of person.” Zara replied with a small smile.

“If Yung-Ko isn’t the one we’re after, and Derrick has been keeping himself busy these days with the tasks I gave him on my first day, who could it be?” Jing-Lee said. “Dan-Li, after you quickly go and see Mallory and Aria, I want you to go back home and go through the database that father used to use. I want every single name of every single security guard or working girl that has ever worked for the Maska Triad. That’s how we’ll find whoever it is who’s trying to fuck us up.”

The three made their way inside the hospital, with the beautiful sunrise in their background when making their way inside. The visiting times for patients had just started for the day, although getting into things wouldn’t have been a problem for them anyway. The ‘three musketeers’ disbanded with Dan-Li leaving to go to the third floor to see his fiancé and child. Jing-Lee and Zara made their way to the ICU ward to check up on Pigbreath and Tarawa-Li. Upon arrival, they were met by nurses which were full of panic and worrisome confusion. The Chairman brushed the fuss off as nominal, and both dodged around the nurses to the rooms where their comrades had been receiving treatment for their wounds. To their astonishment, both had vanished. Their condition must have improved, and they must've been sent to a different ward or perhaps a screening of some sorts. Zara made her way over to a distressed nurse to ask where both Pigbreath and Tarawa-Li had been sent to.

"Excuse me, miss. My friends were here quite recently, have they been moved to a different section of the hospital?" Zara asked politely.

"I-I'm...really sorry...but...we don't actually know where they are. It's hospital policy to work with other wards and to communicate with them about patient transfers, but no one's filled any paperwork to indicate a ward transfer. We've only just came in for our morning shift and this has been dumped on us." The nurse said, getting on her knees and bowing to Zara. "I'm so sorry madame. We'll be sure to get to the bottom of where the two gentlemen went to."

"Don't worry about it." Jing-Lee interjected, "We'll go find them both ourselves. They might have gone to separate wards; I'll search one half of the hospital and you go and search the other half. Meet back here in about ninety minutes if we've found them or not?"

After the two briefly discussed their planned route to find their designated comrades in the massive hallway in the even bigger hospital, and after Jing-Lee threw some more pain relief tablets down his throat with his fiancé waterfalling a cup of water to help him, it was time to find Pigbreath and Tarawa-Li.

A staggering and intimidating fifty-six wards were in this hospital, and the area for each and every one of them were still so spacious and generous. The hospital was so big that the word 'compact' wasn't in their vocabulary. A thorough search through each and every single ward by both would be happening with eagle-vision, so if both were still here, they would be found. It was a good plan that both would be working separately. It meant they could divide their search to twenty-eight wards each, though equipoise, it was still an overbearing amount. One half of the twenty-eight wards may contain no one, but the other half of the twenty-eight wards may inhabit both of the men that were being searched for. The two were hoping for them both to be denizen. Who knows where the two will be found in this gigantic place?

The next ninety minutes were as stressful as you could imagine, rushing hectically through each ward of each floor the hospital had to offer. The way both ran into each ward and scanned every single patient was like they were playing hide and seek, which technically, they kind of were. The noises of their own footsteps on the squeaky hospital floor became an anthem in their heads, their hands became red and irritated from all of the hand sanitiser they had applied from entering each individual section of the hospital, sweat began to pour so profusely in fact on one occasion Zara was mistaken for a patient herself. At this point, after searching each and every ward, room, bathroom, café, everything the hospital had to offer, both met at the starting point empty-handed, with no leads to where both men could be.

“Where could they be?” Zara asked, wiping the sweat off her head with her right forearm.

“Maybe they’re back home? Or at a different hospital? They might be at the same hospital that Tarawa-Li used to work at before I became Chairman.” Jing-Lee replied, gulping down another pain relief tablet with ice-cold water.

The nurse that earlier in the day bowed down to apologise to Zara had walked up to the two, with her innocent green eyes lighting up once she heard both of their voices once more. She had some news to share with both of them.

"Ah, so you're Jing-Lee?" Nurse said, "Here you go. I found a note by the side of the table which has your name on it. Don't worry, I didn't peek on the other side to see what it said. I still don't know where either man are right now, but a man came in earlier and said that it's been dealt with. I think he's the one that left the note there. I hadn't seen it before then."

The bright white note with red polka-dot like shapes was given to Jing-Lee by the nurse, who left courteously to give the couple the privacy that they needed. *It read:*

Watch where you tread,

Because of you, Pigbreath is dead,

The others are alive, but a lot they have bled,

For them to return, get on your knees and beg.

I think it's time that we finally meet, Chairman.

Bring anyone or anything with you, we'll kill them with no second thoughts.

100th Floor, 18:00 hours – no sooner, no later

You shall meet the three leaders of the Takani Triad.

She peeked at the note that her fiancé had held in his weak right hand, there was no way that this could be happening right now. Last night, a home invasion that turned sour once they had realised not one notable target was present. During this, someone came into the hospital and killed Pigbreath? What about Tarawa-Li? What about the word 'others'? Who else could they be talking about? She thought that the note was somehow fabricated, but Jing-Lee knew a note that contained this information was everything but a lie. This note was from the rival Chairman and his two lackeys. Mouse was the only leader he knew. He guessed it was time for him to be properly introduced to the other two.

"Excuse me." Jing-Lee said, raising his voice to grab attention to the nurse that handed him the letter. "The man who came and said everything had been dealt with, what did he look like?"

"If I remember correctly... and I'm sorry if this sounds a little judgemental, but he kind of looked like a mouse." Nurse chuckled, instantly wiping her smirk off her face. "Sorry for laughing at your friend's face. I apologise, sir."

“Don’t say sorry.” Jing-Lee said. “I just wished it was one of the other two who came in to say it to you and give that note in, that’s all.”

Zara and Jing-Lee both left the ICU ward and walked around until they sat in the same café as they had done previously, the morning after the three Takani attacks. They waited for Dan-Li whilst chomping down some chicken and noodles, as the Chairman received a text to say that his brother was still in the hospital looking for the two of them. The café was a meeting point for all three to meet up together once more. Whilst eating the poultry and noodles, both couldn’t help but to think about the contents of the note that was given to them.

‘Pigbreath is dead.’

‘The others are still alive.’

‘You shall meet the three leaders of the Takani Triad.’

These were the three underlying tones that were edged in both of their conscience and memories. The three main questions that followed up in their thoughts were: *Is Pigbreath actually dead? Is Tarawa-Li on the 100th floor bleeding and pleading for mercy? Who is the Chairman of the Takani Triad?*

Thankfully, all of their dreaded thoughts and questions replaying in their minds were shut-off for the time being. This was because Dan-Li had finally approached them both, although the facial expression on his face were more of a physical representative which portrayed their inner thoughts.

"Pigbreath is dead and Tarawa-Li is missing." Jing-Lee said. "Are you ready to go? We have lots of work to do in such little time if we have any chance of getting anyone back alive."

"They're gone." Dan-Li murmured, with tears starting to roll down himself.

"We can't get emotional just yet. It could all be a set-up." Zara replied. "Jing-Lee needs us to hurry though, he does have a lot of work that he needs to do before tonight. Are you ready?"

"Wait, I don't think he's crying about that. I think." Jing-Lee said. "What's happened?"

"Mallory and Aria. They're missing." Dan-Li announced.

CHAPTER EIGHTEEN: THE HUNDREDTH FLOOR

The three were now back at the family property, met by Derrick at the front entrance. The lawyer needed to talk to the Chairman, and vice versa, but there were even more important tasks to be completed first. Derrick and Zara were to keep each other company whilst the two brothers investigated the triad database, scanning through hundreds (if not thousands) of past security guards and working girls. The Chairman was now fully convinced that whoever stabbed the triad in the back was a former employee, it just made total sense for it to be. The first day on the job he made many lose their work and livelihoods because of his actions, and he hadn't even noticed what the potential consequences could have been. Now, already, after such little time gone, this is what was happening. Looking for the double-crosser.

The database of former employees were sorted by first name, last name, age, job role, date assigned, date departed, reason for departure, previous criminal history. Albeit many of the working girls were former prostitutes or strippers, and many of the security guards were previously low-life thugs, there were on occasion other previous crimes committed. Regarding age, the triad were known to recruit as young as sixteen and as old as forty, although the older recruitments were for job roles such as previous lawyers or temporary legal aids. Only now was the time when Jing-Lee was scrolling through this information he realised he should have never given his order to fire these people in the way he did.

After a few more minutes, and using his expertise in computing, the Chairman had managed to sort the database out by nationality. His intent wasn't to racially profile, but he did need to see if any former staff were from Taiwan - the homeplace of their rival triad. Without needing any explanation, nearly the entire workforce they hired had originated from Korea, with a couple of Chinese men (one being Yung-Ko, the other being a security guard that worked with the triad over a decade ago), and you guessed it- a Taiwanese-man. One single man from Taiwan, named: *Chen Jui*. The Chairman looked further into him.

The man in question had worked for the triad when he was recruited at seventeen, roughly five years ago. He worked as a security guard mainly for Atheno-Li himself. He died only two weeks after he started the job, with the database citing that his cause of death was a bullet-wound to the head. There was no way that this former guard could have had anything to do with the current events. It had to be someone with a Korean nationality. He continued his quest and sectioned the database to find the list of people who were still hired until the day they were fired by him. The list narrowed down to twenty employees, split evenly, ten security guards and ten working girls. All Korean, all with a previous history of criminal activity.

Still, nothing really seemed out of the blue when all were compared with each other. That was until one of the names came to light. The triad had only recruited one American ever, but two were found on the database. The two brothers couldn't believe what they were seeing on the computer screen, they couldn't believe the name they were seeing. It was Jason Holland. The teenager who was killed as part of the contract killings. The younger brother of Zara and son of Derrick. The database read: *Jason Holland, Age 18.*

“How is that even possible...just how.” Dan-Li whispered, not wanting to gain the attention of the two members of the deceased boy’s family.

“Did you ever see him working for us?” Jing-Lee asked, also keeping his voice down.

“Never. I never really payed much attention to any of my guards or girls for the last few months though, to be honest.” Dan-Li answered, “How about you?”

“I never paid any attention either.” Jing-Lee replied honestly, “But it says here that he was one of us. Did he really work here? Ever?”

“Maybe it’s a typo.” Dan-Li responded. “Who has control over the database normally?”

“It was Atheno-Li, Yung-Ko and Myself.” Jing-Lee stated. “Oh, and Derrick. He was added as a moderator for it perhaps a few weeks ago.”

Just a few seconds later, the two brothers were met by a chilling and unexpected knock on their door. Acting as nonchalantly as possible, and minimising the database screen of the computer, Derrick had entered the room. The Chairman had a busy day ahead of him, which was bound to be followed by an extreme night.

“Dan-Li, you and Zara check each Maska-owned property in Gangnam. Every house, restaurant, nightclub, everything- from top to bottom. Look for our missing people, any other narcissistic notes, anything you would count as suspicious." Jing-Lee ordered, "Derrick, let's talk in the dining room, shall we?"

The details on how Dan-Li and Zara's search for any clues in properties around the entire district of Gangnam would be revealed later. But for now, there were a serious discussion between the Chairman and his lawyer, a future son-in-law with a future father-in-law, a boss and his employee.

The two sat face-to-face in the dining room, exchanging their words between a serving of chicken and noodles. The Chairman had an appetite, which was good for someone who had previously been so unwell. The lawyer was too tense to eat but did so anyway - he was still a guest in his employer's home. The relationship between the two was rather peculiar, the senior and junior roles were swapped in comparison to a 'normal' relationship between one's son-in-law and father-in-law. The main reason for it was due to Derrick. He couldn't complain even if he wanted to - he would only get blamed for causing a stir by his daughter.

"Before we talk about business. I want to say I'm sorry for accusing you. For believing that you were the one being treachery." Jing-Lee said, "I don't know who it is yet, but I know it's not you."

"No need to apologise, Chairman. I have to admit I was a little disheartened but being in your position isn't easy. It's difficult to trust everyone when you're in such a powerful position and given the status of the triad. The Maska Triad may be the last triad left in Korea, but it's not because there can't be any new ones. The Maska Triad is the only triad left in Korea because of the amount of power it holds on this country. You have the power to do anything, which makes the job of trusting even more difficult." Derrick replied.

"Glad we're on the same page." Jing-Lee replied, "So, what's the reason, why did you need to speak with me?"

"I think you know why. It's to do with the jobs you ordered me to complete, the first day you became Chairman. You wanted me to get an approval for an underground bunker and helipad for the PlaciCorp tower. The bunker is going to be under construction starting from next week; it's been approved. The helipad has been declined four times." Derrick announced, staring at his tattoos. "I'm not incompetent, the helipad is just impossible to build."

“I wasn’t expecting it to be accepted.” Jing-Lee chuckled. “The only reason I set you those two tasks was to see how far you would go to help me. How far you would push yourself not only as a lawyer, but for me. It’s just another piece of proof that you’re on my side. You must have spent nearly all your hours working on those two extensions plans with the district committee.”

“So, you didn’t want me to stop the contract killings or fire your staff either? Or were the PlaciCorp requests sprinkled in to make the orders seem more legit?” Derrick asked.

“I wanted to stop the contract killings; we have enough money. I wanted to fire the security guards and working girls, although I’m regretting that now. The helipad and underground bunker orders...honestly, I was playing around. I had no desire for them.” Jing-Lee replied. “Sorry for giving you a hard time. You’re my senior, you’re part of the family. I know there have been points where you have wanted to scream at me, but you’ve kept your cool because of Zara. I respect that. You’re a great father to her.”

“There definitely have been some times where I thought you’ve been an asshole, but I’m a lawyer. I’ve been able to keep my cool for many years. I also believe that you’ll be able to find out about what happened to my son. Zara and I need to know who killed him, and I know that you'll be able to track him down one day." Derrick said, giving an awkward smile to Jing-Lee, with his gold teeth shining in his mouth.

"I need you to go to the hospital and find some CCTV footage. I'll text you the details, so you don't forget anything. I need to know what happened to my brother and uh, and a long-time friend of mine. Also Mallory and her kid." Jing-Lee said, realising he probably shouldn't mention Pigbreath to Derrick, or at least, try not to.

At this point of the conversation, Dan-Li and Zara were already striding through the streets of Gangnam, driving to each and every property the triad owned. The amount of properties were so many that it were too crazy to try and name them all. But the majority were either apartments or houses, nightclubs or strip clubs, restaurants or bars. Every second felt wasted when the two were driving, so they didn't abide by the driving laws. It's not like they could get arrested anyway. Once they arrived to their destination each time, Dan-Li would stay in the driver's seat whilst his comrade went and explored around each room of each place. He wanted for the roles to be reversed, considering it was his fiancé and child, and one of his brothers that were missing, but Zara was easily the quickest out of the two to complete the task that the Chairman asked them to do.

Even though each time they opened the doors to a different property, unfortunately, the result was still the same. No missing persons. No weird notes. Nothing suspicious at all. Each room she hoped to have found something different from the rest, perhaps a piece of scrap paper that could mean something, a crushed cigarette with still a little flame in an ash tray, an item of clothing that was just chucked on the floor. All floors were sparkling clean, no person to be found in sight, and literally nothing which was out of shape from what it should be.

From the next journey, to the journey after that, to the journey after that, it was obvious the current situation began to take a toll on Dan-Li. His driving especially became erratic, and sweat swam around his face and body, sticking him to his car seat. The rapid increase of blinking, the stuttering of words when the two made small talk to each property, the shaking of his hands on the steering wheel.

The duo went round the entire district of Gangnam to find no clues, no leads, nothing that could help them. The two drove back to the family house, waiting for the night to take over. Only then may the family possibly find out where their missing family members were. Tarawa-Li Maska. Mallory Reece. Aria Maska.

Derrick meanwhile was on his way to the hospital to gain the CCTV footage, looking to find out what had happened to Tarawa-Li and Jing-Lee's "long-time friend". The lawyer had recently acquired even more tattoos on his body, specifically a beautiful clock watch design on his right hand. Tattoos, considered illegal in Korea until a few years ago, meant that he always covered himself up when in public, as he didn't want the negative attention. He forgot to bring his black gloves to hide the art on himself, so he quickly went to his home to grab his gloves and went back on his way to the hospital.

Finally arriving at the hospital, he made his way to the nearest reception desk to ask where he could find the people in charge of CCTV. Told to go to the highest floor and to knock on the door of the 'Security' room. The elevator was broken, but thankfully the escalators were still in use. Going higher and higher, with the first floor of the hospital now giving himself a vertigo reaction, he made his way to the highest floor.

Knocking on the door harshly, he was met by a rather paranoid-looking woman, perhaps in her early forties. She was wearing her security outfit but looked rather shaken from the knock on the door by

Derrick, with the lawyer being a little confused at her reaction. Why would this woman be acting in a peculiar way? Perhaps she had a social disorder and wasn't good mixing with others. Perhaps she didn't like his gold teeth. Perhaps she didn't like foreigners altogether. Before a word was exchanged between the two, she was told to open the door by a voice in the background. She followed his orders, and Derrick was welcomed in the security room by the shaken woman. There, he met the security boss. He knew he was the boss - it literally said so on his badge. *'Security Team Manager – Park Hyeong'*.

"Are you here to apply for the new position?" Park Hyeong asked.

"No. I'm here to look through some CCTV footage. There's a suspected kidnapping that went on in the hospital in the early hours of today." Derrick replied.

"Are you from the police?" The paranoid woman asked, her hands shaking.

"No." Derrick answered. "But if I don't get this footage, then it'll be the police who knock on this door next. It's your choice."

"We have nothing to hide." Park Hyeong interjected, showing Derrick all the hospital security cameras. The manager educated him on how to use the equipment, how to go back hours in time or fast-forward to present day again. “There you go. Use it for whatever you need to. We don’t need the police. If anything, we are the police around here.”

Derrick used the security controls to look through all cameras that led up to the incident. The number of cameras in front of him were astonishing, perhaps a near two hundred of them, all sectioned on one exceptionally large electronic screen. He managed to find the ICU ward where Tarawa-Li and Pigbreath had slept, and the hallways to the wards to where Mallory and Aria were staying. The exact point of time he had replayed to was where the Chairman had just left the room in the ICU ward, when he gave the brutal speech to his brother.

He used the fast-forward function button to speed up time until he could see any of the suspicious activity. There it was, the early hours of the morning, the time when they had both disappeared. The lawyer was glad this was so easy, but he couldn’t be more wrong. Looking through the cameras, suddenly, all cameras became black. Every single hospital camera black. Black for a timespan of twenty minutes. When the twenty minutes went, no Tarawa-Li, no Pigbreath, no Mallory, no Aria.

Time for work. Time for murder. It was now late afternoon, time for the Chairman to meet the leaders of his rival triad. The once beautiful sunrise now was on its way to set in a couple of hours, and the Chairman had planned to watch the sunset knowing that all of his circle were safe and back together. He was prepared for it all. He knew that there was only one of him and a vast number of his opposition, but it didn't scare him. Favourable odds for the side of his opposition never scared him in the slightest. Like his late father once said, gangsters only need two things: fists and persuasion, everything else are unnecessary extras. He was curious to find out the three leaders, but it wouldn't matter who they were to him. Once he knew, he could make sure they would be gone from existence as soon as he could possibly make it so.

There it was, the PlaciCorp tower, looking as tall as ever. The place where he secured the position of Chairman. The place where he lost his external businesses – the place he found out that someone was stabbing him and his family in the back. He couldn't stop thinking about how easy Mouse let him buy the company that day, but now he realised it was all part of their plan. The Chairman wasn't playing dirty today. No weapons, no shenanigans, nothing. Just fists and persuasion, the two elements that created the triad in the first place – although his two broken hands would prefer the persuasion tactic. He began to walk inside the building, where he was met by someone who popped in his mind only a few seconds ago. Mouse. Besides him were two of his henchmen, who grabbed Jing-Lee and escorted him to the elevator with Mouse. The four men were now on their way to the hundredth floor of the elaborate building.

Not a word was exchanged between any of the men, and after what felt like an eternity, the journey from first to hundredth was completed. The same doors that Jing-Lee walked before to gain the position he was in now were right in front of him. It was showtime. The doors were opened from the inside, which held roughly about twenty Takani-men. Well, from the estimate of Jing-Lee whilst he was being escorted by the two beefy men, that is. These twenty men were fully armed, all sporting a pistol in their right hand - like something you would see in a movie. The plan didn't need to be changed, there could be one guard or a hundred guards looking to get in his way, but Chairman Jing-Lee would stick to his ideology.

After walking the 400-metre red carpet, the security let go of him. Mouse made his way to sit in the red leather chair, placing his two legs on the wooden desk. The sight before him was almost Deja-vu.

"Before the other two arrive, let's get to basics. You move, you die. My men will fire their bullets at you."

Mouse stated. "But let's lighten the mood. Shall I confess to you why I'm really here?"

"No matter what I say, you're gonna talk." Jing-Lee replied.

"My brother used to be part of the Maska Triad. His name was *Chen Jui*." Mouse said, which was met by an instant widening of his foe's eyes. "He was killed by Atheno-Li. I don't know how, but he was killed by him."

"You're just making an excuse. My father wouldn't just let one of his men go and die." Jing-Lee replied.

"I even worked for the Maska Triad about a year ago." Mouse announced. "I was fired two weeks after I joined. Your father told me that he couldn't trust me because I was Taiwanese. I'm getting my revenge now. If you want to see me on your database, just look at Jason Holland."

"My father never has racially discriminated – if he kicked you out, it's simply because he couldn't trust you. He was right, because now look at you, trying to take down his legacy." Jing-Lee said.

"I joined the Takani Triad because the founder showed up one night at my doorstep in Taiwan. I moved back there once I was fired from the Maska Triad." Mouse replied, looking straight in the eye of his enemy. "Our goal as leaders of the Takani Triad is to destroy the Maska Triad. It's the reason of this triad being founded. We will take everything you have."

Mouse left his comfortable position in the red leather chair, and quickly excused himself. It was practically like he was about to give Jing-Lee an almost 'gift' of sorts. What would this gift be? After a couple of minutes, it was revealed. He couldn't move, but he could hear behind him. It was crying. The gift was now to the left to the Chairman, two people with bags over their heads, crying and pleading for their life. The bags were released from the two heads, revealing the two almost-dead people to be: *Tarawa-Li* and *Mallory*. No sign of Pigbreath, no sign of the baby.

Before Chairman Jing-Lee could ask where the baby was and if Pigbreath was actually killed in their hands, Mouse sat back down on the leather chair and said "I think it's time you meet one of the other leaders at least, right? Here he is."

The doors opened once again in the distance behind him, and the footsteps grew closer and closer, louder and louder in his ears. The fighting of noise between his crying brother and other brothers' fiancé, the noise of the footsteps behind him. The crying became silent, his pleading family that were bruised and battered, on their knees hoping to survive, were frozen in shock to see who this person was. The man, the second leader was revealed, and he stood beside Mouse. It was revealed. It was Yung-Ko Jang. The man who helped his father through all these years, was now playing enemy only a few days after Atheno-Li's passing.

"You're supposed to be the chosen child to take over the business from your father. Yet, out of the three of your brothers, you're the most gullible." Yung-Ko said, "You accused me to be one of the people behind this grand scheme for you to lose your power, then I say one thing back and all of a sudden you believe me and question your own thoughts. You are the definition of incompetent. Your father really did have three stupid punk sons."

No matter how betrayed the Chairman felt right now, the amount of anger, hatred, and revenge that was boiling in his system - he wouldn't let it get to him. He stayed perfectly still in view of the two leaders and the handful of guards they had on deck. His fists wouldn't get put into use in a scenario like this, (no matter if they were still broken or healed) but he was one arrogant son of a bitch at times. He would use his persuasion to the test. But before that, he was curious to know why a member of the triad for so many years decided to go against them.

"So, you've been behind this from the very first day with the Chairman? You've been a yes-man all your life, I'm guessing it's the same deal with this Takani boss of yours? Should you just bring him in now so we can talk instead?" Jing-Lee asked in a teasing sarcastic tone.

"My first move was setting the hit on Jason Holland. I ordered the contract killing whilst I was in Taiwan. As you know, contract killings were always approved by your father. Luckily enough, though, that day he was having a check-up at the hospital and let me handle the killings for the day." Yung-Ko chuckled, "I'm the reason to why your fiancé's little brother is dead. I even made your own brother kill him. How does that make you feel, punk?"

"My father did nothing but respect you, he gave you a great position and he didn't even worry about trusting you even though you're not a Korean. Are you doing this to go after his legacy or to go after me?" Jing-Lee replied.

"The chandelier back at your house." Yung-Ko murmured.

"What about that stupid fucking chandelier, you fat fuck?" Jing-Lee replied, visually appearing outraged at the Chinaman now. He hated the stalling approach in such a serious situation like this.

“I became a detective because of that stupid fucking chandelier.” Yung-Ko announced, raising his voice slightly for more of a dramatic effect to his former Chairman, “I am Yung-Ko Jang, the grandson of former Chinese President Hui-Ying Jang, who resigned from his position when the chandelier of China was stolen during his tenure. He killed himself due to great shame days later, and I have sworn to gain my revenge to the people who stole the chandelier until the day I die. I became a detective because of the chandelier, and now it’s time to finally take my revenge tonight.”

Mouse and the twenty gunmen that surrounded the Chinaman clapped in applause for the confession that was just made. The noises on the hundredth floor were so loud that any PlaciCorp workers on the floors below could easily mistake it for an electronical-music rave. At least the announcement somewhat answered his question, the Chinaman was looking to destroy his father’s legacy, and he was to do that by taking it out on his three sons. He wasn’t however about to admit these accusations to be truthful.

“Bullshit.” Jing-Lee responded. “What’s your proof?”

“I’m glad you asked.” Yung-Ko sniggered, and aimed a sort of chuckle in the direction of the ever-so-still Jing-Lee. “Many years ago, whilst I was a detective for the KPD, I received a phone call from someone inside the Maska Triad. A whistle-blower revealing all of Atheno-Li's illegal activities. I contacted him, and he invited me over to talk about this situation in person. When I met him, he acted casual and polite, and invited me to drink some coffee, in the exact room where the chandelier was. Sure, I could have just punished him there and then. But hurting the foundation he had built for all these years after his death is more pleasant to witness. I have to give it to the old jerk, he was the most impressive businessman in the world, ever. It's a shame that it's all gone to waste now. The old man trusted me with his life, and in his last dying days he wasn't in any condition to be a Chairman. I was the one who made the decision about the PlaciCorp deal – the winner to become the next Chairman of the Maska Triad. I knew your strategies, and I knew that Jing-Lee would be the next Chairman. It was all part of the Takani Triad's plan. I practically spoon-fed to you that I was the bad guy that day, that I was the snake. The only three people who knew about the illegal businesses you ran by yourself were me, you, Derrick. Do you really think that American punk could devise such a well-thought plan to bring you all down like this? You even knew that his son was killed by the Takani Triad, yet you still couldn't figure anything out."

The doors behind Jing-Lee opened once more, and it was time to see the Chairman of the Takani Triad – the man who founded this organisation to take down the Maska Triad. The footsteps grew closer and closer, louder and louder in his ears, with all the triad's gunmen placing their pistols for the time being in their pocket and bowing to their leader. The broken-down Tarawa-Li and Mallory to his side had now passed out from their wounds. It was now or never for any chance to save his crazy brother and future sister-in-law. He thought to himself that this rival Chairman is probably some hyped-up guy who was hurt by his father, just like Yung-Ko and Mouse. He hated to admit it, considering he did get on well with his old man, but if these accusations were true, he would start to think differently of his father. It wasn't time to think back now though, it was time for the big reveal and then a big rumble.

With Yung-Ko to the left of the chair, and Mouse now standing and to the right of the chair, the Chairman of the Takani Triad took a seat in the red leather chair. Jing-Lee made a mistake, though. The rival Chairman he saw before him wasn't a Chairman. It was a *Chairwoman*.

With her jet-black short hair bangs style, purple lipstick, leather jacket accompanied by leather trousers, crooked teeth, big brown eyes, slim figure and uneasy smile, there she was. He knew exactly who it was just by the way she stared at him. It was his older sister, Wera-Li Maska. This plan to take out the Maska Triad was his sister's doing from day one when she was abandoned – and now, she couldn't stop laughing at her younger brother.

"You may know me as Wera-Li Maska. But rest assured, I no longer use that name anymore. I am Wera-Li Takani, founder and Chairwoman of the Takani Triad." Wera-Li announced, "Takani translates to take, and that's what I'm doing tonight."

"This was all your doing, huh?" Jing-Lee asked, "You were abandoned, is this your revenge then? You're more of a psychopath than my brother who's passed out over there, and trust me, that's not a good thing."

"You really think I'm the bad person?" Wera-Li laughed outrageously, unable to contain her feelings. "I was abandoned by our father when I blew the whistle on him to the KPD. Yung-Ko was at the end of the phone. I waited all these years in Taiwan until we both waited for him to die and take everything he ever created. I'm taking away everything from his 'desired' family members."

"That's it!" Jing-Lee screamed, with droplets of spit releasing from his now enraged mouth, "I've had enough of this bullshit. My father would never do anything like this, so what's the real reason? Do you want money? You know, I'll tell you what, I'll give you 100 billion won right now if you let myself, my brother, Mallory, Pigbreath and the baby go safely. Wherever you put the last two, I want to see them now. Then you can have your money."

"You should know that an older sister never lies to her younger brother. Pigbreath is dead already. In fact, I believe I did you a favour. Why trust someone who would stab their leader's back for their own life to be safe and sound?" Wera-Li replied, in a scarily smooth tone and calmed voice, "As for that little baby, the next generation of your family. I've done the same thing as what our father did to myself all of these years ago. Little Aria is probably being left alone in a basket outside a small Taiwanese church right now."

He couldn't believe what he had just heard from her. His brother's baby was taken away and abandoned abroad in a foreign country just like that. Jing-Lee felt physically sick and outright shaken. The sister just smiled in front of him, with a demonic look in her eyes and crazed laughter that brought an eerie echo in the background. Surely, surely, she couldn't be serious... but in actuality, she hadn't told him one single lie.

He took one step forward to his sister, which was met by the deafening array of clicks of safety catches being unlocked by twenty guns carried by the gunmen surrounded behind him. All twenty looked at Jing-Lee through their trigger-aim sights, ready to shoot if he took one more step forward. The timing still wasn't right for him, so he took a step backwards to where he was originally positioned. He pleaded and prayed for an opening to his benefit. Tarawa-Li and Mallory were still dazed out of it to his left side and Jing-Lee himself was emotionally scarred from the news he had just gathered.

"Don't worry, I won't tell our mother. I know you guys think she's dead, but that was another lie your father told you. I still keep in touch with her now and then." Wera-Li said.

"Stop talking shit now. What do you want from me?" Jing-Lee yelled; his sister had truly psychologically gotten inside his head now. He wanted no more. He knew he couldn't win tonight, all he needed for the night to be somewhat satisfactory would be to rescue his people.

"I challenge you to a fight to the death. A deathmatch, if you will. No weapons, just fighting until the other person is dead. Winner takes all." Wera-Li demanded, her eyes widened in glee as she was announcing her words, "Winner gets rightful ownership of both triads. I'm allowed to challenge to be leader of the Maska Triad as I'm legitimately blood-related to that jerk of an ex-Chairman, and… well… I know you're not going to beat me, so I don't need to explain your side of it all."

He was surprised somewhat. So that was all this night was for? A warning? His sister went through all this trouble to challenge him. The challenge didn't get to him, he was back to being the arrogant Chairman that Jing-Lee was always made for.

"I accept the challenge. I'll take off with these two who are sleeping to my left, and I suggest you say your goodbyes whilst you can. All of these Takani-men are soon going to be bowing down to me." Jing-Lee chuckled.

"You really are a delusional bastard. You really think that's it?" Wera-Li shouted. "I don't think you've learned your lesson after all of this. You're exactly like that wrinkled dead punk. The Takani Triad are better people than those in the Maska Triad, but we're still horrible people. I think you should learn that right now since you think I'm someone you can walk over, just like everyone else in this country. Mouse, Yung-Ko, grab those two over there and sit them up on this table, they're pretty much waking up again."

The two followed the Chairwoman's orders and sat the bruised, broken and death-looking Tarawa-Li and Mallory upwards on the elevated surface. His brother's face looked like it had been trampled by a herd of rhinoceros which was then followed up by a beating via barbed-wire baseball bats, like the same as what Dan-Li used to occupy himself with. Mallory on the other hand looked like she had been forced with injections of many different drugs, with her hair almost falling out without effort and rotten yellow teeth.

Wera-Li looked at her two main comrades and then at her twenty guards. The twenty men once again raised their sights to Jing-Lee, and Mouse and Yung-Ko raised their guns too, but not at him. One gun pointed at the head of Tarawa-Li, and the other gun was pointed to the head of Mallory.

"One's not leaving here alive. You choose who I kill, I'll give you ten seconds to make up your mind. No answer in ten seconds, you'll all be killed." Wera-Li said, being as serious as someone could ever be.

Ten. Nine. Eight. Seven. Six seconds were left, and that's when everything had changed. Jing-Lee still hadn't made his mind, but someone else did. Someone else made the decision for him.

“I volunteer.” Tarawa-Li said barely, unstable as he could be, with Jing-Lee’s eyes in shock at what he had just heard from his brother. “Don’t worry brother, I volunteer. I’ve always been the useless one out of us three. It’s okay. Kill me. I’m the one who should make a sacrifice.”

Printed in Great Britain
by Amazon

52417228R00208